SPACE JUNK

HOUSTON, WE HAVE A HOTTIE

SPACE SERIES
BOOK 1

SARA L HUDSON

STEAMY. FUNNY. ROMANCE.

DEDICATION

For Ken.

ONE
OPERATION A GO

Jackie

JACKIE DARLING LEE IS A BADASS NAME. MY PARENTS DID WELL, bestowing a name that held the promise of fearlessness, hotness, and/or general awesomeness on me. With a name like Jackie Darling Lee, I should be a movie star, a best-selling author of steamy erotic romance novels, or at the very least a Southern belle socialite who lives in a Georgian mansion and can rock a hat as well as those British royals. But no, I am not any of these things. Not even close. I'm a nerd. And not one of those ironic, rock and roll nerds who wear combat boots and Buddy Holly glasses, but a straight-up calculator-carrying nerd.

Okay, so I don't actually carry a calculator around with me. I mean, honestly, there's an app for that these days. I *do* have Buddy Holly glasses, but I had those way before they were trendy. I just got lucky. Even so, Buddy Holly glasses do not a cool person make.

I work at NASA, though, so that's something. But don't get too excited. I'm just a cubicle junky who pushes paper about. It's not like I'm an astronaut or anything. Now *that* would be badass.

I'm on Orbit 2, the 7 a.m. to 4 p.m. shift in Mission Control Center. MCC is always quiet, because we're all on our headsets listening to a constant stream of commands and chatter. I'm FOD, which means Flight Operations Directorate. I'm responsible for all spacesuit- and spacewalking-related tasks, equipment and plans. An Extra Vehicular Activities officer—aka EVA. Not to be confused with the actual EVAs, or space walks, that the astronauts perform up in space.

It's a mouthful, I know. NASA loves it some acronyms.

I began my scheduled EVA procedure review by calling up to the International Space Station. A spacewalk is scheduled tomorrow for maintenance and to look into why one of the external multiplexer-demultiplexer data relay boxes (EXT-MDMs) has been failing. EXTs are like the motherboards of the ISS. However, there are two of these boxes, so no one is in panic mode—yet. But NASA does not like operating without an active backup, and right now we are literally flying on the backup.

"Station, Houston, do you have any open questions prior to the EVA?"

"Houston, Station on 2. I think we're good. We'll take a look at the uplinks and final timeline again, but we should be good to go."

"Station, Houston. All right, conference complete."

That finishes my final run-through for the next day's EVA with astronaut Julie Starr. Yes, that is her name. And yes, she is most definitely living up to it. Youngest female astronaut and Mission Specialist on the crew. On top of that, all the men at NASA like to comment on her universal hotness. Jules is rumored to be making the move to Commander soon and on top of all that, the PR department has coined her NASA's Sweetheart. You'd think it'd be fun to hate her, especially as she has my dream job, but Jules is just as badass personally as she is professionally. And for some strange reason, she likes me. When she is actually *on* Planet Earth, she makes it her mission to get me a social life.

A ring breaks through the chatter on my headset. It takes me a minute to realize my console phone is ringing. No one has ever called me on it before. I'm not like the other guys with spouses or children who check in. And it isn't my birthday or Christmas, so it can't be my dad. And even if it was, my dad is pretty strict about no phone calls at work, no matter the occasion. I get my work ethic from him, I guess.

Preparing to tell someone they dialed the wrong number, I pick up. "EVA console, Jackie speaking."

"So are you going out?"

I blink at the computer screen in front of me a few times. "Jules?"

"Yes, Jules. Now come on, Jackie, you going out, or what?" Jules' voice comes through clearly, but it still astounds me that she's 270 miles up in space and moving over 17,000 miles per hour. And that she's calling me.

"Jules, what are you doing calling me?" I glance around the room nervously. It isn't against the rules to take personal calls, but I've never done it. "You should be prepping for tomorrow's EVA."

"Did you want me to ask you about your social life on the public loop?" She laughs like she could see me cringing from space.

I sigh. "No, I guess not. And no, I am not going out. I'm on call for the front room on your EVA tomorrow." Besides the normal scheduled shifts, there are also people on call in case someone gets sick or for emergencies.

"You need to get laid."

I bark out a laugh. Now everyone in Mission Control *is* looking at me. My face heats. Sean, the Flight Director, frowns. MCC is supposed to be *quiet*.

"Jeez, Jules. We're a bit preoccupied down here," I say quietly.

"You're always preoccupied. You have your hand in so many projects and your mind is always so busy calculating or referencing some quantifiable thing that you'll end up dying a virgin."

The heat spreads down my neck. "For God's sake, Jules, I'm not a virgin," I whisper-mumble.

"Well, you could be. You haven't gotten any since I've known you and I met you on your first day at NASA. How you can go so long, I do not know. You must have one hell of a vibrator."

I'm thankful for the tall console in front of me that helps to hide my now raging blush. Honestly, I've started sweating.

Jules keeps going. "You read those cowboy romance novels, so I know you're not dead down there."

"Jules," I grumble softly into the phone, "I spent my first year at NASA living with my head in reference books and manuals so I could be sitting here talking to you from Mission Control."

"Don't 'Jules' me," she snaps. "What about now? You finished not one, but all three of your certifications in your first year. In record time, you've become a specialist in your field, even getting promoted. Now you're sitting in MCC with underlings to do your bidding."

"Underlings?" I laugh again, earning me another glare from Sean.

"Well, I'm not calling them minions, that's just rude."

"I didn't—"

"No more excuses, girl. I can't take it knowing you're down there, living in that shit apartment, doing nothing but reading about the filthy things you *should* be doing."

"They aren't filthy, and my apartment isn't *that* bad. Besides, my lease is coming up. I'm thinking about buying a house."

"Thinking about and doing are two different things." She huffs out a breath. "Promise me you'll go out tonight."

I start envisioning the crowds, the heat of the room, the noise of a bar and suddenly my blush isn't the only thing making me sweat. "No Jules, I'm not going out. I'm on call. It's not like I can drink." Or have anyone to go with me to make sure I don't pass out from nerves or general social awkwardness.

"Jackie, what am I going to do with you? You're gorgeous. You have that wild blond hair that guys love. You don't even wear makeup and men flirt with you. And when they are flirting with you, you don't have a clue. Or you turn fire engine red and stiff as the carbon fiber on our heat shield. I mean, what the fuck, girl? Wait, you're rolling your eyes at me, aren't you?"

I stop my eyes mid-roll. "Uh, no?"

"Ugh. I wasn't going to do this, but you leave me no choice. You either go out tonight, or I'll call Ian's console, and I happen to know he's working tonight, and tell him you told me you want to bone him. Hard."

Mission Control Center is manned 24/7, with the days split up into three eight-hour shifts. People are always here providing support and more. So even though I've been lucky to get the standard 7 a.m. to 4 p.m. gig today, Ian, also an EVA specialist, will take over after my shift.

"Jules. You can't keep doing this." I turn my head quickly and catch a glimpse of Ian, behind the glass, in the back room, waiting to take over.

Ian is a co-worker Jules thinks is cute. Jules likes to use him to blackmail me whenever the mood strikes her. Ian happens to be hot and single. Seeing as when we do talk, it is about work, I don't freeze and turn into mute nerd statue. This makes Jules think we would be perfect together. He is her only fodder really, as most of the engineers here are either married, in a relationship, or have been here since the Apollo days.

Last time, she blackmailed me into going out to a bar with her by threatening to send Ian flowers from me during one of our

EVA meetings. And that is how I ended up drunk, telling Jules about my romance novel vice in the middle of a rowdy drunken bar crowd.

A request for a flight operations summary comes through on my headset.

"Gotta go, Jules, MCC calls." Saved by the MCC bell, as it were.

"All right, Jackie, but what's it going to be? You going out, or am I setting Ian on you?"

Or not. "Jules…" It doesn't escape me how whiney I sound right now.

"Tick tock, sweetheart. I've got nothing but time to float and scheme until seventeen hundred Earth central time."

The flight op request repeats in my ear. Louder.

"Fine! I'll go out. But that's all I'm promising."

"That'll do, hooker. That'll do."

———

FOUR HOURS LATER, cut to me, sitting alone in Big Texas Saloon, drinking a Coke, surrounded by a flurry of people who are dancing and having fun. My barstool is in the perfect spot for people-watching – behind the railing that encloses the oval wooden dance floor and wedged beside a wooden post. Couples spin, belt buckles glisten and rhinestones sparkle.

A whole hour passes this way. Not a single person asks me to dance. This is a good thing as I don't actually know how to dance. But still, it would've been nice to have had the option of turning someone down. Even one of the older dudes with the crazy big hats.

On the plus side, I did not hyperventilate at the size of the crowd. I feel flushed, but I'm going to blame that on the heat of the place and not my uncontrollable blush factor.

"Another Captain and Coke, ma'am?"

Startled, I look behind me at a petite waitress in a tight black tank top, cut-off denim skirt and black cowboy boots. Her black-ish-brown hair is piled on top of her head, secured with what looks like an office supply of ballpoint pens. I rub the toes of my sneakers together as I take in her expertly applied red lipstick. Sheesh, even the waitress looks cooler than me. And she ma'am-ed me.

"Just a Coke please. And no need for the ma'am."

The corner of the girl's mouth quirks up. "Sorry, a Southern habit. I 'ma'am' everyone, even those celebrating their twenty-first birthday." She jerks her head to the side and I follow the direction. There, in the midst of a large, rowdy group that gives me shivers just to look at is a young woman, head back laughing, tiara on her blond hair and a sash across her chest that reads "Legal."

I smile. "I'll take being called ma'am if it lumps me with her. She seems to know how to have a good time."

"I don't know how much longer you'll feel that way." Her Southern drawl is like the slow trajectory of a rocket into space, every one-syllable word stretched to two. "With the way she's going, it won't end pretty."

"Ah, but that's the joy of turning twenty-one, isn't it?" Not that I'd know. My twenty-first birthday consisted of studying for exams and a Happy Birthday text from my father.

I look back at the waitress, who doesn't seem to be looking at the blonde anymore. Once again, following her lead, I turn back to the group and spot *him*.

Holy crap-o-la.

All rational thoughts leave me. *Him* being a clichéd tall drink of water. He stands toward the back of the group, beer bottle in hand, leaning against the wall. There must be some sort of technical manual all men read—Chapter One: How to lean against a wall and *not* look like an idiot.

He has to be over six feet, with hair cut short around the sides but still long enough on top to feel good if I ran my fingers through it. Not like that would happen. But a girl can dream.

There are flashing lights around the bar, so I can't make out details too well, but I *can* make out the solid block of muscle beneath a long-sleeved Henley—sleeves pushed up his forearms. Though not tight, his jeans are fitted. And of course, cowboy boots.

Sigh.

He reminds me of one of those twinkling stars that catches your eye at night. Even now, with all our telescopes and technology, we have no idea how many stars exist. They are uncountable, the universe so vast. And yet, there are always those that twinkle and draw the eye within the sea of zillions. This guy is like one of those stars.

"Dang."

"You can say that again, ma'am." The waitress laughs, causing her precarious updo to waver.

I cringe, not realizing I said that out loud.

The waitress is smiling at me, so I decide not to be too embarrassed. Instead, I suck it up and think, *What would Jules do?*

I straighten my shoulders. "Okay, I take it back, no more ma'am. I'm Jackie." I thrust out my hand. My dad always stressed the importance of a handshake. The girl looks surprised, but tucks her drink tray under her arm and reaches out with her own.

"Trish." We shake hands once.

"Nice to meet you, Trish."

Trish withdraws her hand and tilts her head, looking over my white Converse, jeans and Stanford T-shirt, before looking to the empty stool beside me. "Are you meeting friends or something, sugar?"

"Uh, no." I look down at my empty glass. "Why do you ask?"

"Just surprised to see a pretty girl by herself. You new here?"

My cheeks get hot. *Pretty.* I decide I like Trish. "Sort of. I've lived here for about a year now, but I haven't gone out much. Been busy at work. But I guess if I'm going to start Operation Social Life, I best make some changes. Maybe even get some boots."

"Operation Social Life?" Trish asks, lips twitching.

"Yep." I nod. "Just made that up. My friend Jules says I'm stuck. Static." I look at the twirling dancers.

"Static?"

"Static. Unmoving, stationary, a body at rest, if you will." I turn back to Trish, who now seems to be holding back laughter. "What?" I glance back down at my shirt. "Did I spill something?"

"No, no, sugar. I just like the way you talk." When she smiles, it isn't the smile of someone laughing at me (and believe me, I know those), but with me. And that feels good.

"I also like the way you talk. It's what I imagine a fixed-width binary code would sound like."

"Uh, thank you?" Trish shifts her weight to accommodate a man with a waist as wide as his hat brim walking by. "Where is this Jules, then? Shouldn't she be here ushering in your new social plan?"

"In space."

"I'm sorry?" She looks at me a bit blankly.

"Space. My friend. Jules. She's in space. Outer space." Trish keeps staring, but now her eyebrows are in the middle of her forehead. God, I suck at small talk. I take a breath, willing myself not to stiffen up and start again. "Jules is an astronaut at NASA. She's currently up on the International Space Station."

Trish looks a little dumbfounded at this, but recovers quickly. "Well, hot damn. That's the best excuse I've ever heard for letting your girl out without a wingwoman." She looks over her shoulder at the growing crowd. "I've got to go make the rounds, but I'll be back with that Coke and you can explain Operation Social Life to me in more detail." Her smile is large and bright when she says, "I have a feeling you're gonna be the most interesting customer of the night." With a wink, Trish saunters off to her tables.

My eyes drift back over to the birthday girl's section, but holy crap-o-la is gone.

Flynn

I feel dirty.

And coming from a mechanic, that means something.

All of Rose's friends are knocking back shots, ordering rounds and preening like a bunch of peacocks in their designer duds in a Western saloon. Like the swarm of cowboy boots really care how much their six-inch heels or Italian loafers cost.

What makes me feel even worse? I used to be just like them.

A few high-rolling twenty-year-olds amble off to the dance floor. I stop one as she stumbles past.

I look down at the blonde in charge of Rose's birthday gathering. "Pam." She blinks a few times, like she's having trouble focusing. "I thought you were the designated driver?"

She wavers on her feet, her head weaving on her shoulders as she looks to my hand around her arm and back to my face. Next thing I know she's plastered against me, her free hand gliding up my side.

Great. Something else to make me feel dirty.

"It's okay, big boy. I got us a limo coming in a bit." She tries to nod toward the dance floor, but her whole body ends up tilting, my arm the only thing holding her up. "Let's go dance off some booze." She tries to shimmy against me, but when I let go of her arm she stumbles back into one of the guys in their group. He doesn't even ask her if she's okay, just continues flirting with the waitress.

"You go ahead." Sweating out some of her drinks has got to be better than passing out at the table, which is probably her other option at this point. "I'm heading home in a bit."

She straightens and runs her hands down her body. "Want some company? Heard you've been lonely."

I scowl in response, but as drunk as she is, Pam doesn't pick up on it. Instead she tries sidling closer. I step back out of her reach.

She pouts. Like a child. Which I guess is exactly what she is. None of the people in this group ever grew up. They're too rich and too complacent. And now I'm afraid Rose will become just like them. Same as I did. Frustrated, I shift my gaze beyond the partiers.

"You can't seriously prefer any of this low-class trash to me?" Pam asks, gesturing to the crowd in general.

Involuntarily, my eyes flick to the dance floor, where the blonde with those thick-framed glasses has been perched all night. I'd caught her glancing over here earlier, and if I hadn't been so busy comparing my past self to these idiots, I might've gone up and said hello.

"I mean, really, Flynn," Pam continues, following my gaze, "remember who you are, for once."

That snaps me back to the moment, and the anger that has been simmering all night surfaces. My anger is more aimed at myself, and I'm aware enough to recognize that, but it doesn't stop me from being pissed at the world in general right now. Especially when I come out to wish my little sister a happy birthday, only to find her friends shit-faced and Rose virtually ignored. The same kind of friends who were decidedly unhelpful after my parents died and then virtually ignored me after one of their own fucked me over. But I guess I owe them a favor. Without that final kick to the balls, I would've never grown up.

"I know who I am, Pam, and I like him a hell of a lot better than the spoiled rich kid with no direction in life."

"Sheesh. Mr. High and Mighty. Beth was right to dump your ass." An evil smile curls up her face before she continues. "Too bad Holt turned out to be just as boring. Looks like neither of the West brothers are any fun anymore."

For a moment I think I'm literally seeing red, until I realize that the flashing red lights from the ceiling are simply mirroring my emotions.

Fuck this.

I shrug my shoulders, knowing the worst thing I could do to her, or any of these posers, is not care. "Well, this boring guy is heading home. Alone." I point my finger directly in her face, uncaring how much of a dick move it is. "You're supposed to be Rose's friend, Pam. So sober the fuck up and get my sister home safe."

I don't wait for her to respond. Really anything she says at this point will just fuel my anger. I simply side-step her and walk over to the table where Rose has stationed herself.

"Rose?"

When my sister sees me she smiles, raising her arms in the air for a hug. Suddenly I'm transported back to when we were kids, when it seemed Rose's arms were always raised, wanting someone to hold or hug her. Anyone to fill the void our parents left.

But really, Mom and Dad hadn't been around much when they were alive, so I don't think much would've changed for any of us West kids.

I bend down and encircle Rose in my arms, pulling her into a tight hug. It's what I should've done every time in the past, but

I'd been too much of a self-important douche to show my sister the affection she deserved.

"How does twenty-one feel?" I ask, straightening and stepping back.

Her eyes are heavy-lidded when she replies, "Same day, different shit."

Her mixed-up words have me taking a closer look. Her legs are hooked in the barstool rungs, back slightly slumped forward, elbow propping her up on the table. "I was going to head out, but maybe I better stay. You don't look too with-it."

She snorts. "It's my twenty-first birthday. I'm not supposed to be with-it. In fact, I think I would categorically declare anyone's twenty-first birthday a failure of epic proportions if they were at all 'with-it.'"

She uses air quotes at the end, which has me smiling. Some of the tension I've been carrying on my shoulders lifts. Rose is her own unique brand of girl. I should trust her not to make the same mistakes I made when I was younger. She's so much smarter than I ever was. And Rose was young when our parents died, so they hadn't quite messed her up the way they did Holt and me.

At least, I hope not.

I tap her on the nose with my finger, chuckling when she glares at me. "Understood." I go to pull out the stool next to her, but she blocks me.

"Flynn, it's awesome that you came to wish me happy birthday. I mean, that *is* why I wanted to celebrate here instead of downtown, but you don't need to stay. Really. I'm a big girl." She points to the sash draped across her chest proclaiming her legal. "All grown up."

"You'll always be my baby sister, Rose."

"Yeah, yeah." She rolls her eyes. "Now stop cramping my style with all the brooding. Get laid or something, will you?"

"Christ, Rose. Don't say things like that."

"Dude. Someone has to. The stick up your ass can't be all that comfortable."

Laughter erupts from my throat and I shake my head. "You sure you're okay?" I lean in and kiss her cheek. "You done drinking for the night?"

"Yes, overlord. Pam and I will have our asses driven downtown. We're heading back to my condo in a bit."

"All right." More tension ebbs once my mind absorbs that I'll be free of these people soon. "Love you, Rose. Be safe."

"You too. I left condoms in the kitchen pantry for you." She smirks. "Remember, no glove, no love."

"Jesus."

———

Jackie

I've never had to take a drunk girl home before. This is not what I had in mind for Operation Social Life, but here I am, trying to haul a semi-comatose birthday girl through the bar. Jules is going to think I'm a lesbian when she debriefs me on my night out. First talking to the waitress and now driving a girl home.

Ten minutes earlier, I found Rose leaning over the sink in the bathroom, having a conversation with herself in the mirror. Something about promising herself to find new friends. Apparently, all hers left without her. She'd been attempting to call an Uber when I told her I'd give her a ride home. I don't know why. Maybe because I know what winding up alone on your birthday feels like.

But beyond that, I seem to have little in common with Rose. The drunk girl.

She's the girl I always pictured as the heroine when reading my cowboy romance novels that Jules likes to harass me about.

Rose has big hair and a short denim skirt that's topped off with a plaid button-down with genuine pearl button snaps. The front tails of her shirt are tied, making the shirt more crop top than anything. What with her high-heeled cowboy boots, she is quintessentially country.

"Put your arm around me," I huff.

Rose is currently slumped against me, and at this point I'm basically carrying her. She isn't heavy, even with her thick-heeled boots, but she isn't light either. My only thought at this point is that I need to work out more. That and a pulley or lever system would be really helpful right about now.

"Jackie?"

I turn too suddenly, and Rose falls to the floor.

"Crap." I look down at the pile of country beauty at my feet.

"I knew you would be the most interesting customer tonight." By the barely restrained laughter shaking her small frame, it's safe to say that Trish is enjoying my current situation.

I put my hands on my hips. "You were right. The birthday girl got sloppy." I wave my hand in the general direction of where Rose was partying. "And her friends all bailed."

Trish glances in that direction then back at me. "That was rude of them." She looks down at Rose. "Need help?"

"Yes, please."

I bend to pick up one arm, thinking Trish will get the other, but she turns around and whistles over a bouncer I've been studiously trying to avoid. "Wait! I don't want her arrested!"

Trish pauses in waving the big guy over. "Arrested?"

"Uh, yeah. Don't people get arrested for public intoxication?"

Trish purses her lips for a moment, still fighting the battle not to laugh. "Oh sugar, if that were true we wouldn't have any customers left." The bouncer she whistled for shows up, looming over Rose.

The look on my face must be comical, because Trish loses the battle and erupts into giggles. "Relax, Jackie. Jimmy isn't going to arrest her, but he can get her to your car."

———

AFTER SOME GRUNTING on Jimmy's part, and laughter on Trish's, Rose is now sprawled across the back seat of my car.

She opens one eye, surveying her position. "I know I'm drunk. But even drunk, I can tell your car is a piece of shit." Then she promptly passes out. Jimmy walks away without a word.

"Well, she isn't wrong." Trish bursts out laughing again.

My car is old. My dad gave it to me for my eighteenth birthday, and it was used when I got it. A small, four-door compact that shakes when I go over fifty miles per hour.

Trish stops chuckling long enough to ask, "You know where to take her?"

"Yeah, she told me where she lived before I had to carry her out of the bathroom."

"Okay then. And since you've been drinking nothing but soda, I take it you're good to drive?"

"Yep."

We both silently ponder the drunk in my car. Me with my hands on my hips, Trish with her mouth twitching.

"Give me your phone." Trish sticks her hand out.

"Huh?"

Trish just wiggles her fingers and waits. I pull my phone out of my back pocket and give it to her.

She looks down, sighs and hands it back. "Unlock it, silly."

"Oh. Yeah." I press my thumb over the button and watch the screen wake up. Trish takes it out of my hands, then starts banging the screen with her thumbs.

"I added myself to your contacts and called my cell, so now I have your number." She hands it back again. "Text me once you get birthday girl and yourself home safely, okay?"

I can feel my face light up, and I stare hard at the phone in my hands so Trish can't see the ridiculous grin I'm probably sporting. Trish wanting to keep in contact makes me way happier than I'm sure it should.

God, I'm such a nerd.

"Sure thing. Thanks," I manage around my smile.

She takes another look at my outfit. "If you want boots, we can get you boots." Once again, she winks and walks away.

A grunt has me turning back to my car.

"Rose?" I ask, peering in the rear side door.

"Slow down! You're driving too fast."

"Um, we aren't moving, Rose. We're still parked."

This gets me a flutter of lashes, like she's trying to open her eyes, but her body's fighting it. "Well shit." She manages one eye again. "You better get a bucket then. This probably won't go well."

Awesome. Just awesome.

———

"ROSE? ROSE! WAKE UP!" I'm driving around Clear Lake Forest, one of the coolest neighborhoods around NASA. All the great astronauts used to live here: John, Gus, Alan and most of the rest of the Mercury Seven. Even some of the Apollo boys. It's one of the few neighborhoods in the area established enough to have big trees lining the streets.

"Rose! What was the house number again?"

She stirs a bit from the back and lurches upright. I brace for vomit, but nothing happens.

Rose looks left, then right, then straight ahead. "Fuck. Where am I?"

"You're in my car," I say, looking at her through the rearview mirror. "I'm taking you home. What is the house number?"

"Huh?" She starts blinking rapidly. "Wait, why are you driving me? Who are you?"

"Seriously?" At the stop sign I rest my head on the steering wheel.

"I'm just playing." She laughs and points between the two front seats. "It's up a few houses on the right. At the end of the cul-de-sac." She slumps back.

I pull up to a one-story house. It has a low-pitched roof, a large picture window in the front and metal scroll work on the sides of the door that is classic 1960s modern. I love it.

"Your house is awesome." I whisper for some reason. When no response is forthcoming, I put the car in park and get out.

But before I can open the door, it's shoved open so hard I think it might come unhinged. Rose heaves herself out and stands next to me. "It isn't my house." She stumbles forward, leaving me to close the door.

"You good now?" No sooner have I said this than she face-plants in the grass. Thankfully she misses the flagstone path.

———

A FEW MINUTES of huffing and puffing later, I manage to get the keys from Rose and muscle her into the foyer and down the hall to the room she slurred is hers. Too bad it's so dark. I would love to see the house in the light. I bet it has original mid-century modern elements throughout. Maybe even terrazzo tile. With one final heave, Rose is face down, yet again, but this time on her bed. With her boots on.

"What the fuck?"

I whirl around to see a guy in the doorway. And not just any guy—it's the holy-crap-o-la hot guy from earlier.

And. He. Is. Shirtless.

His glare is focused on the bed, where Rose rolls over so that she can flip the hot guy the bird.

"You weren't this drunk when I left, Rose. What did you do?"

"Shots." Rose giggles and starts chanting, "Shots, shots, shots, shots…"

I press my lips together to keep from laughing.

"Jesus." Hot guy rolls his eyes and looks at the ceiling. "You said you were cut off. Pam said you were going to dance off the booze and leave." He tilts his head back down and stares at the floor like he wants to pound it. "I should've known better than to listen to any of your friends."

Rose snorts. "Yeah, my friends are lame." She furrows her brow. "But they used to be your friends too."

"And now they're not. And you know why." He widens his stance and crosses his arms, which only serves to enhance his biceps. This must be what people mean by 'nice guns.'

"Yeah. Sorry." Rose closes her eyes for a moment, looking almost contrite. Then she opens them wide. "Fuck. The spins."

Hot guy grunts, but his eyes soften and I swear his lips twitch.

A minute ticks by with Rose and the guy staring at each other. And me being a weirdo voyeur. Time to go.

"Ummm... I'm just going to..." Stupid move. I should *not* have spoken. Because now the hot guy glare is aimed at me.

"What are you doing here?" He turns to fully face me and drops his arms. Smooth hard pectoral muscle over pronounced abdominals. My whole body freezes, except my eyes. They go wide taking him all in.

"Shut up, Flynn." Rose struggles up on her elbows. "Don't be such a douche." Her updo has come down, there's mascara under her eyes and her mouth is set in a grim line that only a country girl could pull off and still look cute. "Jackie helped me get home."

"This isn't your home, Rose. It's mine." He steps closer to her. "And get your goddamn boots off the bed."

Soon the two are yelling at each other, and I have to admit, I'm impressed. Rose has sobered up quickly enough to let loose on the hot guy named Flynn. I'm not sure I'd be able to put together two words to say to him, drunk or sober. Across the bar, he was hot. Up close and personal? I need to change my panties. He has a finger pointed in Rose's direction and with each jab the muscles on his back and shoulders bunch. His hair is all mussed, like he just got out of bed, and the top button of his jeans is undone. Flames race under my skin and I know I've just turned red. Holy Mercury, I need to get out of here. Rose can handle herself. I start inching toward the door.

"And listen, you." I freeze, realizing the hottie named Flynn is talking to me. My skin feels nuclear. "You better not be drunk. Because if I wake up and find out you drove drunk and hit someone else on your way to whatever stupid-ass college party you're heading to now, I will personally kick your ass." With that, he storms from the room.

Time passes. I'm not sure how much, as I sort of zoned out, staring after him, unable to form thoughts. Which is a relatively novel occurrence for me. The non-thoughts part. I freeze in social settings on the regular.

When I finally snap out of it, Rose is passed out, snoring. And her boots are still on.

TWO
BIG BANG

Flynn

I SHUFFLE INTO THE GUEST ROOM AROUND SEVEN THE NEXT morning. Rose is on her back, head tilted up and snoring. Loud. I try to drum up some anger, but I'm just weary. I don't know why my little sister is still hanging out with that crowd. People like that, they're like leeches. They'll latch on to you as long as the good times and money keeps pumping like oil through an engine. But once you say no— game over. They simply move on to easier prey. They tried latching on to my older brother Holt, but he's always been too obsessed with the ranch to care. Me, they got their hooks into. After our parents died, drinking and spending the family's oil money sounded like a far better way to spend my time than wallowing in grief.

Breathing in a pig-like snort, Rose turns onto her stomach. She's still wearing her birthday sash. I glance down and sigh.

And her boots.

Since I'm balancing a mug of coffee in each hand, I nudge her with my foot. "Rose." Another nudge. "Wake up." I give up and place one of the mugs on the nightstand and leave.

I'm sitting at the kitchen counter later when Rose shuffles into the room, hands wrapped around her mug, mumbling. The only thing understandable is a gruff, "Thanks for the coffee," then she props her butt up on the second bar stool. At least she's taken off her boots.

I salute her with my own cup of coffee.

She sighs. "Look, I'm sorry for waking you last night."

That's why she thinks I'm mad? "Rose." It comes out harsher than I want. "I don't fucking care about being woken up. I care about the fact that you were wasted and ditched by your friends. You've been partying with those people since you were sixteen. They're assholes."

Her face tells me I've struck a nerve. "You think I don't know? Who am I supposed to hang out with? They're the only people I know with as much money as we have. It's just…easier."

"I know all about taking the easy road, Rose. And you know where I'd be if I'd kept on it?"

She smiles. "Beth's bitch?"

I laugh. "Uncool, but probably true. I sure as shit wouldn't have started my own business. And a life away from all those high society phonies makes me way happier than hanging with them ever did." I look her in the eyes. "You need new friends."

"I made a new friend last night." Her brows furrow. "At least, I think I did."

"Listen, I don't know who that hot chick was who brought you home, but just be careful. You don't need to be making more of the same kind of friends."

"Hot chick?" Rose tilts her head.

Shit. I shift in my seat. "That's not the point I'm making, Rose. None of your friends are ugly."

"Yeah, but this is the first time you've called any of them hot."

"Rose. Focus." I run my hand though my hair and blow out

another breath. "Who arranged your birthday party? Who paid the tab last night?"

Rose looks down at her coffee mug.

"Damn it, Rose, it was *your* fucking birthday."

"I know, but I didn't have anyone else to go out with." She sounds so small, it kills me.

"I know I yelled last night, but I was really just pissed off at myself for leaving before things apparently spiraled out of control." I take a deep breath. "I thought Pam ordered a limo. Wasn't she supposed to take you back to the condo downtown?"

Rose won't meet my eyes. "Well, Pam said she was going to hook up with some guy…" She starts trailing her index finger on the counter. "… and she wanted the place to herself."

For a minute I just sit there and blink. What Rose is saying doesn't quite compute, but when it finally does all my anger rushes back. "You have got to be shitting me." I slam my mug on the counter, some of the contents sloshing over. "She left you at a bar, on your birthday, after you footed the bill and barred you from your own goddamn home? To fuck some random?" With every question, Rose's shoulders get higher and higher, like she's trying to cave in on herself.

Fuck, I'm an ass.

"Rose." I take a deep breath and lay my hand on her shoulder, waiting until she straightens and looks me in the eye. "I'm sorry. I should've sucked it up and called Holt to arrange a family birthday dinner instead of letting you go out with those ass hats. I should've stayed last night. I just..." I clear my throat. "I fucked up."

Rose shakes her head and smiles before reaching up to put her hand on mine. "You didn't fuck up, Flynn. You shouldn't have to chaperone my twenty-first. It would've been even more of an epic fail if everyone around me was drooling over my big brothers." She rolls her eyes.

There it is. One of the reasons I love my baby sister. She knows I'm feeling shitty, and even though I *should* be feeling shitty, she tries to lighten the mood. Growing up, when Holt was granted custody of us at eighteen, he did the ranch, and I tried helping raise Rose. Though half the time I'd felt like Rose had been raising me.

"And I did have fun being drunk in Jackie's car." She laughs, reminding me of one of the other reasons I love my sister. Ninety-nine percent of the world knows my sister as the badass, take no prisoners, foul-mouthed, confident young woman. Only a select few get to see her drop the act. Although, truthfully, I think my sister is pretty badass all the time, even when she's sad.

Glad she's feeling better, I give in to my curiosity. "So who's Jackie? I've never seen her around before. She go to school with you or something?" I try for nonchalant, but even I can hear the awkwardness in my voice.

Rose tilts her head to the side. She's too perceptive by half when she wants to be.

"Never mind," I say, picking up my coffee cup. "Just another one of your hangers-on, I'm sure." But as I grab a paper towel to mop up the mess I've made, the image of all that blond, wavy hair pulled up, exposing a long neck, and wide, unblinking, brown eyes behind thick, black frames comes crystal clear to the front of my mind.

"Not all women are Beth, Flynn." Rose pats my back. "Or Mom."

I pause mid-swipe. Rose and I have never talked about the woman who burned me. And yet, Beth was one of the reasons I left early last night. Rose's friends, the high society ones that used to be mine, kept mentioning Beth, thinking I'd want to know what she's been up to since I found her in my brother's bed. But really, I don't care. She did me a favor. Now she's just the woman who fucked me for family money and then just fucked my family for good measure.

And Mom? She was just fucked up. Then she died.

———

Jackie

"What happened after you left?" Trish asks.

Trish called to go shopping as she said she would. We're wandering around Cavender's, a Western shop mid-afternoon. I've never been, even though this place is a staple among Texans.

See, in the dark of Big Texas Saloon I can pretend to fit in, even though I know I'm no cowgirl. But in the bright light of day, helped along with rows of fluorescent ceiling lights, I know there's no way in hell I can pull off shopping here on my own. Floor-to-ceiling shelves grace the outer walls and chest-level shelves make up the aisles on the floor, all of which showcase various styles and colors of boots.

Then there are tables piled with jeans that have pockets so blinged-out, Liberace could go cowboy and still maintain his look. Don't even get me started on the racks of shirts with pearl snaps and fringe, or the jewelry cases filled with brick-sized belt buckles.

Today, as I'm with Trish in her skinny jeans, complete with rhinestone pockets, and a leather purse so big that I figure a whole cow had been sacrificed in its making, I figure I fit in by association.

I answer Trish's question with a question. "What do you mean?"

She pauses in her perusal of belt buckles. "I mean that I've been waiting, patiently I might add, to hear all about how you got Miss Birthday Girl home last night."

"Oh, that."

I'm currently caressing a pair of snakeskin cowboy boots with dark brown leather uppers. They are beyond amazing. Like Crocodile-Dundee-meets-badass-cowgirl amazing. Paul Hogan is on my celebrity list. But you know, a *young* Paul Hogan.

"Yes, that," Trish says, hands on her hips.

I squat down, searching the shelf for my size. As usual, a hopeless endeavor. I straighten in defeat and put the shoe back on its perch.

Trish gestures to my whole person and continues, "You come in, cute as can be, order a Coke in a bar, talk about 'Operation Social Life,' and the next thing I know I'm helping you pour a drunk blonde into the back of your clunker." She settles her hands back on her hips. "What gives?"

"Cute? Uh, did you not see my Chucks and T-shirt?" I look down at myself and realize I'm basically in the same thing today, only my T-shirt is of the periodic table. Hmmm… New clothes might have to be added to Operation Social Life's agenda.

Trish shakes her head. "Not everyone in Texas needs boots and big hair." She stares pointedly at my ponytail. "Though I have a feeling if you let that loose, you might be one step closer to country."

I like Trish. She's just as cool now as she was in Big Texas, so that allays my fears that she'd just been working a big tip. There is also something refreshing talking to someone outside the NASA world.

"My work is kind of demanding…" I stop, the usual excuse falling short. "Actually, it's more like I *make* my work so demanding."

"Well, you work at NASA. That's a bit more demanding than hustling drink orders."

"I'm sure waitressing is hard work," I say quickly, turning red again.

"Relax, sweetie. Cocktail waitressing and bartending suit my life. I'm quite happy." She pats my shoulder before turning to the boot racks. "I'm just saying that NASA requires a bit more dedication, I'm sure."

I shrug. "It does, I guess. But I… well, I've come to realize that my lack of social skills may be negatively affecting my professional trajectory."

Trish pauses in reaching for a pair of super high heeled, red leather boots with fringe on the sides. "Say again?"

"Um, I need a life outside of work?"

She nods, dark hair waving. "That, I get." She kicks off her shoes and slides into the red boots. They looked ridiculous on the shelf, so I'm immediately jealous when she stands up, gives them a test walk and looks implausibly amazing in them.

"But I thought you were friends with Julie Starr? Or do you just hang out at work?" In these boots, her eyes are on the same level as mine.

"I am and not exactly. She's really cool, but super busy. You know, either in space or doing some sort of PR travel to DC. And it isn't that I don't like the rest of my co-workers, I'm just sort of…"

"Shy?"

"Well, I was going to say an extreme introvert with no social skills, but we'll go with shy."

Trish laughs.

"And even the ones I do talk to, it's all me explaining the proportionate weight ratio needed to achieve optimum minimal buoyancy force. Or the negative side effects of drag time in water as opposed to the zero G of space."

Trish replaces the red boots with her own and I can see clear over the top of her head again. "You're like a genius or something, aren't you?"

My ponytail falls over my shoulder when I look down at my

feet. I don't like talking about being smart. I mean, I'm not stupid, obviously, but when people hear about my degrees and what I've done they tend to think of me differently. Been there, done that, got the heartbreak to prove it.

"Anyway," I say, waving her question away with my hand, "I thought, as an experiment, I'd change my natural environment to see if such a simple change would be enough of a catalyst to spark a reaction. Kind of 'Big Bang' my own social life, if you will."

"Big Bang?"

"Yeah, the Big Bang, the more commonly accepted scientific explanation of the birth of our universe. The singular explosion that acted as the catalyst in the universe's creation."

"Ah, *that* Big Bang," Trish drawls.

I can't tell if she's messing with me or not.

"Yeah, that one. Then I made the mistake of telling Jules about my social experiment." I pick up a pair of all-black boots. Even the stitching is black. Very Johnny Cash.

"Why was that a mistake?"

"Because the stupid astronaut blackmailed me, that's why!" I slam the boots down, causing the plastic display shelf to fall.

"Okay, you lost me again," Trish says, helping me pick up the boots as I right the shelf.

"She said if I didn't go out and execute my plan she was going to tell Ian that I want to have rough sex with him."

And that is when Trish erupts into a fit of laughter so hard she has to bend over and rest her weight on the bench in the middle of the aisle. She finally just sits down on the floor. While she recovers I see that the Johnny Cash boots are also not available in my size. Figures.

"You like rough sex, huh?"

We both turn to see Rose in the next aisle over. Trish struggles to her feet.

"Rose?"

"In the flesh, darling." She leans forward, resting her elbows on the top of the shelving. "Thanks for the ride last night."

"You're welcome." I look at Trish and then back to Rose. "This is Trish."

"I know. She helped haul my drunk ass into your car last night."

"You remember that?" Trish asks. She sounds as surprised as I feel. Who knew Rose hadn't been completely comatose last night?

"Yep. People rarely think I'm paying attention when intoxicated. But I do." She's wearing large black sunglasses and her hair is one step away from birds being able to inhabit it.

"How did you know we'd be here?" I ask.

"As I said, I was paying attention. Heard you two talking about boot shopping last night. And as this is *the* place to get boots, I took a chance."

I raise my eyebrows. "The probability of us meeting here at the same time isn't very likely. I mean, how did you know what day we would meet up, or what time to come? Or if Trish would actually call me?" I run through some numbers in my head, but there are too many variables and possible outcomes to calculate.

"Well, girl, the probability was increased by the fact that I paid the gentleman at the cash register a hundred bucks if he'd call me when a short brunette and a tall blonde with geek-chic glasses showed up." She raises her glasses up on her forehead, revealing a surprisingly fresh looking, makeup-free face. "I'd say money well spent for the looks on your faces alone."

"I'm not short." Trish pouts. "I'm just a petite Southern woman."

"Hey, there. Nothing wrong with a petite woman. Good things come in small packages. Especially if that package is Tiffany blue." Rose purses her lips and looks up at the ceiling. "I take that back. *Some* good things come in small packages. If you're a dude, and your package is small? That's just sad."

Their conversation fades while I contemplate Rose's approach to finding both of us. "You solved a complex problem with a multitude of probable outcomes, due to nearly unquantifiable variables, by introducing the concept of capital gain."

They both stare at me for a beat. I fiddle with my glasses.

"Don't you just love the way she talks?" Trish asks Rose.

"I truly do." Rose nods, taking her glasses completely off and resting her head in her hands.

Face flushed once again, I change topics. "Anyway, I hope your boyfriend wasn't mad at you this morning."

"Boyfriend?" Rose's forehead creases.

"Mr. Holy-crap-o-la hot guy from the bar." My body stiffens. "I mean..."

Trish and Rose laugh loud and hard.

Rose recovers first. "Did you just say—"

"Never mind. Don't repeat it." I cut her off and look at Trish, mumbling, "He was the guy leaning against the wall at Rose's party last night."

"Oooo." She squeals while turning her eyes to Rose. "Well done, sugar." She holds out a fist to Rose.

"You mean Flynn?" Rose bumps the fist with her own in a way that is somehow cool and not ridiculous. "So, you think he's hot, huh? Even after he yelled at you, and quite unfairly I might add?"

"Wait, what? How am I just hearing this?" Trish looks at me accusingly. "I asked you what happened and you made no mention of any hot guy drama." She winces slightly in Rose's direction. "I mean, Flynn."

Rose waves Trish off while lifting her brows at me. "Hmmm. Now why wouldn't you mention dear old Flynn?"

"It's nothing. It was nothing. No big deal." Damn it, my face probably looks like I had heat stroke. "*Anyway,* I'm just glad I got you home okay."

"In her piece of shit car, no less."

"Thanks a lot, Trish."

"Oh, speaking of your car. There might be a problem," Rose says as she meanders around to our side of the shelving.

"What do you mean? Did you leave something in it?"

"I definitely left something."

"I didn't notice anything. Maybe it rolled under the seat. Was it your phone? Wallet? We can go look now if you want. My car's just out front." I start making my way past her toward the door, but Rose stops me with one hand, and gives me a business card with the other.

"What's this?" I ask. She's given me an automobile mechanic's business card. "West Auto?"

"Yeah, that thing I left? It wasn't last night. It was ten minutes ago." For some reason, she looks quite pleased with herself. "It's a big-ass dent."

————

THE CAR STUTTERS as I park it at the garage Rose directed me to. She had hit the side of my car, right by the back left wheel. I still don't understand how she did that pulling into the space next to mine. She would have had to drive straight into my car. When I explained that her accounting of events didn't match the basic trigonometry of the accident's angle, Rose just shrugged.

Next to me is a white luxury car that only seems to highlight the decrepit nature of my own vehicle. It might be time to get a new one. I grab my bag and haul myself out. Maybe I'll get an SUV so I don't always feel like I'm climbing out of a hole. I pass what I now see is a BMW, and a vintage sports car with a For Sale sign propped on the dash. Now, I don't know much about cars, but I do know this particular car is badass. It's a cherry red convertible. It has that classic, boxy look to it, with the initials GTO on the front grill.

Wowzers.

I walk up to the driver's side and peer in. White leather seats with a red dash. Stick shift. Hmmm, I don't know how to drive a stick. Maybe Trish or Jules knows? With the way Rose apparently drives, I don't think it's a good idea to ask her.

A loud clank brings my attention back to the garage. It's off NASA Road 1, about two minutes down the road from my apartment. Though it's in the opposite direction from NASA, I still must have driven by it quite a bit. Funny what you miss when you're not looking.

The auto shop is comprised of several open bays, most of which have more luxury cars in them. Even with my limited car knowledge, I know that my POS does not belong here.

I enter the glass-front office situated to the right of all the bay doors. A guy about my age, maybe younger, is standing behind a hip-height desk clacking away at a computer. I stand for a moment waiting for him to look up, but he doesn't. Instead he keeps 'typing,' which is really him just pounding two index fingers at some keys. Who doesn't know how to type properly these days?

"Hello?"

He pounds a few more keys and looks up. That's when a smile spreads slowly across his face as his eyes drop to my feet and make their way up to my eyes. Again—slowly. It isn't the most seductive moment of my life, but as he has a nice smile, and he doesn't actually leer, so I appreciate his appreciation. Jules always says that a little innocent appreciation does a body good.

"Hello there." He leans forward, resting both forearms on the counter. It does nice things for his biceps as they flex to take on some of his weight.

"Hi, yes. I'm Jackie. Rose sent me. Told me to ask for the owner, a Mr. West? Said he would know who I was."

"Rose, huh?" His eyes travel over me, his eyebrow quirking when he gets to my Chucks. "Unusual."

Before I can figure out what that means, he walks away. What the heck? I stand there for a few minutes and am about to leave to find my own mechanic when the office door opens and *he* walks in.

I can't be this unlucky. Or lucky, I guess, depending on how you see it.

He already looks angry. I wonder if he's perpetually pissed, or if there's something about my general appearance that puts him off. Maybe hot guys are only nice to hot girls. And he is definitely a hot guy. Why didn't Rose mention that her boyfriend owns the place?

Flynn, that *is* what she'd said his name is, has grease-stained coveralls on. Coveralls that are universally unflattering on any man, woman or child, and yet there he is looking like sex. Just straight-up sex. I'm peering over the counter to see if he has cowboy boots when he speaks.

"You wanted to see me?"

I snap my gaze up. He's caught me checking him out. Crap. At least he doesn't look angry anymore.

"Uh, yeah. I mean, yes. Sorry." I will myself to relax enough to rifle through my bag and emerge with the card Rose gave me. "You're Mr. West?"

"I'm surprised you don't know that, as you were in my house last night." He places his palms on the desk and leans forward. I endure yet another perusal of my person. This one leaving me a bit breathless.

I hear a snicker and realize the guy from before is behind him. I feel my face flush.

"Well," I start, clearing my throat, "I was just getting Rose home. You never really introduced yourself, now did you?" I don't like how he's looking at me. It is... I don't know, confusing. I don't like being confused.

"Oh, I remember you all right. Just another college student home for the summer, I'm sure. Going out, getting drunk, being stupid." He shakes his head like a father scolding a child.

I am *not* a child.

"Excuse me? I believe *I* was the one who got Rose home last night. Not you, her *boyfriend*, who was at the bar and then conveniently left when it was obvious she needed to go home." I put my hands on my hips and lean right back into him.

He seems to pause at this, so I keep going before I lose my nerve.

"Here are my keys." I slam them down on the counter between his palms. "My car is parked out front." I jerk my thumb towards the parking lot. "Apparently, thanks to Rose, who was nicer to me in a state of complete intoxication than you have been stone cold sober, I have a nice-sized dent on the side of my car. She gave me your card and told me to come here, that I would be... let's see, how did she put it? 'Treated kindly,' as a favor for getting her home safely last night." I even use air quotes. I'm on fire.

Flynn has the decency to cringe at my words. It's like I'm having an out-of-body experience. My mind can't believe that I am actually talking to a hot guy. Angrily. Coherently. Without stuttering or freezing up. And still I keep going.

"Now I don't care if you fix it or not, but what I won't do is stand here and listen to you blame me for doing nothing but care for your girlfriend while you were home doing God knows what."

His brows pinch together and he opens his mouth, but I raise my hand.

In. His. Face.

I have no idea what has come over me, but it's like I'm a bitch on a roll and I'm kind of enjoying it. I grab the pen on the desk that's attached to a chain and flip over the card Rose gave me.

"Now." I slam the pen back on the counter and thrust out the card. "Here's my number. If you want the job, fine, let me know when it's done. If you don't, fine, let me know when to pick it up." When Flynn doesn't take the card, I reach around him and hand the card to the other guy, who is now staring at me with a wide smile. He takes the card with a wink. If I hadn't already been red with anger I probably would have blushed.

A rumble comes from Flynn's direction. He might have actually growled. I can't be sure, as he's looking at the other guy. But I do know I've poked the bear enough. I turn on the heel of my Chucks and beat it out of there.

THREE
EVENT HORIZON

Flynn

"Did you just growl at me?"

"Shut up." I snatch the card out of Mike's hand then grab up the car keys Jackie slammed down. There are at least five pounds of keys on the ring. Who has this many keys? And fobs. There's a weird fob with a digital readout of numbers on it. One more thing to add to the list of questions I have about this girl.

"You did. You actually growled at me," Mike says, laughing. "You're hilarious."

I glare at him. "I wasn't the one winking at the girl, now was I?"

"I always flirt. That's why you have me out front." He puffs out his chest. "Women love me."

"It sure as shit isn't for your typing skills," I say, gesturing to the computer.

Mike flips me off.

"Be careful, princess, that's your good typing finger."

"Har, har," Mike says with an eyeroll. "You better get going if you want to catch up with her. Being a dick to a customer is not good for business, bro."

I shouldn't have been anything less than appreciative to Jackie from the start for getting Rose home safely. I don't know why this girl brings out the jerk in me. Thinking of the flush that spread down her neck when she was angry, I say, "Even if that girl was a few seconds away from ripping me a new one?"

"A few seconds away?" Mike barks out another laugh. "Dude, all I have to say is you better take it easy next time you take a seat, maybe invest in one of those circle pillows — she didn't need any more time. She ripped you one good."

"Whatever." I pocket her number and head out the door. Leave it to Rose to send her late night designated driver in for car repairs. Fucking Rose. When the heck did she have time to dent the girl's car? Now I probably have to pound out an expensive car door and eat the labor cost in addition to apologizing.

Out of everything, though, the fact that Jackie thinks Rose is my girlfriend pisses me off the most. 'Cause that's just incestuously disturbing. No other reason.

The front parking lot has three cars. A BMW M3 Manhart, a 1957 Pontiac GTO that I personally restored, and a rusted-out Honda of unidentifiable age, except to say *ancient*. The BMW is a Space Ex executive who came in earlier for a tire rotation. That leaves the clunker.

A bad feeling starts churning in my stomach. None of Rose's rich-ass friends would be caught dead driving this junker. Maybe this isn't her car. But when I step up to the driver's side door and insert the key, the lock pops.

Shit.

Okay, plus side, Rose isn't making friends with any more privileged asses. Con, once again I've been a complete dick to Jackie, this time by assuming she is a rich, privileged ass.

I look down the highway to the right. Nothing. To the left I can just make out a blond ponytail swishing back and forth a few blocks away. Damn, the women can move fast. I pocket her keys and get out my own, jogging over to the GTO.

This baby needs a drive anyway. It's just convenient and practical to take her for a spin.

Nothing to do with impressing the enigma of a girl with the sexy as fuck glasses.

———

Jackie

My anger lasts two minutes outside in the Texas heat. It might be cooler than normal for June, but cool in Texas means 82 degrees. Not counting the heat index. I have about three miles to walk to my apartment. Uncool.

One, I cannot believe I yelled at the hot guy. Kudos to me.

Two, he will now only be referred to as Hot Guy, or even better, The Asshole That Shall Not Be Named. He doesn't deserve a name. Especially not one as cool as Flynn West. I mean, honestly, who's named Flynn West? It's almost as ridiculous as Jackie Darling Lee.

Three, he, at least, has lived up to his cool name potential. He's a hot mechanic who owns his own business and lives in a house worthy of John Glenn.

Argh.

Angry again, I stomp one block closer to my apartment. A horn beeps close behind me.

I turn to see the freaking Asshole That Shall Not Be Named driving the bad boy car from the garage parking lot.

Of course he is.

He pulls into the Whataburger parking lot I'm currently bypassing. Some say they can hear a car purr, but this car doesn't purr. It growls. And I feel that growl in my downtown so fiercely, I shiver.

ATSNBN climbs out of the car and jogs over to where I'm standing.

One, why is he following me?

Two, who can jog wearing folded down and tied coveralls without a wardrobe malfunction?

Three, why am I severely disappointed when the aforementioned wardrobe malfunction does not occur?

Four, why am I still counting things?

"Yo."

This is how he greets me. Not 'I'm sorry for being such a douche canoe,' or 'Please let me give you a ride as it's hotter than hell outside and you're too pretty to sweat,' or even a polite 'Hello.' No, I get, 'Yo.'

I cross my arms and let my cocked eyebrow speak for me.

"I..." His mouth seems to stall.

I'm about to try and harness my earlier kick-ass-and-take-names attitude, but I'm distracted when he runs his hand through his hair. It does seriously wonderful things for his arms.

The hair he pushes back falls forward again when his arm drops to his side. "Look. I'm sorry. Okay?"

I'm a little surprised that he has it in him to apologize, and I almost say 'okay' out of some ingrained habit, but I don't. Because his apologetic face mirrors his mad face, and though the expression does nothing to dampen his hotness, I'm mad that he seems mad that he's apologizing. Magnificent arms be damned.

Am I even making sense anymore?

He steps closer, bringing our proximity down to a nerve-racking two feet. My earlier forwardness gone, my body freezes on me.

"You forgot these." He holds out my keys.

I stare at his outstretched hand a minute, until what the keys mean seeps in, unlocking both my mind and mouth. "Fine. You don't want to fix my car that *your* girlfriend dented—fine. Just fine." I snatch the keys, smart enough not to short circuit my brain again by touching his hand. I make a move to go around him back toward the garage. At least now I won't have to walk.

His fingers wrap gently around my upper arm to stop me. "No, it isn't that."

My breath catches at the feel of his callused fingers on my skin. His hand is large enough to wrap completely around my bicep. I find this wildly erotic for some reason. It must be the heat.

"I took the car key off. You should never leave house keys with someone else. It isn't safe." He reaches out and fingers one of the fobs on my ring. "Plus, this looked important."

Holy crap. I actually left my NASA token, the off-site security key clearance, behind. It enables a two factor authentication that allows me to access classified government information remotely. I mean, unless someone knows how to access NASA's secure server it's probably useless in another person's hands, but even so, I never should have left it.

"Yes." I wrap my hand around it, grazing his. "It *is* important."

I turn my attention from my keys to Flynn's face and immediately wish I hadn't. Without the look of anger I'm so accustomed to seeing, he is ridiculously handsome. It's like staring at one of my cowboy romance covers come to life. The sides of his eyes crinkle and a small smile plays on his lips. I shake my head a bit. Why won't my brain work properly?

"Th-thanks." I move to pull the keys out of his reach but his fingers close on mine and he gently pulls me closer.

Oh. His eyes aren't just blue. They have flecks of green and a thin ring of amber around the iris like an event horizon around a black hole. I've always been drawn to black holes. They're misunderstood. People think of them as destroyers, ominous orbs sucking life into the depths of their nothingness. But black holes aren't nothing. They are *everything*. Still waters running deep. Their strong gravitational pull attracts stars, particles and light. So strong is the pull of a black hole that stars will actually orbit it, drawing close to its force. Though unseen by the human eye, when a black hole and star get in close proximity, a high-energy light is made. From a telescope, this light is spectral in its beauty. Looking into Flynn's eyes, I feel as if *I* am the star, desperately trying to wallow in the pull of his gravitational singularity. Heat is radiating from us, and for once I don't think it's from the Texas sun.

"Jackie?"

I take a deep breath, trying to clear my head. But the smells of oil, sweat and musk only compound my delirium.

It's the sound of David Bowie singing that finally pulls me back to reality.

"My phone," I mumble, stepping away from Flynn to pull my phone from my bag. "Space Oddity" is my work ringtone. I clear my throat.

"Jackie here."

The words coming through sober me from Flynn's spell, firing my brain back online.

"I understand. When is the emergency briefing? I see. Yes. I'll be there." Shoot. Ten minutes. I look down the long road toward work. There's no way I can get there in time. But *Jules.* I close my eyes and take a deep breath. No, I *will* get there.

"Jackie?"

I jump, startled out of my reverie. His unruly dark hair falls forward into his beautiful eyes as he looks down at me.

I blink away all thoughts of his hotness and focus on the task at hand. "Listen, I hate to ask, but there's an emergency at work and I need to be there, like, now. Is there any way you can drive me?"

He stays quiet, his eyes probing mine.

Panic rises.

"I'll pay you," I add.

This might have been the wrong thing to say, going by the affronted look on his face. "You think I'd take your money for a ride? What kind of guy do you think I am?"

Well, that is *definitely* the wrong thing to say to *me*. Anger mixes with my frustration and panic. I feel the woman I'd become in the garage rise and I give in to it because it's easier and probably more efficient than giving in to the others.

"What kind of guy? I don't know, the kind who instead of thanking the person who got Rose home safely yells at them and then threatens unwarranted violence against their person? The kind of guy who gives that same person a hard time when coming to them for help with their car after their girlfriend dented it? That kind of person?" I huff out a breath. "Never mind, I don't have time for this. I'll hitchhike." I spin on my heel and stride toward the road. But before I have time to stick my thumb out, I'm lifted off my feet and thrown over a muscular shoulder.

"What the heck?"

"Calm down. I'm taking you to work." Flynn's arm is anchored under my ass, which is pointed skyward and jostling with every step he takes toward his car.

I'm being manhandled. I've never been manhandled.

I have no idea what to do. So I do nothing. This seems to suit Flynn just fine. He crosses the lot, opens the passenger door with his free hand and flops me down onto the seat. How he manages to do all that without breaking a sweat, or my head on the car, is beyond me.

Flynn gets behind the wheel and wastes no time bringing the

car to life. He looks over at me, eyebrow cocked. Him mirroring my earlier expression is not lost on me.

When I get myself and my lady parts under control from the unexpected hum of the engine, I answer his unasked question. "Follow NASA 1 under the overpass toward Saturn Drive."

While Flynn maneuvers out of the parking lot, I make use of my phone. I also make use of my Kegel exercises as the car continues to growl.

"Ian? It's Jackie. Yeah, I heard. Listen. I need you to come get me at the badging office. The, uh, guy who's giving me a ride doesn't have clearance." I cut my eyes over to Flynn. He raises his eyebrows at 'clearance.'

"Thanks."

Ian does not sound pleased. Apparently, I'm inconveniencing everyone today.

"Take a left on Saturn, then stay in the right lane."

"Where do you work?"

I don't answer, but he does as asked.

The car is silent. I don't bother trying to fill it, I'm too busy trying to contain my hair in the wind whipping around the convertible.

"Turn here."

"NASA? You work at NASA?" Clay, one of the security officers, approaches Flynn's window, preventing me from reacting to Flynn's apparent shock. I grab my security badge from my purse and lean across Flynn to show the guard.

"He's just giving me a ride." I motion to Flynn with my thumb. "I have another NASA employee picking me up to take me in. We just need to pull into the badging office." Clay nods and waves us over.

The badging office is right next to the security post. This is common protocol for non-employees. Everyone is required to have a badge to go any farther on NASA property, even guests of employees.

I lean back and loop the lanyard attached to my badge over my head, pulling my mess of hair through it. Flynn makes the immediate right into the parking lot, cutting confused, side-eye glances at me as he does. Ian's already there, leaning against his car. I've never really noticed cars before, but I do now. Maybe it's because I've gone from driving my junker to riding in Flynn's bad boy car. Who knows? But right now, as I open Flynn's car door with a distracted "thanks" and hop out, I realize Ian has a really nice car too. Whereas Flynn's is all muscle, Ian's is what I would call sleek. The cars seem a perfect match for their owners.

"Who's this?" Ian's head jerks in Flynn's direction.

Hmm. Maybe good looking men are incapable of polite greetings.

I glance back to see that Flynn has gotten out of the car. He makes his way around the back end to stand next to me, arms crossed, jump suit still tied around his waist.

I wave my hand in Flynn's direction. "This is Flynn. He owns West Auto. He's fixing my car." I realize that might not be true after my little hissy fit. Justifiable hissy fit, but still. The question must have been evident in my voice because even though he keeps his eyes on Ian, he nods. I clear my throat. "Yes, well, I had just dropped off my car to be fixed when the call came in about the EVA problems," I continue. "Flynn was *nice* enough to give me a ride." I don't think anyone missed the sarcasm I laid on there.

Flynn grins. I have to actively look away so my brain doesn't shut down again.

And although Ian is one good-looking guy, my brain seems to function just fine around him, even when we aren't talking shop, as it were. Ian simply looks annoyed. Which is understandable as

I've called him out of the office during an emergency. The EVA results must be worse than I thought.

It takes me a second, but I realize that neither of the men are particularly interested in me, or even aware of me. They're staring each other down like boxers before the bell.

Men (insert eyeroll here). String Theory is more easily understood, I swear.

Moving closer to Ian's car, I try and break the stare down. "We should go. I want to take a look at the footage from the ISS cameras. I need to ascertain the extent of the corrosion so we can get an emergency spacewalk operational as soon as possible."

Ian finally looks at me. He's what I like to think of as Polo Guy. The all-American, Ralph Lauren model kind of man. Sandy blond hair, blue eyes, straight white teeth. I've never really let my thoughts wander too much in his direction as he's my co-worker, no matter what Jules has said. But if what she says is true and he likes me? I have to admit, that would be pretty darn flattering.

"Sure thing, hon." Ian sweeps his arm in the direction of his car. He's never called me hon before. It's unprofessional. I decide it's best not to think on that and deal with the more important things happening at the moment.

I turn back to Flynn. "Uh, thanks?" He smiles again and funny things happen to my stomach. "Call me." Crap. "I *mean,* call when you have an estimate on my car."

The heat is getting to me. That is the only excuse I'll accept for my moronic behavior.

In answer, Flynn steps closer. He places his hands on my shoulders, leans down and kisses me.

Kisses. Me.

It is light. Barely there. A whisper, really. I can almost pretend it didn't happen. Almost.

"Yeah, I'll call you."

And then he gets in his car and growls out of the parking lot.

———

THE SHORT RIDE to MCC is quiet. Ian must be worried about the ISS. I should be too, but I'm really thinking about that kiss. I can still feel the whisper of him on my lips. Why would he do that? Wait, what about Rose? True, the girl has been nothing but trouble, but I like her, and I let her boyfriend kiss me. Guilt has me trying to focus back on the recent EVA.

"It'll be okay, Ian, we'll fix the main computer. I'm sure we can bypass the main cable, or even replace it with another onboard."

"What are you talking about?"

"The corrosion Jules' EVA uncovered." I take in his tense jaw. "Isn't that why you're upset?"

"No, Jackie. That is not why I am upset. It should be why I am upset. But it isn't."

"Is it because I asked you to come get me? I'm really sorry, it's just that—"

"Really?"

Okay, now I'm getting a little mad—again. Ian seems to be projecting his bad mood onto me.

All this anger is disconcerting. I'm not an angry person. In fact, I rarely raise my voice. I don't often curse. I'm rational. Logical. But ever since I stood in a space-race era bungalow and had my butt erroneously handed to me by a drool-worthy mechanic, my anger seems to be set to a constant simmer.

"Then why are you giving me the stink eye?" I huff, too late realizing that crossing my arms after I ask makes me look like a child having a tantrum.

His lips twitch. "Stink eye?"

"Yes." I face front and lower my arms as he pulls into the MCC lot. "I don't like it."

A long sigh escapes his mouth before he switches off the ignition with a button. A button ignition. That is so cool. Maybe my new car, which is inevitably in my near future, will have a button starter. But Ian's doesn't growl like that GTO. In fact, it is oddly silent. Which makes Ian's inspection of me now all the more uncomfortable.

"You're a beautiful woman, Jackie."

Startled with Ian's thought process, I answer, "You too. I mean, man. Beautiful man." I feel my brow furrow. Can a man be beautiful?

Ian laughs.

I smile, feeling some of the tension dissolve. "What do our aesthetics have to do with the EVA failure?"

Still smiling, Ian shakes his head. "Know what? Never mind. Just be careful, okay?"

Huh. I usually don't do well with implications, but evidence might suggest Ian is referring to Flynn and not the EVA when he says 'be careful.' I guess, if I look at this logically, it makes sense, if what Jules said about Ian wanting to ask me out is true. I'm not sure how I feel about that. It isn't that Ian isn't attractive. He is. Very. As one may deduce from my previous Ralph Lauren model comment.

But I've gotten involved with someone I worked with before. It didn't end well. And even with all of Ian's handsomeness not a foot away from me, I'm still thinking about that next-to-nothing kiss from a guy I'd been so sure didn't like me.

"Sure thing," I say, as it seems I need to say something to get us past… whatever this is.

Ian rolls his eyes. "Let's just get to the Flight Investigation Teams meeting."

On our walk to Building Five, I try to focus on the meeting ahead.

But that *kiss*.

I shake my head hard. Rose is my friend. I think. And as a

friend, I should be indignant on her behalf. I will simply ignore the aftershock panty tingles my downtown is currently experiencing. They must be from the muscle car's engine. Not the kiss.

My phone vibrates as I scan my badge into the security door after Ian. A text from an unknown number pops up.

BTW, thanks for getting my sister home safely last night.

Sister? Rose is his *sister*?

The tingles shall not be ignored.

FOUR

MAIN ENGINE START

Jackie

SEAN IS NOT HAPPY. AS THE FLIGHT DIRECTOR IN CHARGE OF THE EVA who explains why the EXT-1 is failing, he is the fan that the proverbial shit hits. Everyone is sitting at the table but Sean. While slamming down what must have been his fifth cup of coffee, he mans the slide show of photos Jules was able to take while out on the EVA this morning.

"This was supposed to be a normal maintenance EVA." He clicks his keyboard hard and the slide changes. "And now we are dealing with this."

Jules did a good job of focusing in on the bundle of wires running up one of the main panels. Astronauts on EVAs wear special gloves, attached to their space suits. The primary focus of the gloves and suit is to protect astronauts from the pressure and conditions of space. That means bulk. Taking detailed pictures in a giant marshmallow suit is hard work, but Jules has done it and done it well. Small holes can be seen on some of the wires, and one looks so bent that it could be a moment from snapping. That means a meteorite or a piece of space junk hit the ISS.

NASA monitors the orbits of thousands of larger pieces of space junk floating around in the Earth's orbit. Some of it is man-made—pieces of satellite, tools dropped by astronauts during space walks, and leftover debris from Star Wars tests in space. Then there are natural particles—meteorites. Small meteorites can travel faster than a bullet.

Sean looks around the room. "We knew that EXT-1 was starting to give failures and the thrusters were hit or miss on taking commands, so we switched all power to EXT-2. Unfortunately, during the spacewalk, Astronaut Starr discovered that the fix was not as simple as powering cycling."

The EXT-MDMs are the external computers set up on the truss of the ISS which control the functionality of station components such as the solar arrays, radiators, cooling loops and other systems.

Ian speaks up. "EXT-2 is running without problems?"

"Yes. EXT-2 is in full working order. That's why we're not talking evacuation. We have the CHRONUS group monitoring them." Sean shifts through more slides and shakes his head. "The station simply got hit in a bad spot."

The ISS is as large as a football field. And though, in the beginning, a lot of wires had been exposed and running along the exterior of the station, most of them, especially on the US side, have been moved internally. Computer failure due to a space junk hit is relatively low on the probability scale. And in the grand scheme of things, hitting wires isn't as bad as if the space junk had hit a window or penetrated the hull.

But this is still bad. Not life threatening. At least not yet.

Sean flips to another picture. It shows a small section of thickly insulated wires on the exterior of the ISS.

"Does ADCO anticipate the need for any complicated maneuvers anytime soon?" I ask.

"They've conferred with TOPO and Space Command and say we are clear for the foreseeable future. The Russians are also helping," Sean answers.

Attitude Determination and Control Office manages the station's orientation and calculates any needed maneuvers to avoid large debris. I've worked with them a few times during EVA planning. Trajectory Operations Officer and Space Command are responsible for the station trajectory and maintaining data regarding the station's orbital position.

Another click on Sean's computer. "You can see by Starr's photos that what we think was a tiny meteorite, too small to be picked up by TOPO, hit the space station here." He points to the center of the screen, where damage to the wires seems localized. "This small section is only about 12 inches long, but there are leads to the US computers in this bundle. We have an old EXT on board the station. We'll get the crew working on refurbishing it with the parts available so we can swap it out with the damaged one." Sean looks to Ian and me. "The next spacewalk's primary task will be the removal and replacement of a data relay box. In the meantime, the EXT-2 is operational and all ISS components are in working order."

Ian and I look at each other, then nod.

"Listen," Sean continues, speaking to the room at large now, "I know the EXTs are crucial, vital even to sustaining life on the ISS, but we're still good. We still have an operational computer, six of the smartest astronauts with degrees in shit I can't even pronounce, an old computer we can install and we *always* have the option to depart. But discussion on that is a few failures away."

The Soyuz "lifeboat" is always docked to the station. If needed, the astronauts can evacuate inside the Russian capsule and clear the station in the event of an emergency. At the moment, we have a few critical failures, but NASA always has more than one fail-safe.

We *should* be good.

————

FOR THE NEXT few hours it's nothing but blueprints, slide shows and conferences with different departments. The Russians are on the telecom, calling in from their flight control room in Moscow.

Among all this, Rose has texted me quite a few times.

How she knows about Flynn giving me a ride, or my hot co-worker Ian, I have no clue. For someone so young and sweet looking, she's kind of scary.

My eyes keep drying up. Sealed and secured government buildings are known for their dry, recycled air. It's like working on an airplane. It also doesn't help that I've had a long day. After a long night. And I hate coffee.

Sean doesn't have that problem. He pours himself another cup. I've lost track of how many he's had, but the pot has been refilled more than once. "Look, a usual EVA takes weeks to plan, if not months. So I know this is a lot to cram in, but let's not rush and make mistakes. The astronauts are sleeping at the moment. Let's reconvene early tomorrow and get them in on the discussion as well." He gets up and stretches. I can hear his bones creaking from across the room. "For now, we continue with the plan to load The Progress up with replacement software when it launches to resupply the station in two weeks."

Despite what a lot of movies or books say, you can't just tell an astronaut to suit up and head out the air lock into open space. Suits have to be charged and oxygen tanks hooked up. Space walks need planning and engineering teams need to be consulted. Ten days is about the fastest a spacewalk could be safely scheduled. At NASA, no one messes with safety procedures.

————

I'M WALKING AGAIN.

And though it's dark outside, it's still hot. I didn't feel right asking Ian for a ride home. He sat next to me the entire meeting and brainstorming session. That's normal, but it didn't feel normal. Not since the Flynn and Ian stare down.

I jump up over a curb and run my hand along the twelve-foot-high chain fence, topped with barbed wire, that marks the perimeter of NASA. There are only two exits and entrances to the site. One on the east side, and one on the west. My apartment is west, so I'm walking my way back to the security entrance by badging.

I take a left onto the road by the security huts, hitting the side-walk. The guards are busy with cars coming and going. NASA never sleeps.

"Yo."

I stop mid-step. *It can't be.* Slowly, I let my foot drop to the pavement and pivot, the worn bottoms of my Converse smoothly making the turn.

But it is. Flynn is leaning against a car, his arms crossed. This isn't the car from this morning. This one is green, but just as badass. More badass, really. Bigger. It's another vintage car, and I recognize the Mustang emblem on the front. That much I know. Though the BOSS 429 inscription on the side means nothing to me.

It isn't even running. No growl to set off my tingles. And yet my downtown is wide awake just looking at it. Who knew I had a thing for cars?

I walk over to him. "What are you doing here?"

He straightens up beside the car. "I heard from a little birdie that you were gonna walk home." He saunters forward, erasing the distance between us. "At night."

"Rose," I sigh. She's continued to text me throughout the day, wanting updates on when I'd be finished working. I should've known she had ulterior motives.

"Yep."

"Listen," I start, trying to find the courage to look into his eyes and failing. "It was really nice of you to drive down here," I tell his shoulder. "But I'm a big girl. I can walk a couple miles to my place."

"Uh huh." He points to the tingle-inducing car. "Get in."

His brisk attitude finally draws my gaze to his. "Excuse me?"

We have a bit of a stare down until he breaks eye contact to run his hand through his hair, clearly exasperated with me. "I'm sorry I was such an asshole earlier, okay?"

When I still don't move, this time from speechlessness, he sticks his hand out in the direction of the car and jiggles the keys. "Please?"

"Fine." I wave my hand in acquiescence and accidentally hit his outstretched arm. The car keys fly out of his hand.

And down a storm drain.

"That didn't just happen." I look from the grate to Flynn then back again. "That can't have just happened."

Flynn tilts his face up to the sky and sighs.

There is a beat of silence before I go into fix-it mode. "I'll call Triple A," I say, fishing in my bag for my phone.

Flynn lowers his chin back down and cocks an eyebrow, watching me rummage through my purse. "If you were going to walk home, your phone should've already been in your hand. In case something was to happen."

"You mean like a disgruntled man lying in wait for me in the parking lot?" I ask.

Flynn surprises me by barking out a short laugh. "Disgruntled," he snorts. "Yeah, that about sums me up." Then he smiles, like *really* smiles.

And oh sweet Neptune, if I'd deduced him as being a chronically angry guy from all our earlier interactions, this new evidence completely destroys that once logical conclusion. Because Flynn's smile outdoes both his cars *combined* in the creation of downtown, happy dance tingles. I'm so focused on his smile, I don't really notice he's moved closer until his fingers brush along the side of my jaw.

"Touché," he says, his voice low. Not quite a whisper, but low enough the timbre resonates in my chest, creating a warmth inside that not even the Texas heat could mimic. His smile turns softer, his touch lingering a moment, before stepping back and walking toward his car. "Put your phone away, darling. I'm a mechanic. You'd seriously wound my already bruised ego if you called Triple A."

He moves around the front and opens the passenger side door. I follow him while taking a moment to ponder the fact that one, he called me darling, and I don't mind. At all. And two, smiley Flynn is just as disconcerting to my brain as angry Flynn. More so, really.

He sprawls across the seats, then turns, getting his upper body under the steering wheel on the other side, while masterfully avoiding the gear shift. As he stretches out on his back, his shirt creeps up. His abs are golden, tan from the sun.

I think I'd willingly give up my Buzz Aldrin signed NASA T-shirt to see Flynn without his.

A small line of dark hair travels down behind a silver belt buckle into his jeans. A sudden urge to trace that trail with my fingers rears its head.

I clear my throat. "So…what are you doing?"

"Hot wiring the car."

I glance around the parking lot and over to the guard station. "Hotwire?" I whisper. "Isn't that illegal?"

He laughs again. "Only if it isn't your car, darling."

"Oh." I'm glad he's tucked under the dash and unable to see my face flood with embarrassment. I may be queen of the nerds, but it would seem my street smarts need work. I should add that as a goal in my Operation Social Life.

"How do you hotwire a car?" Whenever feeling lost, focus on the academic, I always say.

He shifts up, doing a small crunch that contracts the cords of muscle on his stomach. "Wanna learn?"

My brain once again stutters before rallying. "Really? You'd teach me?"

"Sure thing. It's the least I can do." The sheepish look on his face makes him appear younger, less intimidating.

"That'd be so cool, thanks!" And once again, I'm a little late in realizing that jumping up and down while clapping isn't the most mature of actions.

But it does earn me another smile.

"Holy Mercury," I whisper.

———

Flynn

I can't help the smile that spreads over my face at Jackie's obvious excitement. Or the fact that her little jump set certain body parts of hers moving. So even though I have to cut the wires on my 1969 Boss 429 Mustang, I just can't bring myself to get mad.

Especially as it seems I'm forgiven for being such a dick to her today. And last night.

I swear I'd been planning on being a normal, nice guy when I picked her up from work. I'd even spent the drive over here thinking of charming apologies and ways to prove to both Jackie and Rose I'm not a complete asshole. But then I saw her. Blond ponytail swaying, walking alone, at night, her sneaker-clad feet bouncing like a kid off to kindergarten, not a care in the world. Something about her not taking her safety seriously had me grinding my jaw and snapping.

Again.

Jackie opens the driver side door and kneels down on the pavement. How different Jackie is from all the women I've known before really hits me. She works, for one. And at *NASA*. Plus, she doesn't even flinch at getting her pants dirty.

"What do we do first?" Jackie licks her lips and leans forward.

Jackie on her knees with an eager expression on her face blanks my mind from the task at hand. I take a calming breath before I begin.

"Okay," I start, focusing on the car, "because this car is a '69, it's pretty cake to hot wire. Nothing's computerized." I remove the panel under the steering column while I talk. "Turning the key really just connects three things: the battery, the ignition and the motor. Hot wiring just means we have to do all that manually." I separate out the wires we need. "Red is always battery. The others can vary depending on the make and model of your car. Though more often than not, on cars of this age, the ignition wire is yellow."

I reach in my pocket and fish for my pen knife, holding back a hiss when my hand brushes up against my dick. The dick that has been in a perpetual state of semi-hardness since I brushed my lips against hers earlier. The dick that only got harder since Jackie gestured toward my car, glasses sliding down her nose, knocking my keys down the grate. Basically, my dick needs to calm down.

"You need to cut and strip down a half inch on all three

wires," I narrate, trying to get my big brain to outthink my little brain.

Which isn't easy. There's some kind of deliciousness emanating from her hair. Probably from whatever shampoo she uses. Then, because it's summer in Texas, there's the light scent of sweat on her skin. Clean sweat. Gets me thinking of sex sweat. My dick gets harder.

Not helping.

She's leaning as close as she can without touching me, but that doesn't stop tendrils of her hair that have escaped her pony tail from tickling my skin. *So soft.*

"What next?"

I refocus on what I'm doing. "The battery and ignition wires get twisted together." I motion to her by jerking my head up. "Turn the lights on, see if it's a good connection."

Jackie reaches up with her left hand, bringing her neck closer to my face. All I'd have to do is arch back and maybe stretch a bit and I could kiss it. I've never been a neck person before. Because honestly, who's a neck person? There are boob men and leg men and ass men. I've always liked to think of myself as an equal opportunist when it comes to a woman's body—I like it all. But for some reason, the sight of Jackie's long slender neck does things to me.

"They're on!"

"Huh?"

She looks down at me. "The lights. They came on."

"Oh yeah. Right." I shift in the seat, willing my dick to behave. "So the next step is to touch the starter wire to the battery and ignition bundle. But you have to be careful. The starter wire is live. You don't want it to touch anything metal or it could short. And since this is a manual transmission, you need to push in the clutch."

"This is the clutch, right?" She rests her long, delicate fingers on the far left pedal.

"You don't know how to drive stick?"

"No." She frowns as she says it. I have a feeling Jackie Darling Lee doesn't like not knowing things. She sets her jaw. "But I'm going to learn. That seems like something one should know how to do."

I smile at the serious expression clouding her sweet face. "I'll teach you how to drive stick."

Her face brightens. "Really? You'd do that?"

Her excitement both pleases me, 'cause it means she wouldn't mind spending more time with me, and makes me feel like an ass, since she's so surprised by my offer. Well, in for a penny... "Yeah, I'd love to get your hands on my stick."

She turns bright red.

I can't help but chuckle. As pretty as she is, I can tell she isn't used to flirting. I shouldn't fluster her, especially after being such a jerk. But God damn, when she blushes it spreads down that pretty neck of hers and all I want to do is follow its trail with my tongue. Why I'm having such a strong reaction to this woman is a bit of mystery. Even when I thought she was one of Rose's directionless friends, I'd still clocked the way she looked and moved.

Giving both of us a breather, I get back to work. "Now, I need to touch the starter wire to the battery and ignition bundle. With the wires exposed and ready to go, I can get in the driver's seat now. I've got to push in the clutch and rev the engine so it doesn't stall out."

"Okay."

I curl up and get out of the car. We both circle around to opposite sides and get in.

"Is there a procedural order? Does one wire have to be cut and exposed before the other? Do you have to push the clutch in first and then touch the wires, or is the clutch like the accelerator and you just have to rev it?"

I feel my lips twist in a smile. She's so fucking cute. "Procedural order?"

She blushes again and looks down at her feet. "Never mind."

Fuck. Somehow, I've embarrassed her again. "Hey?" She doesn't say anything so I reach over and tuck two fingers under her chin, lifting her face to mine. Her blush intensifies but I can tell it's not from embarrassment when her eyes dart to my mouth, her tongue licking her bottom lip.

I'm about to lean in, drawn to this girl who's busted into my life so unexpectedly, when a light flashing into the car breaks the moment.

A security guard is standing at my lowered driver side window. One of his hands is on his flashlight, momentarily blinding me, the other on the gun by his side. He does not look happy. And in Texas, an unhappy man with his hand on a gun does not mean good things.

First, I raise my hands for him to see I'm unarmed. When that's done, I'm about to speak, but Jackie beats me to it.

"Hey, Clay!" The officer dips down, jerking the flashlight to Jackie, who raises a hand to her eyes. "It's me, Jackie."

"Oh. Hey, Dr. Lee." He lowers the light and takes his other hand off his gun. "You okay?" His eyes go from Jackie to me.

"I'm good, Clay. This is my friend Flynn. He's giving me a ride home." She reaches over and pushes my arms down.

Clay chuckles. "Car trouble again, Dr. Lee? I've told you to get rid of that old thing."

Jackie rolls her eyes. "Yeah, yeah." She cuts her eyes to me. "You're not the only one who thinks that, I'm sure."

Clay tosses a wave in our direction and walks off.

"*Doctor* Lee?" I ask when Clay is out of earshot.

Another blush. "Uh, yeah," she mumbles.

"That's pretty badass."

"It is?"

I don't get why she finds that surprising. "Yeah, it is. I did the basic four years." I can't remember a damn thing I learned at Baylor. I'd been too busy coasting on my family's name with drinking, women and spending the opposite of hard-earned money. "But afterwards, I went to trade school. Cars were more my thing than books."

"That's great." Jackie is nodding her head as she talks. "I think trade schools are vastly underrated."

I can't tell if she's fucking with me or not. She looks sincere, but this is a PhD I'm talking to. I really would've thought I'd get a condescending look when I mentioned trade school. I sure as shit did from my friends back home.

I nod, then reach back under the dash, while pushing in the clutch.

"Wait!" Jackie says, putting her hand on my arm, ducking her head down, trying to see what I'm doing. "What's next?"

"Sorry, forgot." I sit back so she can see my left foot on the clutch. "The clutch should be pressed all the way down before you touch the wires." Then I reach back under the dash, the steering wheel pressing into my shoulders and chest to finagle the bundled set and the starter wire together. The engine ignites, making Jackie's expression light up. I touch the gas a few times, causing the engine to rev and vibrate the whole car. "Then you rev the engine afterwards so it doesn't stall."

The first time I revved the engine, her lips parted slightly. The second time, her eyes close and she looks like she's on the verge of coming. Without thinking, I touch the gas pedal again.

She moans so softly I almost don't hear it. But that red-hot blush spreading across her face and neck tells me I'm not imagining it.

I love vintage cars. The sight, smell and feel of them. My

blood might as well be motor oil. It's why I got off my ranch horse, said good-bye to the suit jobs and into the car restoration business in the first place. There have been no regrets since I made that decision.

But now, with this shy, standoffish, hard-to-pin-down girl close to ecstasy from the V-8 engine I personally rebuilt? I'm grateful all over again.

Something tells me Jackie might like more than just a lesson on how to drive stick.

FIVE
GREEN FLAG

Flynn

JACKIE HADN'T BEEN LYING WHEN SHE SAID HER APARTMENT WAS close by. It's also a shit hole. The sign out front says Regatta Apartments, but it's been nicknamed the Reghetto by the locals. I pull in through the broken security gate, my hands tightening on the wheel.

"*This* is where you live?"

She blinks a few times, as if waking from a daydream. "Yeah."

"Why here?"

She frowns, like she's confused by the question. "Why *not* here?"

"Have you looked at this place lately?" I ask, prying a hand off the steering wheel to gesture outside.

She moves her head left and right, her eyes taking in the worn-down apartment buildings before her. "Oh." She takes another look and sighs. "It's been a while since I've looked around. It *is* a bit run-down, isn't it?"

She doesn't seem put out by the complex's lack of care, but

rather surprised that its decrepit nature has escaped her notice. It's hard to picture the gorgeous NASA engineer living here. Or maybe I just don't want to. Jackie may not be wearing all that froufrou stuff Beth had, or even any makeup, but no one can ignore her kind of pretty. She either tries to hide it, or doesn't even know she has it. My bet's on the latter.

Nothing can cover up the high cheekbones, large eyes and full lips. Not even her glasses. In fact, the thick frames only highlight the delicate nature of her bone structure. She's like a well-made race car, whose sleek lines are accentuated with racing stripes running down the hood. Then there's her brain. She works with some of the smartest minds in the country. Even if she didn't, with the way she talks, I don't need her to tell me she's been educated up the ass.

"Run-down is one word for it." Unsafe is another. But I'm trying to rein in my inner caveman, so I leave it at that.

"When I moved here from back East, my car barely made the journey. So I thought it would be appropriate to live somewhere close to work." She shrugs. "You know, in case I needed to walk?"

Before I can respond, she motions me to park in an empty spot. As soon as I put the car in park she has the door open. She's out before I turn off the ignition.

"No need to get out. This is fine," she says, leaning into the car. "Thanks. See you around." With a slam, she closes the door and leaves me behind.

That's new. I'm used to girls doing the whole "I can't find my key" thing or starting some inane conversation, stalling long enough for me to make a move. And I know Jackie and I started out rough— okay, *I* started out rough, but I thought we'd had a moment. A few of them, actually.

Damn it. I sound like a girl.

Still perplexed and a bit amused, my eyes follow Jackie as she walks away. Her jeans are a bit baggy, and her T-shirt shapeless, but there is just something about her that rings my bell. Maybe it's because she seems so unlike the woman who raised me. So unlike my ex and her friends.

I'm thinking about what my next move might be when I see two men leaning against a lamp post farther down Jackie's path. One has a bandana tied across his head, a wife beater tank top on and jeans so low I'm pretty sure the guy has to waddle so they don't fall down when he walks. The other dude is dressed pretty much the same. There isn't a lot of gang activity in these parts, but I recognize enough colors and symbols inked on their arms and neck to know these guys have done some time.

No longer amused, I climb out of my car and jog over to Jackie. I catch up to her just as she's passing the men. She's so preoccupied with getting her keys out she doesn't notice them. The wife beater guy steps away from the lamp post and I tense.

"Hey, Jackie."

"Hmm?" Jackie glances up. "Oh hey, Paulie. How's Tiffany?"

Wait. She *knows* them?

"Good, thanks. Said to say hi. It was cool of you to help Alex with his homework. He got a B on the assignment."

"That's great. Tell Alex to come find me if he needs more help." She smiles again at Paulie. I don't like it. I put my hand on her lower back, causing her to jump.

Paulie stares at me, brows drawn.

"Oh! Guys, this is Flynn." She turns to me. "Flynn, this is Paulie and his brother Jorge." We all nod at each other, none of us smiling or shaking hands.

"Nice tats," I say.

Paulie just smirks while Jorge narrows his eyes.

"I tutor Paulie's son sometimes," Jackie says.

"Yes, we consider her *familia*." He looks me in the eyes and I get what he means. Apparently, Jackie is well taken care of here at the Reghetto.

Jorge nudges his brother's shoulder, breaking our stare-down.

Paulie smiles at Jackie, looks over to my car and back to her. "You need help with your car again?"

"Not this time." Jackie smiles at him. "This time it wasn't my car's fault. Someone backed into it."

Paulie frowns. "You get a good look at who did it?"

"Yeah, my sister," I say, not really sure why, except I don't like being left out of the conversation.

"But she's having it taken care of," Jackie puts in quickly, resting her hand on Paulie's arm. I *really* don't like that.

Paulie's quiet for a bit, before he nods hard once. "Okay, *chica*. But you let me know if you need any help." He finishes this off by glaring at me, giving me the feeling his version of 'help' might be hiding my dead body. "Take care, *dulce nina*," he says before walking away, his brother following without a word.

Jackie continues walking toward an unlit stairwell, like she didn't just have a pleasant conversation with ex-convicts and possible gang members.

"You tutor, huh?" This girl. The more I find out, the more questions I have. I want to understand her, pop her hood and figure out what makes her run. I was so sure she'd be like all the other assembly-line women I've met in the past. Yet at every turn, Jackie proves what a unique model she is. And I've always had a thing for unique models.

She shrugs. "A bunch of kids live here. Sometimes they need help."

"You tutor more than one kid? In what?"

"Alex needs help with science. Diego and I like to talk about astronomy, but he's hopeless in math, so we're working on that. And sometimes Amy needs help with her history. That's Jorge's girlfriend. She's taking all her prerequisites at San Jacinto

College, and the history classes throw her with all those dates." She delves into the shadows by the stairwell and stops. "They have quite a tight-knit group of friends and family that live here. I came across Alex and a few of his friends outside one day, struggling with a science project. They had to create a carrier that would hold and protect an egg when dropped from fifteen feet. When I asked if he needed help they laughed at me." Jackie smiles. "So I went to my apartment, made my own and ten minutes later snuck onto the roof and dropped it right next to Alex and his friends. All twelve of the eggs I dropped from over thirty feet were intact." She pushes her glasses up the bridge of her nose. "They didn't laugh so much after that," she says with a chuckle.

We both stand in silence for a moment before she shakes herself and steps back. "Okay, well, my apartment is up there, so no need to walk any further," she says, pointing up.

The dim lighting makes everything a bit more intimate, a bit more real. Her ponytail has swung around over her shoulder, the end resting on her chest where, no joke, an image of the periodic table is printed on her T-shirt. She slides her glasses up her nose and something inside me shifts. What started as me trying to prove I'm not an asshole has morphed into something else entirely.

Beautiful women in the past have always meant high society — expensive and social climbing. But Jackie is a different kind of beauty. She helps drunk college girls get home safe, works with astronauts and genuinely likes helping kids with their homework.

"Listen, I don't want to be pushy, but the broken lights above the stairwell have me feeling twitchy." Once again she looks up, as if seeing her surroundings for the first time. "The least I can do is make sure you get home safely, after I basically threw you out of my house last night."

Her brows draw together, shifting her glasses. "Okay, but it's on the third floor."

She says that like it's a negative, but I'm happy about it. Third floors are usually the last to be broken into because criminals have to carry stolen goods down two flights before they can make a getaway. I guess it might be cumbersome dragging groceries up three flights, especially as I'm sure this dump doesn't have an elevator. But safety first.

Waving her forward, I let Jackie lead the way. Either she works out, or she's been walking a hell of a lot due to her rundown car, 'cause the girl doesn't walk up the stairs, she bounces. It does such wonderful things to her ass while her pony-tail swings like a pendulum that I don't even mind the burn in my thighs from jogging up the stairs in my heavy work boots. But I can't fully appreciate it, as my mind is stuck on something.

"You let Paulie work on your car?"

"Yeah. I would've had him repair the dent, but Rose was pretty adamant she pay for it and I take it to your shop."

Something I'll have to thank Rose for later.

"Plus, I'm not sure Paulie has the equipment for body work." She pauses at the first landing, head tilted, like she's thinking this revelation over more fully. "Maybe he does. Hmmm... I should ask—"

"What shop does he work in?" I cut in, not wanting her to take her car to someone else. Least of all someone who may have done time.

"Huh?" She blinks, looking back at me. "Oh. Nowhere at the moment. He has trouble getting a job because of his record."

That confirms it.

"Listen," I say, leaning on the railing below her. "I'd be happy to fix your car whenever you need. You don't need to take it to an ex-con."

"He isn't just an ex-con. He's my friend." She doesn't look angry, just perplexed.

Which makes me feel like the judgmental asshole I used to be. The one I thought I'd left behind.

"Well, still," I mumble, "the offer is open, if you ever have car trouble."

She nods once, her glasses again shifting down her nose. "Thank you." She pushes her glasses back in place with her index finger, then continues walking up the next set of stairs.

"Also, if you ever want to take me up on the offer to learn manual transmission"—I use both thumbs to gesture to myself— "I'm your guy."

She laughs and some of the tension lifts. "Good to know." Jackie crests the top landing. "And thank you for the hotwire lesson and driving me home. I appreciate it." She walks over to her door, keys in hand. "Good night." She unlocks her one lone bolt and opens the door. "Thanks for the ride."

I lean in and kiss her cheek, which immediately blushes.

"Anytime, darling."

Eyes wide behind her glasses, Jackie keeps eye contact until the door is shut. I wait until I hear the bolt lock before turning and bounding my way down the steps.

SIX

LINE OF SIGHT

Jackie

SLIDING INTO MY DESK CHAIR AFTER A BRUTAL MEETING WHERE
Sean had obviously been going through caffeine withdrawal, I
check my phone screen. This is a new habit of mine since Operation
Social Life began. Usually my phone doesn't make an appearance
unless I need to adjust my schedule or check work emails on the fly.

Two text messages from Flynn.

One at 4:55 p.m.: *Car won't be ready*

Another at 5:15 p.m.: *You better text me when you're heading
home*

"What has you smiling?" my cube-mate, James, asks. "I heard
most of the EVA crew got their asses handed to them at the
meeting by Sean. Didn't think anyone would be smiling for a
while."

It's true. Sean was his usual uptight self. Only a few seem to
be immune from his exacting tendencies, and I'm one of them.
Probably because I have the same work ethic he does. Unfortunately, he's been even more on edge than usual, as EX-2 had a

random malfunction. It's probably a one-off, but without a back-up or the ability to power cycle, everyone is stressed.

James looks at me expectantly. I'm guessing that means his question isn't rhetorical.

I place my phone down on my desk and gather my stuff together in my purse. "Uh… nothing. Just a YouTube video."

He snorts. "What, another cat video going viral?"

I make a noncommittal sound, somewhere between a grunt and a hum, but it seems to work, as he turns back to his own desk. James is a good cube-mate. He never eats stinky food in our space and keeps his desk rather tidy. Even so, I'm not about to tell him I'm smiling like an idiot because a super-hot mechanic texted me. And he has been *all day*.

Though, oddly, I really, really want to.

"Don't forget, leftover kolaches in the break room," he says, eyes locked on his computer screen.

Another hum/grunt and then I'm walking out of our cubicle, phone in hand.

On my way out

Flynn sends a thumbs-up emoji in response.

Ugh. Emojis. Yet another language I'll need to learn how to decipher. I'm good with NASA acronyms, Russian and French. I'm hoping this new modern-day version of hieroglyphic writing will be easier to manage than that of the Egyptians.

Thumbs-up seems pretty self-explanatory, thankfully.

A few people wave as I walk by, some reminding me about the leftovers. I nod, but though I slow my steps when passing the breakroom, inhaling the savory sweet smell of kolaches, I keep moving.

When I told Flynn, via text, about my usual choice of meals, if you can call me scrounging for leftovers meals, he insisted on taking me out for a proper dinner after work tonight.

I was too shocked that he had actually shown up to drive me home to argue.

Not to say I didn't think he wouldn't show up when he said he would … but still. I'm having a hard time believing that auto repair shops make personal chauffeur services de rigueur. And definitely not dinner. I'm not sure what Flynn is up to, if anything. Maybe he's just a good guy doing a good deed. Why must I always question men's motives? I hate that my past has made me so paranoid.

Even so, I push open the security-locked door and speed walk toward NASA's west entrance with a smile on my face.

The sun is low in the sky, hovering over NASA as I walk across campus. It's still light out, so I don't know why Flynn wants to pick me up. It isn't like I'm going to be mugged with the sun out. Or even when it's down. The area around NASA is usually pretty safe.

But I'm not about to point that out. One, I'm sure he'd blow off my valid argument for some reason or another. Two, on the off-chance that he didn't, I'd be denying myself another ride in his kick-ass car. And three, you know, *Flynn*.

High humidity causes a mist of sweat to dust my skin and I'm thankful it's only in the high seventies. I won't be a complete sweaty mess by the time I reach Flynn. Just a somewhat sweaty mess.

The trees from the Challenger memorial throw shade over me as I walk by.

"Jackie. Need a ride?" A sleek silver car slows down beside me. Ian is looking quite nice in his white button-down shirt, silver tie and aviators.

I work very hard not to drop eye contact, but I can't help the blush that rushes under my skin. "Uh, no thanks. I'm, uh, meeting Flynn." I wave ahead of us. "In the badging lot."

"Is that right?" Ian's nostrils flare as he fights a smile. He loses the battle.

"Oh shut up," I mumble.

Ian just laughs. "You two drive safe, now."

Before I can respond, he pulls away and around the corner.

Since the Ian and Flynn episode the other day, Ian has been far more relaxed at work. I'm not sure what that is all about, but it's brought a sense of relief, as I'm no longer looking for nonexistent signs of attraction anymore. I can just focus on my job. Stupid Jules and her stupid innuendoes and blackmail. I knew Ian didn't like me that way.

Turning the corner, I have to pause and catch my breath. Not due to my power walk or the heat, but because my eyes are filled with the ridiculously breathtaking sight of Flynn leaning against his car, arms across his chest, biceps bulging. The same pose I found him in the other night.

"Yo," he calls out, making my smile widen.

"Hi, Flynn." *Sheesh.* I have to fight the urge to roll my eyes at how breathless I sound. Let's hope Flynn chalks it up to my walk.

"Lookin' good, darling." He pushes off the side of his car and walks toward me. The smell of him surrounds me when he leans down to kiss my cheek.

The heat radiating from under my skin has nothing to do with the temperature, but I'm going to pretend. I blame a lot on the weather in Texas. I'm also not sure if he's making fun of me. True, I traded in my usual T-shirt and jeans for a button-down and khakis, but it isn't glamorous by any means. I'm still sporting my well-loved Chucks.

He takes my bag from my hand, walks me around to the passenger side, and opens the door. He waits until I'm situated before placing my bag at my feet, closing the door and rounding the car again to slide in behind the wheel. I must be a pretty bad feminist, because I find his chivalry wildly attractive.

"You didn't eat yet, did you?" he asks, hands on the wheel.

"No. I remembered."

He nods, one hand drifting down to the ignition. The action has me sitting up straight, legs perfectly perpendicular to the seat, feet flat on the floor mat, palms resting on my thighs. The optimal position to make the most out of this moment.

This moment being when his hand cranks over the ignition, and the rumble from the engine filters through every point of contact I have with the car, sending chills and vibrations through me like the jet propulsion of the space shuttle in lift-off.

"You like sushi?"

"Hmm?" I blink, having to fidget on the seat to stop from coming right here in his car, parked at my work. *Get it together, Jackie.*

His lips do that twitching thing Ian's had earlier when he fought a smile. Paranoia sets in. People are always doing this around me, and I am *not* that funny.

"I said, 'you like sushi'?"

"Oh, ah, no." Shoot. Maybe I should've said yes?

"Thank God."

His response is so illogical that I can't help but laugh. "Then why did you ask?"

He shrugs, looking sheepish. "I don't know, the girls I knew usually liked sushi."

"Oh." Well, there go all the good feelings from the engine.

He clears his throat. "Never mind that, then. This is Houston, there are five restaurants on every corner. What would you like? French? Italian? We could go to Perry's. It's a Tuesday, pretty sure we won't have trouble getting a table."

I look down at my khakis. There is no way I want to go to the exclusive steakhouse in my work wear. Flynn's in jeans and he doesn't seem to care, but hello? Why would anyone object to him wearing jeans when he wears them the way he does? All sexy-like and stuff. Me in khakis? Not so much.

"What about Jimmy Johns?" I ask.

"Jimmy Johns," he repeats slowly. "The sub shop?"

I warm up to the idea. "Yeah, they have a killer Italian Hoagie." He just continues to look at me. Crapola. Now what did I do? "I mean, you *did* mention Italian," I mumble to my lap, twisting my fingers together.

His chuckle has me looking up. His hand lifts off the gear shift and I watch it as it ascends, his long, masculine fingers grazing my cheek lightly before dropping back down.

"Italian hoagies it is."

————

Flynn

"I'll have the number eight please, with salt and vinegar chips and a small drink," Jackie declares, bouncing on the toes of her sneakers.

It's true I've never really dated. Never took the time to get to know someone and how we'd fit together. Growing up, it was more like I'd hooked up with people in my social group, and some hookups lasted longer than others. And the only requirements were each other's family name and net worth. But I would've thought that adult dating would at least mean a sit-down restaurant with waiters, not a chalkboard menu with a pimple-faced cashier.

Jackie glances down at the rack of chips before her, missing the way the teenage boy at the counter checks her out. She grabs the bag and turns to me.

"Did you want an Italian hoagie too, or did you see something else you like?"

She says this with a straight face, brow creasing at my answering smirk. I don't think Jackie does innuendo. But it still makes me smile, because I *do* see something else I like— her. I don't know much about her family, how much she makes, what she'll inherit, and yet I like her.

"I'll have a number eight too. Plain chips, large drink," I tell the teenager, moving closer to Jackie so he can draw the correct conclusion that we're on a date.

And that is when I know I have it bad, when I feel the need to broadcast the fact I'm on a date to a pubescent teenager with wisps for a mustache.

Jackie digs in her purse for her wallet, but I stop her with my hand.

"I hope you don't find this forward, but where I grew up, ladies don't pay on dates."

Jackie blinks at me as I hand the cashier my card. "This is a date?"

The boy laughs, but he's nice enough to try and cover it up with a cough. Damn, this girl sure knows how to cut a man down at the knees. "Yes, Jackie. This is a date." My voice is a bit rougher than I meant it.

"Oh." She stares at me for a minute before the biggest, sexiest, most beautiful smile lights up her face. "Really?"

All the embarrassment fades in the face of the most clueless genius I've ever met. "Yes." I lean down, brushing my lips across hers, savoring her gasp at the contact. "Really."

We stare at each other, the moment broken when the cashier thrusts my credit card and our receipt with our order number on it toward me. Looking envious now instead of amused, he motions us to the side counter.

It only takes a minute for our number to be called. Jackie snags the last available booth while I fill up our drinks.

We eat in comfortable silence until I catch two guys across the room checking Jackie out as she licks the salt from the chips off her fingers. When she leans forward to sip her drink, wrapping her full lips around the straw, I know I'm not the only guy in here sporting wood. I chuckle at how oblivious to the attention she seems to be.

"What's so funny?" she asks, swiping her mouth with a napkin. She glances down at her shirt as if looking for spilled food.

"I was just thinking of something my grandfather used to say."

She uses her index finger to push up her glasses. "What's that?"

"He liked to tell my father that he couldn't see farther than the end of his nose."

She nods, grabbing another chip from the bag. "Ah, from Pope's *Essay on Man.*"

I blink. "Huh?"

"That saying." She pops the chip in her mouth, chewing softly before continuing. "It derives from Alexander Pope's *Essay on Man.* I think the quote is 'Onward still he goes, Yet ne'er looks forward farther than his nose.'"

I don't know why her brain continues to surprise me. She told me about her two masters degrees, one in physics, the other in aeronautics and astronautics, which she'd then followed up with a PhD. All before age twenty-nine. But every time she opens her mouth I'm astounded by her knowledge. It's so fucking sexy.

I try unsuccessfully to adjust myself under the table. "I think Grandpa will be sorely pissed he didn't come up with it himself, as much as he liked to throw it around."

Jackie laughs, and the sound soothes the rough edges from my hectic day at the shop. Being with Jackie is calming. No drama, no games. Just Jackie.

"Unless your grandfather was around in the early seventeen

hundreds, I don't think he can take credit." She smiles, reaching for another chip. "You'll have to let him down easy next time he says it."

"Gramps passed away. But I'm sure he's grumbling in his grave right about now."

"Oh." Her hands still. "I'm sorry."

I wave away her apology. "That's okay. It was quite a long time ago. He went out the way he wanted, riding horses. Old man never did know when to quit. Still tried wrangling horses at seventy-eight. Got thrown off a particularly angry stallion named Angus who didn't appreciate Gramps' attempts at breaking him in."

She's silent for a bit before asking, "Did you have to put the horse down?"

"Angus? Oh hell no. Gramps would've hated that." I take a long pull on my straw. "Good old Angus roamed the ranch until he passed."

"Ranch?"

"Uh, yeah. My family... they own a ranch. Northwest of Houston."

Shit. Dread pools in my gut. I hadn't realized how much I'd wanted Jackie to get to know me without the family baggage and riches until now.

"Wow," Jackie breathes, her eyes round, and the heaviness in my stomach grows. Our table shakes as she bounces her leg a mile a minute. I wait for her to put together my last name and the ranch and come to the million dollar conclusion. She'll ask about oil rights, beef prices—

"So you know how to ride a horse then? Rope a steer?"

I stare blankly at her, my mind not making the jump.

She blushes and the color travels down her neck. "I, uh...just wondered if you were, you know...a cowboy?"

I laugh, the release of all that dread making me feel lighter and happier than I'd thought possible. My laugh cuts off abruptly when Jackie looks down at her lap, shoulders hunching in.

"Sorry," I manage, trying to cover my laugh with a cough. "Sorry. It's just that…" I struggle to find words, not wanting to bring up money or my past experiences with women. "Here in Texas, being a cowboy isn't such a big deal. Your enthusiasm just threw me for a second." Her head stays down. Leaning over, I tilt up her chin with my hand, waiting until she meets my eyes. "I wasn't laughing at you, darling. Promise."

She nods once, but still averts her eyes as soon as I drop my hand. *Damn it.*

I take her hand, and she lets me, though her eyes stay down. "If your definition of a cowboy is someone who can ride a horse and rope steer, then sure, you can call me a cowboy."

Even with her eyes averted, I see her teeth bite down on her bottom lip, and I fight a groan as my jeans tighten further.

"Really?" With her free hand, she slides her glasses up the bridge of her nose.

"Yep." I take another sip of my cold soda, trying to cool down the surge of lust her fidgeting caused.

She looks up again, wonder in her eyes. "That is so cool," she breathes.

And then she's off, asking me questions about horse riding, roping, and cattle. Even asking if I wear a cowboy hat when I ride. I try to keep up with her quick mind and rapid-fire questions as best I can.

When she's finally exhausted all her questions, her breath comes in short bursts and her bottom lip is swollen from her teeth. And it hits me.

Holy shit. Jackie's got a thing for cowboys.

I can work with that.

SEVEN
BLACK FLAGGED

Jackie

WOW. FLYNN IS A COWBOY. A *COWBOY*.

He didn't even mind when I fan-girled over it earlier. Instead, his eyes softened and both sides of his mouth widened when he smiled, scattering my self-conscious thoughts from my mind like a meteor shower through space. It was almost peaceful going witless for a moment. Like a well-deserved nap for my brain.

"Are all the men in your family cowboys?"

"My brother is the most cowboy out of anyone in my family. He runs the ranch." Flynn runs a hand through his hair. "I was raised roping cattle and riding horses, but I took after my dad and fell in love with the horsepower in engines instead."

"Is your dad a mechanic too?"

Flynn's face blanks for a moment. "Uh, no. He wasn't. He raced cars, actually."

My stomach drops. "Was?"

"Yeah, he and my mom died in a car crash a while back."

I close my eyes and sigh. Really, how many times can I put my foot in my mouth on one date. My face must mirror my inner turmoil, because Flynn's quick to reassure me. "Really, it's okay. You didn't know." He squeezes my hand. "We weren't that close, really. They were always off on the racing circuit. Gramps was the one to raise us. After Gramps and my parents died, Holt stepped up and got custody."

Silence deepens for a moment.

"My mother died right after I was born," I blurt. "Cardiomyopathy. They didn't know she had it. It wasn't until her heart failed twelve days after I was born that they realized."

He's quiet for a minute, giving my hand another squeeze. "Jackie. I'm so sorry."

I nod. I don't usually tell people that, but I figure if I know about his parents, he should know about mine.

"It's really okay. It's hard to miss someone when you don't have any memory of them."

"But you can still miss not having a mom." He brushes his fingers across my face, tucking a tendril behind my ear.

"I guess." I'm not sure of what else to say. Leave it to me to bring out the depressing stuff on my first ever date.

"What about your dad?"

"My dad? Oh, he's great. I mean, we don't talk a lot or anything, but we have scheduled check-ins. He is *very* regimented. Once every other week, with additional calls on our birthdays and Christmas if they fall on the alternate weeks. Otherwise it's just email." He gives me a look, so I rush to explain. "He's really busy with his work. He's a chemical engineer back East where I grew up." I smile, hoping he doesn't think my relationship with my father is weird. I get that others might think it is, but it works for my dad and me. And really, Flynn doesn't need to think me any weirder than he probably already does. "We may not talk as much as other families do, but he's never made me feel bad about being different."

"Different? You mean super smart?" he asks, his tongue slipping out to catch the straw in his mouth. My mind momentarily blanks.

"Huh? Uh, yeah, I guess that's a good enough descriptor." I concentrate on folding up my sandwich wrapper. Wondering if it would be too weird to fold it into something.

"Was it a problem being that smart?" He reaches for another chip. "I can't even imagine."

I talk while folding down the corners of the wrapper. "At first it was just frustrating. It was like I knew everything before my teachers taught it. I was, and *am*, a voracious reader. I've always had my nose in a book." I fold the right and left sides back up, making a diamond shape. "And when teachers would catch me reading instead of paying attention, they'd try to call me out on it, asking me questions. But I only made them mad because I could answer any question they asked." I pause to push my glasses back up, then press down on the folds, sharpening the creases. "I mean, it's not like I'm *that* smart. I—"

"Jackie."

Flynn's voice startles me and I look up into his serious expression.

"You *are* that smart. And there's nothing wrong with that. You should be proud—it's cool." His fingertips graze my cheekbone. "And super sexy."

I cough on my own inhale like the super smooth person I am, and go back to concentrating on my wrapper folding. "Well, it isn't cool when you get skipped up two grades and no one wants to be friends with the twelve-year-old who can outsmart them. And it isn't all that sexy when every dance, football game and weekend, I was home alone because I didn't have a date or friends." I shrug and fold the bottom part of the wrapper up to meet the diamond, then flip the whole thing over. "Then when I entered college at sixteen, people mistook me for the professors' kid, when I was, in fact, their T.A." I tuck the top folds down into the pocket I made from the bottom fold and flip it over once more.

"Wow, Jackie." Flynn picks up what is now a somewhat grease-spotted, but expertly folded, heart-shaped sandwich wrapper. "Can I keep this?"

"Uh, sure." I shrug, my embarrassment lifting in the face of Flynn's surprising awe over a bit of origami. "I can make you a better one, though, if you want. You know, with non-greasy paper and all."

Flynn reaches back and pulls out his wallet. "No," he says, while carefully sliding the heart inside. "This is perfect."

I smile. He really is. Perfect.

―――――

BACK AT MY APARTMENT COMPLEX, my nerves resurge. Flynn has the ability to both calm my mind and get my electrical synapses firing, all at the same time. It's a unique gift of his that defies all scientific logic and leaves me, frankly, bewildered. He is uniquely gifted that way.

He's been nothing but a gentleman. Driving me home, walking me to the door, leaving after what I am sure was a platonic kiss on my cheek. But tonight he mentioned a date. That we were definitely on a date. That changes things. Once you classify an object there are certain details and assumptions to be made based on the definition of that classification.

Such as kisses. Dates usually have kisses, don't they? And not the cheek kind.

I should've read up on this.

"Wait," he says, jumping the last two steps onto the landing.

I pause, not realizing I have basically run up the stairs to my door. "Oh. Sorry." I'm out of breath again. I run up these stairs all the time without issue, but I'm still blaming them for my lack of oxygen.

Flynn steps closer to me, his hand pushing back the end of my ponytail. Goosebumps blanket my skin.

"I'd like to see you again."

"Really?" Had he not been on the date I'd been on? I'm pretty sure bringing up multiple family deaths, traumas of my childhood and crafting with trash at the table are not the standards to which Flynn should hold his dates.

He steps back, running his hand through his hair. "I mean, if you want to. I don't want to force you on another date. Especially as it didn't seem you knew you were on the first one."

"No!" I half-shout, while jumping up on my toes. His head jerks back. "No, I mean, yes," I say quieter, "I would like to go out on another date with you." Somehow my head is bobbing along to the bounce of my feet.

Holy Mercury. What is *wrong* with me?

A large smile overtakes Flynn's face and now I couldn't care less if I'm doing the Macarena in front of him. He has the *best* smile.

"Good." He steps closer again. "That's good."

Then his nose is nuzzling the side of my neck, skimming upward to my ear.

"This okay?" he whispers.

I nod my head once, trying to remind myself to breathe.

"You smell so good, Jackie."

"Pheromones."

Flynn pauses, pulling back a bit. "I'm sorry?"

"Pheromones." I look up at the ceiling, trying to focus my thoughts. "Men and women send and receive subconscious odor signals. These odor signals are called pheromones, which are airborne chemical messengers released from the body that have a physical or emotional effect on another member of the same species."

From the corner of my eye I see Flynn tilt his head to the side. "I'm smelling pheromones?"

"Yes." I nod. "You are probably sensing my pheromones through the vomeronasal organ, which is then relayed to the hypothalamus, which, as you know, is responsible for emotions, hormones, and sexual behavior."

"Ah yes." Flynn dips back down to my neck, inhaling again. "The hypothalamus."

I shiver. I don't know if he knows he's doing it, but ever since he's encroached on my personal space, Flynn's Southern twang has deepened. Between his proximity, the vibrations of his accent and the gentle scrape of his stubble against my neck, I'm going to need to change my panties ASAP. My hypothalamus is definitely working overtime right now.

His left hand cups the side of my head, the touch forcing my gaze to his.

"I'm going to kiss you now."

I feel my eyes widen. I'm ninety percent sure he doesn't mean on the cheek.

"You okay with me kissing you?"

I can't find my voice in order to seek clarification on the placement of said kiss, so I simply nod.

He leans in slowly, eyes not leaving mine until the last moment, right before our lips meet and I close my eyes. The kiss is gentle, light, like the ones I've felt before. But then he presses deeper and my whole body jolts, stiffening with shock. He pulls back, a question in his eyes.

"Uh, sorry?" I say, not entirely sure why I'm apologizing, except for the fact that he's probably kissed more girls than I have guys. Girls who probably don't overthink and freeze up when they're turned on. Girls who know what the heck they are *doing*.

Instead of being annoyed, or worse, laughing at me, Flynn smiles softly, his eyes gentle. Then he makes me giggle when he rubs the end of his nose against mine. I love Eskimo kisses.

"Want to try that again, darling?"

With his playful kisses and kind words, some of the tension drops from my shoulders and my nerves float away. I want this. I want *him*. I somehow need to show him how very much I want him, even if my kissing technique is unpracticed.

Keeping my eyes on his, I drop my keys, the metal clanging on the concrete. Slowly, but firmly, I drag my hands up his arms, along his neck and up into his hair, my fingers lightly digging across his scalp, angling his head lower.

"Yes," I whisper before I press my mouth to his. My touch probably lacks finesse, but Flynn doesn't seem to mind. And when his tongue slides across the seam of my mouth, something breaks inside me and I moan.

Suddenly my hands are everywhere. Gripping his shoulders, dragging down and up under his T-shirt. My God, the feel of his skin, it's indescribable. I don't have long nails, and I'm thinking that is a good thing for Flynn, otherwise he'd have claw marks all over his torso by now.

Flynn brings one hand to my ass and hauls me against him. This time the moan rips from his throat. My glasses are skewed when Flynn finally draws back from our kiss. Gently, using the tips of his fingers, he rights them before once again touching his nose to mine.

"Never thought a genius could kiss like that."

All good feelings vanish. Suddenly I'm transported back to college, overhearing the boys outside of my class asking my new boyfriend if the nerd he was banging was any good. How he'd laughed and said, "Not yet, but she will be when I'm done with her." There hadn't been any question about who they were talking about. Who the nerd was. I'm always the nerd. The genius. The odd one.

I look down at the toes of my Chucks, peeking out from the hem of my khaki pants. "I see." My voice is stilted, my body back to being rigid.

Sensing the change, Flynn frowns, ducking down to try and meet my eyes.

I don't let him. Instead I squat down, swipe my keys up from the floor and pop up in one quick move.

"Now that you've satisfied your curiosity, I'm sure you have more important things to do than kiss the nerd." I unlock my door, thankful I get the correct key on the first try. I step inside and turn back, the vision of Flynn burned into my mind right before I slam the door.

Stalking into my bedroom, I sit on the edge of my bed, listening to him knock on my door and call my name a few times, mumbling about this not being over. Thankfully, I soon hear his boots stomp away from the apartment.

At that moment all I can think of is that I really should move as the doors don't seem very secure if you can hear so well through them.

But later, when I'm in bed, running through the whole date, looking for the signs I may have missed about Flynn being disingenuous, I find nothing. Instead, I see his face, right before I slammed my feeble front door on it.

He hadn't looked smug or satisfied. He'd look confused and upset.

And I have a horrible, sinking feeling that I'm not as smart as I think I am.

EIGHT
POWER CYCLE

Jackie

"Houston, we have a problem."

I sigh. Tom Hanks' voice from one of my favorite movies, which I'd turned into my text notification, is quickly becoming the most annoying sound in the universe. This is the second day since we kissed that Flynn has blown up my phone. I haven't gotten any work done today. Flynn, it seems, does not know when to quit. And still I don't know what to make of our kiss.

The text messages started out innocuous enough. *What'd I do?* and *I'm sorry.*

When I didn't answer, the texts changed. *Earth is the largest planet, right? Elon Musk should run NASA.*

It's getting harder not to respond.

Flynn: *What's your favorite planet? Mine's Pluto.*

He has to be joking. Tom Hanks speaks again.

Flynn: *It was named after my favorite Disney character.*

Okay. That's too much.

Jackie: *Pluto was discovered in 1930, before the creation of Mickey's canine companion. This is a moot point anyway. Pluto was stripped of planetary status in 2006 and reclassified as a dwarf planet by the IAU.*

Jackie: *Stop texting me.*

I don't get it. If I was right, and he was just messing with me when he kissed me, then why bother texting? Has his pride taken a hit because I called him on his game of 'kiss the nerd'? *And* if I was wrong, which is highly improbable but still statistically possible, then why would he want to talk to the crazy girl who kissed him like a porn star then slammed the door in his face? There is no way a guy like him—tall, sexy, and immensely cool—would want to be with a clueless, inexperienced geek like me. It just doesn't make sense. I don't like things that don't make sense.

My phone sounds again.

Flynn: *IAU? The Interstellar Astronaut University?*

I roll my eyes. He has to be messing with me.

Jackie: *No. International Astronomical Union.*

Jackie: *And stop texting me.*

"Jackie, what did you think of the EVA proposal I emailed you?"

Startled, I jump in my seat, causing my chair to roll back a few feet from the desk. Ian is leaning up against the edge of my cubicle.

Another reason to be aggravated with Flynn. He's taking away time and brain space I need for work. I use my heels to walk my chair back to my desk and turn to Ian.

"Sorry. I didn't get a chance to read it. What'd it say?"

One of Ian's eyebrows arches up. "I sent it first thing this morning."

Seeing as it's past lunch, I should have read it.

"Sorry, I've been, uh, really busy with the..."

"Don't worry about it. I'll run it by Sean."

"Sorry. Really. I'm just a bit...preoccupied."

Ian grins and turns back into my cubicle. Or, as I like to think of it, my personal command center. James is nowhere to be found. Another reason he's a great cube-mate.

I'm lucky in that our cubicle backs to an actual window. Windows at NASA are like a rare hybrid eclipse. They exist, but no one really believes it until they see one. Especially in the older, space race era buildings, when the U.S. thought the Russians were spying on them. Which, you know, they were. But still, now it's like working in the Bat Cave.

"I was just thinking about The Progress supply shuttle going up soon," Ian explains. "I know we have new software going up to install on the old EXT, but I made an additional EVA plan should we want to incorporate a procedure to attach a protective panel to shield the external wires."

"Yes." I nod, thinking through his idea. "Totally agree. The odds are astronomically against this happening again, but we thought that before the main computer wires got hit too. I'm actually surprised there's any external wiring left on the station, let alone these two vital computers. We should reposition and run everything internally."

Ian nods as I speak. We're often in agreement on space-related updates.

"But good luck getting Sean on board, or the higher-ups to fund the materials or the EVAs needed to accomplish that," I continue, letting my exasperation show.

He chuckles and sighs. "Yeah, I know. The odds of that happening are probably lower than wires getting hit with more space junk."

We share a familiar smile. It's nice having someone who speaks my language, so to speak. But looking into Ian's pretty face, I can't help but wonder if he knows how to hotwire a car.

———

"BEEP. BEEP."

I've finally given Flynn his own personal ring and text tone. He'd been destroying my love for one of the best movies ever made and the voice of one of the finest actors. I can't let that continue. I don't watch car movies. Or I hadn't. Yet. I might have bought a few on Amazon this week. *Fast and the Furious. Gone in Sixty Seconds. American Graffiti.* For research. No correlation to a certain mechanic. Nope.

Anyway. I don't know any car movie quotes. So Flynn gets a car honk for his ring tone.

Flynn: *The moon landing was a hoax.*

He. Did. Not.

Jackie: *High definition photos taken by the Lunar Reconnaissance Orbiter have shown evidence of the Apollo landing site and the actual tracks left by the astronauts. In addition, the photographic evidence also reveals that five of the six flags put up by the Apollo 11 crew still stand on the moon today.*

Flynn: *Photoshop.*

Jackie: *Seriously. Stop texting me.*

―――――

ROSE AND TRISH have stayed in contact all week. Though I'm careful not to tell Rose when I get off work, in case she decides to tell Flynn. I don't need him showing up again. At least, I tell myself that, even though I miss his car. Just his car.

I'm thinking our recent texting is safer than face-to-face contact. Even if he is the world's most annoying texter.

I've actually had to call my cell phone provider and change my plan to unlimited texting. The phone guy was astounded that I hadn't already had that plan. Like I'm the only holdout in the world of continuous texting under the age of thirty.

Rose says she's turning over a new leaf, which includes

ditching toxic friends. I'm not entirely sure what that means, except that I must not be toxic as she's declared us new besties. This both delights and frightens me. Trish is new to the area and seems amused to be besties with a twenty-one-year-old co-ed and a NASA geek.

I guess I'm turning one over myself. I've started looking at houses for sale in the area, and even called my financial planner about liquefying some of my investments. A new car and a house don't come cheap.

Jules would be so proud of me if she wasn't too busy being distracted with the potential failings of the ISS. Luckily, there haven't been any more random failures with the EX-2 since our last meeting.

I keep thinking about the cherry red GTO and Flynn's Mustang. I've done a bit of research, and though not necessarily expensive to buy, the upkeep on vintage cars is a pain. My research also shows that although relatively new to the area, Flynn's garage is the best reviewed and most trusted in a sixty-mile radius for rebuilds and maintenance on vintage cars. I'm not sure any car is worth putting myself in Flynn's hands, albeit mechanical, in the future.

Rose never mentions Flynn. Part of me wants to ask her, "What the heck is with your brother?" But the bigger part of me doesn't want her to take sides. 'Cause I'm pretty sure family trumps the girl who drove you home after getting shit-faced. Declared bestie or not.

Work is stressful, but the girls keep me amused via group text.

Trish: *Did you ever get boots?*

Jackie: *No*

Rose: *How do you not have boots?*

Trish: *She's an engineer. Engineers don't have cowboy boots.*

Rose: *That's racist.*

Jackie: *I'm pretty sure that is not the definition of racist.*

Rose: *It should be.*

Trish: *You can borrow mine. See how you like them.*

Jackie: *That's okay.*

Trish: *What? My boots not good enough for you?*

Jackie: *No. That's not it.*

Trish: *Then what is it? You don't like my style?*

Rose: *You've gone and pissed off the Southern midget now, Jackie.*

Trish: *I'm not a midget, damn it!*

Rose: *Tell me the truth, did you stomp your tiny foot after you texted that?*

Trish: *I hate you.*

Jackie: *Calm down, both of you!*

Jackie: *I have big feet, okay? They won't fit.*

Trish: *Oh.*

Rose: *If you were a boy, big feet would mean a big ding dong.*

———

MY THUMBS HURT. From texting.

I can't decide whether to be disgusted with myself or proud. Stretching my arms overhead, I push myself deeper into the couch, while also flexing my sore thumbs. Doors slam, people pound up and down the stairs... the white noise of my apartment complex washes over me, allowing the stress of my day to drift away.

"Beep. Beep."

I close one eye and squint at my phone, which is lying face down on the coffee table. I can feel my heartrate accelerate.

Studies have shown that every time a person receives a call or a text, their brain releases a shot of dopamine into their system. Dopamine is created naturally in various parts of the brain and is critical to thinking, moving, sleeping, mood, etc. Dopamine also causes you to want, desire, seek out and search. It increases your level of arousal and is most powerfully stimulated when given small amounts of information that doesn't fully satisfy the system, i.e., a text message. Text messages are akin to drinking alcohol, doing drugs and having sex.

So it isn't my fault that in six days I have gone from frustration to excitement at the sound of Flynn's ringtone. And that even though I know I shouldn't, I reach out and pick it up off my coffee table, eyes glued to the screen.

It's science.

Flynn: *I love when you talk smart to me.*

I'm losing whatever game he's playing. Because a big part of me *really* wants to believe him. Another part of me knows from experience that he's so far out of my league it's astronomically unreal.

"Beep. Beep."

Flynn: *It gets me hard.*

Annnnnd…brain shutdown.

I can do nerdy. I can lecture on astronomy and combat the musings of weird conspiracy theorists. But what am I supposed to do with *that*?

I switch the volume off my phone and shove it between the cushions of my couch.

NINE
JUMP START

Jackie

Whisper-light touches lick my body.

"Please," I beg.

"Please, what?" His voice is soft, but rough. Chills race down my neck.

"Please." I raise my arms, wanting to touch him. But he isn't there.

"Tell me what you want." His voice is harder now, demanding.

"Flynn..."

Bang! Bang! Bang!

I sit up so fast I nearly roll off the couch. What's that noise? My heart? It could be. I mean, I can feel it pulsing against my rib cage, audible even with all the heavy breathing I'm doing. That dream. Heck, *all* of the dreams. My Flynn fantasies have put my vibrator out of commission.

Bang! Bang! Bang!

Oh, it's not my heart. It's the door.

"Open up, slut!" A familiar voice accompanies another round of door banging.

"Rose?" I call out.

"Yeah, and I've got Trish-the-Dish with me."

"You're calling me Trish-the-Dish now? Really?"

"Would you prefer Southern Midget?"

I struggle up from the couch as their argument, clear even through the apartment door, helps chase away the remnants of my dream. I take a deep breath and slowly let it out, slowing my racing heart. Once I'm satisfied that I don't sound like a marathon runner, I unlock the door. Before I can open it an inch, it's thrust back in my face and both Rose and Trish march in.

"Um, hello?" I ask, stepping back to accommodate them.

"Girl, we're here to rescue you." Trish is holding multiple shopping bags on each arm. She turns one way and then another, looking over my apartment and nearly knocking me back on the couch in the process.

"Sweet sofa," Rose says, gesturing to the comfortable, mid-century modern piece of furniture I just napped on.

I don't have much in my apartment. I guess I've always thought of this place as temporary, even though I've been a bit too preoccupied with work to move. But what I do have I splurged on. The green tweed couch is something John Glenn would've sat on, and my white, marble-topped, circular tulip table barely fits next to the galley kitchen. But it's awesome, so I got it.

"What are you doing in this place if you can afford things like that?" Trish says, gesturing to the kitchen table.

"I don't know. Never got around to finding another place, I guess." I run my hand down the sofa's arm. "But I always thought that when I did, it would look like…" I trail off, not wanting to admit the truth, my face heating with embarrassment.

"That it would look like something out of the space race era?" Rose asks, clearly catching on.

I lower my head, studying the clean but dingy carpet. "Uh, yeah."

"Cool. Very you," Trish says.

I jerk my head up, wondering if she's making fun of me, but Trish's usual sincere expression relieves that worry.

"You'd love my brother's place then," Rose says.

This piques my interest. I didn't get a good look inside Flynn's house the night I dropped Rose off. All the lights were out, and honestly, I was too distracted by a shirtless Flynn.

But before I can sort out a clever way to ask what Rose means without being completely obvious, she changes the subject.

Rose thrusts a finger in my direction. "You've been working all week and blowing off our texts."

I blink, unprepared for the accusation. "I have not. I texted back." I flex my sore thumbs as proof.

Trish rolls her eyes at me. "What about the ones from today? You never answered us."

I turn and dig my phone out from under the couch cushions. Ten texts and four missed calls. None from Flynn.

Not that I'm keeping track or anything.

"Oh. Sorry. I didn't see them."

"Yeah, well, just so you know, your apartment complex is a shit hole. It matches your car." Rose opens my bedroom door and leans in to flip the switch.

"Wait!" But it's too late.

"Holy shit, Jackie," she says, standing in my bedroom doorway, looking in.

"What?" Trish shakes the shopping bags off her wrists and hurries over to Rose, who has now walked into the room.

Great. Just great. I follow after them.

When I moved in, I'd known it wasn't the best apartment. But it was close to work and the landlord had seemed to like me, which could be because I paid a year's rent in advance. One less thing to have to think about and all that. This in turn had made my landlord deliriously happy. Happy enough to let me redecorate a bit.

With his permission, I'd set out to make my bedroom my haven. My nerdy, hopelessly romantic haven.

Almost everything is white. White walls, white curtains, white pillows, and the fluffiest white down comforter I could find.

"They let you paint the ceiling?" Trish asks.

I shrug.

Everything is white but the ceiling. That I painted black, swirled with the darkest, deepest midnight blue I could find, with a hint of burgundy and a light swirl of silver. Then splattered with high-end, glow-in-the-dark paint. It took a week to get the colors melded the way I wanted. And another to get all the glow-in-the-dark paint out of my hair.

Research proves that people who get a solid night's sleep have a stronger memory recall. When your brain rests, regions for making and storing memories talk to each other. Good sleep promotes consolidation, the process of transferring memories from temporary memory storage in the hippocampus to long-term storage in the neocortex. All of which is why I spent so much energy on my bedroom.

And maybe also because the all-white color pallet makes it easy for me to pretend that I'm an astronaut up in the International Space Station, staring into the abyss of space.

Rose is looking over the multiple stacks of books I have around the room. Besides the ceiling, they are the only splash of color in there. I have books stacked into the shape of a nightstand next to my bed, as well as the large, floor-to-ceiling bookshelf along one wall. Trish comes up beside her and I start to sweat while they peruse my book collection in silence.

This is the one place I let my nerd flag fly free. I love books. I love learning new things. A lot of my books are on topics like astronomy, math, and engineering. But mostly, I love all the dirty, sweaty, cowboy sex fantasies between the pages of my romance novels.

Trish's fingers linger over one of my favorite romance series by Audrey Cole. She looks back at me, hand still on the romances, and winks. I can't decipher Rose's expression. She may be young. She may look country sweet. Though I have a feeling all of that is just a façade, and Rose is the architect of many machinations.

"Damn, girl." She kicks the side of her mouth up into a grin.

I let out a breath I didn't know I'd been holding. I'm not used to having anyone in my apartment. In fact, I'm pretty sure no one has been in my apartment since I moved in over a year ago. And no one on this green Earth knows about my romance novels. Jules doesn't count, as she's currently in orbit.

Rose looks at me in that calculating way again, but as I brace for whatever she might say, she spins away and heads to my closet.

"Let's see what we have to work with," she says, opening the doors. She throws me a look over her shoulder and shakes her head. "Seriously?"

"What?"

Trish moves next to Rose. "Oh, sweetie, this is so sad."

"*What*?" I repeat. I have clothes. Good clothes. All my T-shirts are in my dresser. The closet is reserved for work apparel. I've spent a good amount of money on some of those dress pants. I even have a nice shift dress that the lady at Joseph A. Banks called "classic." I mean, I've never worn it, the tags are probably still on it, but Rose and Trish don't know that.

"It's like a cross between *Working Girl* and *Revenge of the Nerds*," Rose whispers.

Trish leaves the room and returns with the shopping bags. "No worries—we've come prepared," Trish sings, all sunshine and roses as she dumps the bags on the bed.

"Makeover!" Rose and Trish exclaim together, like they've practiced or something.

My immediate reaction is to hide. Literally walk into my closet, close the doors on myself and wait for them to leave. But that would be weird. Right?

I force myself to I think about Operation Social Life. Then I look at the pile of sequins, boots, cosmetics, spaghetti straps, and is that... yes, that is a thong.

I flex my sore thumbs, plaster a smile on my face and manage, "Yeah. Makeover. Whoo hoo."

Death row inmates have sounded more chipper, I'm sure.

————

"SO HOW DO you feel about blow jobs?" Rose asks.

I cough on the sip of rum and Coke I've just taken.

"Or sex on the beach?" she continues.

I look to Trish, thinking the question must be for her, but she's eyeing me expectantly. Well, so be it.

Squaring my shoulders, I adjust my glasses and reply. "I think maybe the logistics of having sex on the beach would be counter-intuitive to the ultimate goal. I would think intimacy would be hard to achieve if one was in pain from the abrasive friction from sand in one's nether regions."

Rose looks confused for a second, then bursts out laughing. "I mean *shots*. You know, a Blow Job, the one with Baileys and whipped cream? Or Sex on the Beach, made with vodka and schnapps?"

We're back in Big Texas Saloon. I'm having a bona fide girls' night. Operation Social Life is succeeding. I can't believe it. It's enough to make me forget what my two new friends have dressed me in. Well, almost. It's hard to forget when you have a piece of lace wedged up your backside.

Unexpected new information has been gathered tonight: thongs are the devil.

"Oh." My face heats. "I've never had one of those before."

Rose's mouth falls open. "Never?" She turns to Trish. "You work here, why aren't there shots on this table?"

"I'm off tonight, sassy pants."

"So? Use your connections. For heaven's sake, this is an emergency."

"How is this an emergency?"

"Because this girl"—Rose thumbs in my direction—"has turned down not one, but two men who asked her to dance. She won't stop fidgeting in her new outfit, *and* she is determined to ignore my brother who has called and texted her like, a bajillion times this week." She slaps her hand on the table. "We need shots."

I don't know if I'm supposed to respond or not, but I feel the need to defend myself. "I don't know *how* to dance."

I tuck the fact that Rose knows about my Flynn situation away for later.

"Fine." Trish stands up on the top rung of her bar stool, which is quite a feat considering the four-inch heels she's wearing, and waves both arms overhead like a ramp service agent flagging down a plane on the tarmac. She gets the attention of the bartenders all right, along with everyone else. "We need three Blow Jobs and three Sex on the Beaches over here!" she yells, arms still overhead.

One of the bartenders laughs and nods in our direction.

Trish sits back down, ignoring the commotion she's just caused. She eyes my chest. "I'm telling you, if I had known what was under those T-shirts and jeans you wear, Jackie, I would've worn my push-up bra." Trish reaches into her dress and pulls her breasts up in her bra. A few men stumble as they walk past.

I laugh. "Trish, I think you just gave that man a mild coronary."

Trish winks. "I still got it then."

"Don't think I didn't notice how you ignored the Flynn comment," Rose says, redirecting the conversation. "And I know you're not gay, 'cause even my slutty ass was intrigued by the filth you had on your bookshelves."

"It's not filth! And don't call yourself a slut. I swear, between you and Jules, you are both setting womankind back decades." I peer over the edge of my glasses and try to look admonishing. She rolls her eyes, so I'm thinking I need to work on that.

"Jackie likes herself some cowboys," Trish puts in. "No wonder you like it here."

"These guys aren't really cowboys." Rose waves in the general direction of the bar and dance floor. "I'll take you to the ranch sometime. You'll be in heaven."

"Ranch?" Trish asks.

"Yeah, my family's cattle ranch is about two hours from here."

"Wait." Trish puts her hand up. "Your family has a ranch?" Trish's light expression has changed to one of concentration. Maybe Trish has a thing for cowboys too. "West. Rose West." Trish's eyes go round. "You mean your family owns *the* West Ranch?" At Rose's slight nod Trish's mouth falls open. For the first time since I've known her, Rose looks uncomfortable. And once again I'm confused.

Rose looks visibly relieved when the bartender comes by with our tray of shots.

"Now ladies, you just let me know if you get another craving for a Blow Job or Sex on the Beach. I'll be more than happy to oblige."

Bouncing back from the awkward moment, Rose laughs and playfully slaps his arm. "You'll be the first to know, sweetie." She checks out his ass as he walks away.

Trish makes a face. "Ew. No. That's Craig. There isn't a hole he hasn't plowed around here."

"Then he should know what he's doing," Rose mutters under her breath as another man walks up to the table. He's tall, and good-looking in an older man sort of way.

Without asking, he takes my hand and moves to usher me to the dance floor.

"I'm sorry, but I don't dance." I pull my hand from his grasp. His nice smile vanishes before he walks away.

"What a douche. Didn't even ask, just *assumed* you'd want to dance with him." Rose snorts. "Men."

I'm too amused to be annoyed. I find it funny how, in just a week, I've gone from being alone at a bar, with no friends and no one asking me to dance, to turning down men and sitting with friends.

Operation Social Life for the win.

"What are you thinking about with that smile?" Trish asks.

I pick up the least dangerous looking shot on the table, the overhead lights illuminating the red liquid. "Just thinking that I'll have to thank Jules for blackmailing me the next time we talk."

"Hell yeah, you do." Rose raises her own Sex on the Beach shot and clinks it to mine. "Drink up, bitches!"

I watch her and Trish swallow the contents in one gulp.

"Why didn't you drink? It's bad luck to cheers and then not drink," Trish informs me.

"It is?"

"Well, if it isn't, it should be." Trish gestures to my drink. "Knock it back, girl."

"Here here!" Rose pushes the glass closer to my lips.

It smells like cough syrup, so I'm dubious. Still, I take a

deep breath, tilt my head back and let the liquor slide down my throat. My eyes water a bit, but besides that, it tastes sticky sweet.

"I may need to rethink Sex on the Beach," I say, licking my lips. "It's delicious."

Rose laughs. "Girl, you just need sex, be it on the beach or up against the wall over there."

"I just need a new vibrator," I mutter.

Trish and Rose laugh so hard they lay their heads on their folded arms on the table to try to catch their breath.

Trish lifts her head slightly and wipes the tears from under her eyes. "Listen, I am the first to praise the invention of the vibrator —I've got three all in different shapes, with different settings. One for every occasion, as it were. But, sugar, you're smart and lovely. I don't see any reason why you can't let a man, a man who knows what he's doing, pick up the slack in the bedroom department."

The warmth spreading over my body is probably a combination of embarrassment and liquor. But I'm pretty sure it's just the liquor that has me sharing, "Men suck."

"If you ask them nicely, they might." Trish's mouth curls up at the side.

"And bite too." Rose mimics a cat, clawing the air.

"Whatever," I huff.

"Did you just 'whatever' us?" Rose looks at Trish. "The great and glorious smarty-pants NASA engineer 'whatever'ed us."

This time the warmth definitely comes from embarrassment. "Never mind."

"Oh, no you don't, Jackie," Trish butts in. "I've been waiting for your man-story ever since I clapped eyes on you sitting alone in this bar. Give it to me, girl."

"Man-story?"

"Don't deflect," Trish scolds.

I sigh and take a big sip of my drink. "Nothing to tell really. I just don't see the appeal of men."

"You realize that's a crock of shit, right? Especially after we saw those slut books you like," Rose says.

"They aren't slut books! They're *romance*," Trish says, sounding surprisingly defensive on my behalf.

Rose puts both hands up. "Okay, okay. Ix-nay on the lut-say."

I study the swirl of whipped cream mounded onto the other shots on the table. "Did you know Pig Latin predates Shakespeare? But it used to be called Dog Latin." Rose and Trish just blink at me. "Anyway," I drawl out, "I'm smart enough to know the difference between romance novel fantasy sex and reality."

"Oh, girl. If you think good sex is just a fantasy, then you truly do need to get laid. And STAT." Rose leans over and pats my hand. "But before that you need to tell Auntie Rose all about it."

"Let's just do another shot." I reach for the complicated Blow Job, but Rose smacks my hand away. "Hey!"

"No shot until you spill."

"Fine." I straighten my shoulders. "When I was in grad school, I was a T.A."

"Tits and ass?" Rose gasps. "You were a stripper!"

Trish rolls her eyes at Rose.

"A teaching assistant! Sheesh." I push my glasses up. "Anyway, I taught what a lot of people called the Jock class—remedial math. It's the course all the athletes took hoping for an easy A."

Rose smirks. "Were they hot for teacher?"

Trish shoves her shoulder. "Let the girl finish."

"Sorry." Rose waves for me to continue.

"It's okay. I guess you could say they were hot for teacher. Or I thought one of them was at least." I pause, thinking back.

"What do you mean?" Rose asks.

"Growing up, it was always hard to make friends. I skipped

two grades, so I was always a lot younger than my classmates. But in this class, I was pretty much the same age as all the students." I watch the mirror ball rotate above the dance floor. "He was a baseball player named Brian Hampson."

"Holy shit." Trish slaps the table. "*The* Brian Hampson?"

"You know him?" I hadn't taken Trish for a baseball fan.

"I know *of* him. The Houston Astros just signed him as their shortstop. And, I mean, did you *see* that underwear ad he did for Nike?" She fans her face. "He is *hot.*"

"Yes. He's definitely hot," I mutter.

"So what happened?" Rose pulls us back to the story.

"He was the first person I ever slept with."

"You gave up your virginity to Brian freaking Hampson?" Rose yells.

"Shhhhh!" I admonish.

"Hell, girl, if you were going to wait that long, I say Brian Hampson was the way to go." Trish salutes me with her drink. "Well done."

"I guess if you look at it that way. But it was all just a game to him."

"What do you mean?" Rose asked.

"All leading up to it, he acted sincere. He took me out. Introduced me to his friends. Held my hand at parties. It was... it was great. I felt like..."

"Like what, sweetie?" Trish's voice softens.

"Nothing." Both open their mouths to speak, but I cut them off. "It was a joke. A real, honest-to-God joke. He'd made a bet with his teammates. The day after we slept together, I heard him talking to them before class. They asked if the nerd was any good. It was all part of a bet. He got the nerd to spread her legs."

It's quiet for a while. The music keeps blaring, the dancers keep twirling, but our table is silent. I stare at the dance floor, unable to meet my friends' eyes. Trying to focus on not embarrassing myself further by crying.

"Like I said. It's nothing," I say, blinking a lot.

"Well, I think you're an idiot," Rose says.

Trish jerks her head in her direction. "What the heck, Rose?"

"That guy was a dick. A legit dick," Rose says, shaking her head as she talks, her big hair swaying. "In fact, I think we can all agree on his uber level of dickdom, can we not?" Rose looks to Trish, who nods, and then to me. I'm too shocked to say anything.

"Okay, so that guy was a dick. It's agreed," Rose continues. "But Jackie, how many men are there in the world?"

Her question catches me off guard but allows my mind to snap back to the present, running through numbers. "There are about seven billion people in the world. So roughly, and by no means should this be taken as a hard fact, it would be safe to say that there are around 3.5 billion males on earth."

"And of that 3.5 billion, how many are in a datable age range?"

"Datable age range? That's trickier. On the whole I do know that the Baby Boomer generation created a shock to the world population, and in turn created Generation X and then in turn the Millennials. I'm thinking that's who you're referring to when you said 'datable'; however, you also have to take into account—"

Rose cuts in, "Babe. I love you. You're super smart and you rock the sexy nerd vibe for sure. But just guesstimate for me, will ya?"

"Oh, okay, sure. Let's see, I would say, taking into consideration we would only be dating men in the U.S., then I could give a safe guesstimate, although I want it on record that I truly do not like to guess, about forty million datable men." Trish smiles and Rose rolls her eyes at me. She must give herself headaches with how often she does that.

"And, not counting Flynn, how many men have you slept with and or dated?" Rose ask.

"Um, one?"

"And you, who love probability and all things mathy—"

"Mathy?"

"Yes, mathy. Don't interrupt." Rose gives me a look. "As I was saying, you who love all things *mathy*, decided that you would let one man, albeit a huge dick of a man, speak for the rest of the forty million dudes on this planet."

My mouth drops open.

"Now does that sound like a good, logical rationale to you?"

When I continue to stare at her, she turns to Trish. "Blow Job?"

TEN

ORBITAL RESONANCE

Flynn

I stroll into Big Texas thinking I need to buy Rose a second birthday present. Maybe some new riding boots to go with the saddle I'd gotten her. She deserves them for texting me Jackie's whereabouts. I've been trying to connect with her all week, but unless I count the times she's replied to my texts in total exasperation, I'm finding it hard to draw her out.

Speaking of hard.

I spot her across the bar, sitting at a table with Rose and a brunette who must be Trish.

Jesus.

I try to shift subtly. Anything to ease the semi I've just sprouted.

Some douchebag comes up to their table and takes Jackie's hand. I see red for a minute before Jackie tugs her hand out of his and shakes her head. Only when the guy walks away do I release the breath I've been holding.

When Rose texted me, *@ BT with Jackie and Trish. Help me fight off the man-whores circling your girl*, I thought she was just playing, trying to stir up my jealousy. I didn't know she meant it literally.

I mean, it's not that Jackie isn't freaking hot. She is. But a lot of men are stupid, only interested if there's enough skin on display. Jackie presents herself in a way that doesn't invite attention, but I love it. I mean, who wears periodic table T-shirts? Jackie does, that's who. It's original, just like her. She's also freaking smart as hell, and some men lack the confidence to break through that I-have-better-things-on-my-mind shield Jackie probably doesn't even know she throws up.

Good thing I have experience looking under the hood and even after the disastrous end to our kiss the other night, I've never lacked in the confidence department.

Tonight, though, even with that shield in place, the men are coming at her. And it's no wonder. Her hair is pulled back from her face in the front, the rest loose and long down her back. Though the multicolored lights change with each spin, I know those locks to be a captivating mix of white, blond, gold and chocolate, swirling together like the iridescent shimmer of motor oil. The wavy ends trail lightly on the seat of her stool. Her chub-inducing glasses on full display.

She's wearing a dress. And it has to be short, because sitting down as she is, it's hiked up high on her thighs, giving the guys in here a look at those long, toned legs. Legs likely toned from all the walking she does when her car kicks out on her and the three flights of stairs she jogs up. She has on a leather jacket. It looks like a biker jacket, but it's cut tight around her body. That, in addition to the black studded high-heeled cowboy boots, is enough to make any man start fantasizing about hot librarians.

Lord knows I've spent the past few days with enough of my own smart-girl fantasies.

Her glossy lips shine in those cascading bar lights. Lips I want to stare at while she explains some complex, scientific matter. Or moaning my name. Or wrapped around my cock. I wonder if I ask, if she'd give me a lesson on the history of blow jobs. Fuck, she'd probably call it fellatio, all proper and academic like, while pushing her glasses up on her nose.

I shift again.

Jackie's head tilts back, probably laughing at something inappropriate Rose said. Her laughter makes me oddly happy. Jackie seems like such a serious person, or better, a person who's used to being serious. Rose hadn't told me much about Jackie, claiming the girl code or something, but I've gleaned what I could since Jackie stopped talking to me. Jackie's a workaholic, recently looking to expand her social life. Apparently, Rose finds her both hilarious and fascinating, and for once, I agree with my sister's choice of friends. I just wish I knew what I did to piss her off.

I head over to the bar, claim a seat and order a beer. I'm thinking a bit of recon might help me out. That and letting the girls have another drink. I'm not afraid to play a bit dirty; I mean it has been a while since I've done this. And I've never been interested in someone like Jackie. She is so far away from the ditzy, spoiled, self-indulgent women of my past.

Thank God.

———

TEN MINUTES LATER, I'm still staring. I probably look like a creeper, but seeing as most of the men in here are staring at Jackie's table as well, I'm not alone. Luckily, the girls are too wrapped up in their conversation to notice.

Jackie seems lit up tonight—hands waving, long hair swishing, index finger pushing up her glasses. At times looking embarrassed, others like she's lecturing.

Professor Darling Lee. Oh, I could definitely see that.

On a side note, wooden bar stool seats do *not* feel good when you have dick situation going on.

Rose says something to Trish, to which the brunette smiles and nods her head. Rose drops her arms to her sides and shouts, "Blow Jobs!"

Shit. They're going to get kicked out before I can make my move. I scan the bar for the bouncers, but though they heard my sister—who didn't?—they're just shaking their heads and smiling. I guess even they can see the girls are bringing them business in the guise of men drinking while checking them out, so they're willing to let a few things slide.

Rose and Trish jump off their stools and stand by the table, hands behind their backs. They motion for Jackie to follow. She does, sliding carefully off her seat and running her hands down her body. No amount of pulling is going to make that dress any longer, but Jackie sure is trying.

Rose starts imitating throwing her head back, but it isn't until I see the whipped cream topped shots on the table that I realize what's really happening. *Holy, fuck-no.*

I stand up, pulling my wallet from my back pocket so I can throw money down for my drink and stop this nonsense.

Fucking Rose. This has to be her idea. No boots for her. She'll be lucky if I let her keep the damn saddle after this.

A cheer sounds. I glance up in time to see Trish and Rose wiping their mouths with the backs of their hands. I drop some bills next to my beer bottle and maneuver around the bar in their direction. Through a break in the crowd that's gathered around them, I see Jackie leaning over the edge of the table, her brows drawn in concentration. Then she raises her neck up, aligning her lips directly on top of the whipped cream topped shot. She lowers her face straight down, mouth wide, inhaling the cream and wrapping her full lips around the rim of the shot glass.

I freeze in place.

In one move she tilts her head back, arching her neck and back in the opposite direction, turning the shot glass over 180 degrees, the contents draining into her mouth. I can see her neck working to swallow from where I stand.

Jesus.

She releases her hands from behind her back, plucks the shot glass from her mouth—*did I hear a pop?*—and bangs it down on the table. Rose and Trish gawk, open-mouthed, as does everyone else in the room. Jackie's smile is radiant. And I don't use words like radiant.

When everyone keeps staring, her smile falters.

Until Rose shouts, "Fuck yeah, bitch! That's how you do a Blow Job!"

The bar erupts in a pandemonium of cheers, leers and beers.

And now I don't know whether to kill my sister or buy her a fucking pony.

————

Jackie

Holy Mercury. That. Was. Awesome.

My heart is pounding, my face feels flushed and, going by that reaction from Rose, I'm pretty sure I rocked the hell out of that Blow Job shot. It was tricky—the mound of whipped cream, in addition to the height of the table, made it a challenge. But by gauging the angle, helped by the forward pitch from the high heels of my new boots, I'd been able to tilt forward at the pelvis and—oh fuck it. Who cares about the science? Blow Job shots rule!

Also, I might be buzzed.

Unfortunately, not buzzed enough to forget about the wedge of lace strangling my nether regions. This thong has to go.

Not that I'm not grateful to Rose. According to Trish, Rose kidnapped her earlier today and took her on a shopping spree aimed at updating my look. The catalyst being that my feet are too big for their boots and no one wants to share underwear. That's just weird.

Trish said that Rose hadn't even looked at price tags, just went around gathering things up and whipping out her credit card. It's sweet that Rose wanted to help with my apparently lacking wardrobe, but a stop at the ATM is definitely on my agenda so I can slip some cash in Rose's purse. I'm not about to have a college student go into debt because my usual attire read more *Revenge of the Nerds* than *Sex in the City*.

And now I have boots. Real cowboy boots.

Okay, so I haven't exactly seen any of the heroines on my romance covers wearing studded motorcycle/cowgirl boots... but still. They count. Rose bought them, and she grew up on a ranch. That makes them legit.

I wave to the crowd gathered around us and tell the girls I'm heading to the bathroom. Trish hops down to follow, but Rose stops her. She's motioning to something behind me, but when I turn to look all I see is a blur of unfamiliar faces.

I push through strangers and make it to the bathroom. For once, there's no line. That's a relief.

No, I take that back. True relief is when I close the stall door and shimmy out of the lace dental floss.

Much better.

I shove it in the pocket of my jacket and exit the stall, stopping when I catch myself in the full-length mirror.

I bend one way and then another while looking at my reflection. If I keep from squatting or bending down to touch my toes, which I'm pretty sure are not normal girls' night out maneuvers, I think I can limit the free anatomy lessons made possible by the removal of my underwear.

I feel for my phone in my other pocket. Still no text from Flynn. That's good, I tell myself. That's what I wanted.

Right?

I open up my texts and thumb our conversation open. His last text, *It gets me hard,* stares back at me. The alcohol is vibrating through my veins to the rhythm of the two-step I can hear blaring from the speakers. My thumbs fly across the screen.

Jackie: *How hard?*

Oops. Is this what people mean when they warn not to drink and text?

The three period ellipse pops up under my text. Oh my God. Flynn just read my text.

Panic builds until I catch my eyes in the mirror. True, I might be out of my element, and in unfamiliar surroundings. But I'm a woman, who, if I believe even a smidge of what Trish, Rose and Jules say, is at least mildly attractive. I can text a good-looking man. I can be sexy. I can *sext.*

The booze and heels may have gone to my head.

Feeling quite pleased after my pep talk, I nod at myself in the mirror and pull the door open, a little extra sway in my step. Crossing the threshold, the heat from the packed bar and the pulsing beat of the music hit me, making me pause.

"Hello, darling."

I spin around, hand on my chest.

Flynn's leaning against the wall, eerily reminiscent of the first time I saw him. Except this time, he notices me. This time he's actually talking to me. When he sees me notice the phone in his hand, a smile curls up on one side of his face.

"I got your text."

Forget my earlier pep talk about being a confident woman. My whole body burns with humiliation. I clear my throat, trying to find words that will make me want to die a little less. Not able to meet his eyes, I address a spot over his right shoulder. "Yes, well, the appeal of that particular text was that it lacked the complexity and messiness of a personal, face-to-face interaction." I move to adjust my glances but pause when Flynn takes a step closer. The smell of his cologne, subtle but intoxicating, fills my lungs, and I hate to say it, but I may be regretting getting rid of that thong when I feel myself dampen. Pheromones. Those damn pheromones.

Flynn reaches out a hand, tilting my face to his with two fingers. "Yeah, but the appeal of face-to-face interaction is the simplicity of you putting your hands on me so you can feel exactly *how hard* I am."

I open my mouth. I close my mouth. My mind simply blanks.

"I need a drink." I turn away and make for our table. Rose and Trish are there grinning like idiots. "More shots?" I ask when I get there.

"Honey, you may need to keep your wits about you with that one," Trish says.

I glance back to see Flynn sauntering after me. "I don't know. My wits never seem to help me out in these situations."

Unhelpful, Trish and Rose just smile.

Two hands rest on my shoulders.

"Let me take your jacket." Flynn has it half slipped from my arms before I can stop him.

I try raising my elbows to stop the progression, but it's too late. The leather falls away into his hands.

"Christ, Jackie."

"You got her to take off the jacket—well done, bro." Rose raises her fist for him to tap, but he leaves her hanging. I can only imagine it's because his eyes are still glued to the particular bit of me now on display courtesy of the dress Rose and Trish made me wear. The only reason I'd agreed to it was because they'd promised me the biker jacket. One, because I've always wanted a leather jacket—very badass and all. And two, it matches my boots. Third, and most importantly, it covered the top half of the dress.

Until now.

Yes, the dress is short, but the most scandalous part is the back. The front dips to a V, nothing too indecent. It's the back, or rather *total lack* of a back, that makes the dress so scandalous.

Needless to say, I had to go braless.

Feeling his eyes on me from behind, I slowly turn around. Flynn swallows. The realization that without the thong, the only thing covering me is a pale pink swatch of stretchy fabric has goosebumps traveling over my skin.

Flynn's gaze locks on my chest, where my braless state has made it clear I may be feeling a bit chilled without the jacket.

"We're dancing," Flynn states, tossing my jacket on a chair before guiding me to the dance floor with one hand on my exposed back. The brand of his hand is enough to shock me into moving forward. But I come to my senses at the edge of the dance floor.

"I don't dance. I've never two-stepped before." I lean back on his hand, trying to reverse directions. "This isn't going to work."

Flynn pushes back and helps me step onto the raised wooden planks. "Dancing is just two planets orbiting the sun." He turns me around and takes me in his arms. My hair, which had been scattered around my shoulders, floats down my back again, covering most of my exposed skin.

I stiffen further. "Are you making fun of me?"

He looks genuinely confused. "No. Why would I do that?"

"Huh." I remember what Rose had said. Maybe Flynn *is* different. Statistically, he makes good odds. But his dancing analogy is all wrong. "Planets orbiting the sun isn't quite right, is it?" I say, trying to ignore the tremor running through my body as he leans in. "I mean, planets orbit the sun, but no two planets orbit simultaneously while orbiting the sun. Each has its own rotational path, which I guess can be compared to that of the couples on the dance floor." I look up over his shoulder, lost in thought. "Really, the two-step seems more like the orbital resonance of Jupiter's moons, specifically the Galilean moons."

"Orbital resonance?" Flynn smiles. He has such a sexy smile. It does wonderful things to the corners of his eyes.

"Hmmmm?"

"You mentioned orbital resonance?"

"Oh, yes. Orbital resonance." I'm thankful for the flashing lights and general dim atmosphere that hide what is probably my beet-red complexion, and look back over his shoulder, away from his distracting smile. "That's when two orbiting bodies, such as you and myself, exert a regular, periodic gravitational influence on each other. That way, as we maintain our rotational path around the dance floor, as the moons do around Jupiter, we also create our own orbit. A circle circling in a circle, if you will."

"You mean like this?"

Suddenly, I'm spinning. Before my thoughts can trip me up, or my feet, Flynn's hands come back to me, guiding me toward him again.

"I'm dancing!" It hits me that I've been dancing ever since Flynn had me talking about orbits. "You tricked me!"

But I'm not mad, far from it. I laugh long and hard at the thrill of actually being one of those couples orbiting the dance floor. I can feel my center of gravity being controlled by one of his hands on my hip while the other clasps my right hand. The flashing lights blur as he takes me around the floor, navigating through and around the other couples like one of his muscle cars weaving through traffic.

I'm still laughing when I tilt my head up to his.

He isn't smiling anymore, though his eyes are soft. He has a look on his face I can't name, but whatever it is makes my breath quicken. I'm aware of how small my hand feels in his. Hands that can build things, create and restore. They're large and callused against my own and I suddenly want them everywhere. The hand at my hip flexes and drifts a shade lower—one finger dipping beneath the fabric at my back.

I stumble.

"Whoa, I got you." He moves in closer, until our bodies align like magnets. The push and pull of our forces dance against each other to the rhythm of a country song I can't name but will never forget.

All that exists is his body moving against mine. Pushing forward, swaying, pulling back. I can't think, I simply react in tandem to his movements. I'm lightheaded. I take a deep breath, which pushes my breasts further into his chest. He smells good. God, so good. And he's hard.

So very hard.

ELEVEN
COUNTDOWN

Jackie

I'm in Flynn's car again. The green one. But the difference a dance and the absence of panties makes is significant. Like discovering ice on Jupiter significant.

Then there's the alcohol. Sweet Neptune, the alcohol.

I blame Flynn. And Rose. And Trish. In fact, all my new friends are bad influences.

Wait a minute. Is Flynn a friend? I can't help but glance down as his thigh muscles bunch and flex whenever he changes gears.

Operation Social Life hadn't included hot guys. Just friends. Learning to be more social. Helping myself become more normal in social settings so that I can get past those last hurdles on my way to becoming an astronaut. But I'm not sure I can categorize Flynn as a friend. You don't get turned on by your friend's thighs or imagine tracing the contours of a friend's abs with your tongue. Do you? Not to mention our date, or the kiss. The one with tongue.

I could just chalk up my Flynn fascination to alcohol. But even I can't ignore the fact that I've been hyper aware of him since he barged into Rose's room shirtless and angry. Or how I attacked him like cesium on water. Boom.

Hmm, I'm thinking about dangerous chemical reactions. How many drinks did I have? Let's see, there was the initial Captain and Coke, then Sex on the Beach and the Blow Job. After dancing, the bar crowd tried enticing me into an encore show of my Blow Job skills, but Flynn shut that down.

I giggle.

"What's so funny?" Flynn asks.

"Blow Job skills."

The car swerves slightly. "Fuck, Jackie."

I giggle again.

After some water and another dance, Flynn helped me back into my jacket and hustled me out to his car. I was going to put up a fight. Honestly. But one look at Rose and Trish, who'd been high-fiving each other at Flynn's initiative, and I knew I wouldn't be getting any help from that quarter.

Okay, let's be honest. I hadn't really wanted help.

True, I've been pushing Flynn away after that thoroughly confusing kiss, but after a makeover, learning the two-step, coitus-named shots and my very first sext, I've owned up to the fact that I don't really *want* to push him away.

Plus, Rose had called me out on my faulty logic. Faulty logic is just the worst.

Flynn is older than Brian was, more mature. He's worked hard to be one of the best in his field and runs a successful business. That takes real dedication and drive. Focus. Commitment. All those things are just as hot as the muscles he's packing. Or, you know, close to it.

A passing car's headlights illuminate Flynn's face, making the hollows under his cheekbones more pronounced. He lifts his hand from the gear shift and runs it through his hair, pushing back the locks that have fallen forward. His shirt sleeves are pushed up, revealing the tendons in his forearms. He drops his hand back on the gear shift while the other rests over the top of the steering wheel. Pumping the clutch and pressing the gas, he shifts gears, his movements fluid.

From context clues in some of my romance novels, I understood the concept of arm porn, but it isn't until Flynn that I truly *got it*. A good reminder that theory and practice are two *very* different things.

He's so fine.

But I'm discovering so much more than that. He has a sense of humor. He's confident, but not cocky. And he seems to like me, even when I nerd out on him. Actually, *especially* when I nerd out on him. No one's ever really liked that side of me before.

Plus, he's Rose's big brother. I like Rose, and Rose likes Flynn, therefore, I'm safe in liking Flynn. There's a lot of faulty transitive logic in that statement, but I'm going to actively ignore it this time.

There's more shifting, more muscle flexing. I fidget in my seat, but freeze when I feel my dress scrunch higher. Warm leather caresses my ass cheeks.

Flynn's hand stills on the wheel. He's looking straight ahead at the road, but I'm pretty sure he's tracking the upward progression of my dress in his peripheral vision.

He lets out a long, slow breath, then makes the left into Clear Lake Forest, winding through the neighborhood to his house. His awesome, awesome house.

"When did you buy this place?" I lean forward to get a better view as he pulls into the drive. While also trying to covertly pull down my dress.

The dress is not cooperating.

Flynn reaches an arm over to my visor and presses the garage door opener clipped there. I take a deep breath, enjoying his scent. Whereas I probably smell of booze and sweat, he smells delicious. The sexy scent makes me want to research whether or not cologne companies are bottling pheromones. But I'm pretty sure what I'm breathing in is all Flynn.

"About two years ago. A little after I opened the shop."

"What made you want to open—wait. Is that my car?" The garage door fully opens, revealing my old, rusted Honda. Minus the dent.

"Yeah, I..." Flynn shakes his head and smiles, pulling up alongside it in the wide three-car garage. "I kind of forgot I had that here."

"You forgot that you had my car parked in your garage?"

He nods.

"Why would you have my car here?"

"Well..." He runs his hand through his hair again. "I thought you might try and sneak into the shop when I wasn't there to get your car back. So I brought it home when I was finished with it." He snorts. "That way you'd *have* to talk to me."

I don't have a response for that. First, that's a brilliant plan. Second, it shows he really does like me. It takes me a moment to realize I'm staring at him, my mouth slightly open.

Flynn leans in and cups my cheek with his large hand. "And I really wanted to talk to you again." His thumb sweeps across my bottom lip. *Oh my.* I'm sure he's going to kiss me until he leans back and exits the car. I blink a few times, trying to clear my head, while Flynn rounds the hood and opens my door. He's holding out his hand for me.

I place my hand in his and swing my legs out of the car, trying to keep from flashing him, but I'm ninety-nine percent sure that when I stand, it takes my dress a second longer to fall down over my ass cheeks than I'd like.

How do I know this? I know because Flynn takes in a sharp breath before he hauls me to him.

———

Flynn

A man can only take so much, and I've reached my limit. Hell, I reached it when Jackie took that Blow Job shot. I reached it again when I slid the leather jacket down her bare arms, revealing the great expanse of skin left visible from her barely existent dress before she proceeded to inform me on the correct orbital metaphor for two-stepping. And I reached it when she'd giggled, *freaking giggled*, in my car while thinking of blow job skills. But now, now that I've seen that bare, milky white ass cheek sliding against the tan leather of my car, I've definitely hit my fucking limit.

I lean down, the descent made easier because of her heels and the shocked expression on her face. Her mouth already open, I delve, my tongue stroking hers. My palms slip under her leather jacket and up across her bare back, pulling her tight into my embrace. Each arm wraps around her until my fingertips brush the sides of her breasts, so easily accessibly in the scrap of fabric she's wearing. She's lithe but solid, like a Lamborghini built for the curves of a racetrack. Her arms fold up between us, palms resting on my chest, her fingertips curling into the neck of my T-shirt.

Jackie tastes sweet, a mix of those damn shots she drank and whatever flavor of lip gloss she's wearing. I pull back far enough to drag my lips across her jaw and down her neck.

Fuck, I'm hard.

What is it about her that drives me so nuts? It doesn't matter if she's talking, sulking, yelling or silent, I just *want* her. Want to be around her, in her.

Remembering the way our last kiss ended, I slowly lean back, taking in her flushed face and tilted glasses, waiting for her reaction. Her eyes are still closed and a Mona Lisa smile spreads across her face. I can't help it, I dip back down to rub the tip of my nose against hers. The gesture is more sweet than sexy. But her smile spreads wider afterward, so fuck it, I guess I'm sweet now.

Her eyes open. This close they take on an owlish quality behind her lenses. Brown eyes. I'm not poetic or anything, and I'm not sure if there is anything sexy about the color brown, but right now, they are the prettiest eyes in existence.

"Jackie." I touch my nose to hers again. "I need to get you inside before I rip that damn dress off you and do something to you on my car that other vintage car collectors would kill me for."

"That sounds like fun."

"Going into the house?"

"Well, yes. But also, the thing on the car."

I squeeze her tight and groan. "Jesus, darling. You're gonna be the death of me."

She sighs and sinks into the hug, turning her head to rest it on my chest. "I don't even mind when you call me that."

"What?"

"Darling. I usually hate it when people call me that. But I like it when you do it."

I drop a light kiss on the top of her head. "Oh, yeah?"

"Yeah." The word blows out of her in a breath, the tendrils around her face dancing.

"Darling, there are a good many things I'm hoping to do that you'll like." I close my eyes for a moment, gathering the strength I need to step back. But when I do, I grab hold of her hand, unwilling to completely surrender her touch.

Fingers entwined, I lead Jackie out of the garage and through the side door to the house. When I flip on the lights, she stops mid-stride, tugging my arm back.

For a minute I'm worried she's having second thoughts, until I catch the look on her face. Eyes wide, mouth open, gaze sharp, seemingly undimmed from the alcohol, she scans every surface.

She still seems turned on, but it might be because of my house.

Part of me is proud, similar to the feeling when people appreciate a particularly meaningful restoration I've done. And there's this weird caveman-like satisfaction that the woman I'm into openly admires the home I've worked so hard on.

The mid-century era has been on my radar ever since I first got my hands on my elusive 1969 Boss 429 Mustang. People usually think I bought my house because of the popularity of the show Mad Men. They'd probably all laugh if I told them I bought it 'cause it went with my car.

"This is beautiful, Flynn," Jackie says, her eyes roving over the large ribbon windows and floor-to-ceiling sliding glass doors that make up the entire back wall of my house.

"And look at the ceiling!" She actually jumps up and down and points to the pitched roof's exposed beam.

Damn, she's cute. "I think I may have lost you. You aren't supposed to be looking at my beam." I step closer. "At least not the one up there."

She laughs, but cuts it short, exclaiming, "Is that a Noguchi table?" She walks over to the living room section of the open floor plan. "An original Eames lounge chair?" Running her fingers over the Brazilian rosewood and leather, she breathes, "No way."

This stirs up the other part of me. The part that isn't proud, but rather is waiting for the other shoe to drop. Waiting for Jackie to show her true colors and start talking about money and—

"I think your dining room table cost more than my yearly rent." She laughs.

There it is.

I try to laugh with her, but her words feel like a punch to the gut and she tilts her head at me when an incoherent sound barks out of my chest.

I find myself rubbing the back of my neck, joking, "That isn't saying much."

"True," she says, still smiling. "And I just love this neighborhood, but the houses usually need a lot of work."

I want to ask her how she knows all about this stuff, but I'm afraid of the answer. This girls ticks all the boxes and then some, pulling me into an immediate, all-consuming awareness and need. Which is scary enough on its own, but the conversation we're having now is digging up too many ghosts and painful memories.

"I gutted it after I bought it." I look up at the ceiling and down to the terrazzo tile floor, anywhere but at her. "I had a crew come in for the heavy lifting, but mostly I did it myself."

"You did? That's really impressive." Her eyes focus on me again, and the way they heat as they travel over my body eases some of the tension I've been feeling. Well, almost all the tension. A part of me is still just as tense now as it was when I saw Jackie at the bar.

"Yeah, I'm good with my hands," I say, lifting them up for her to see, distracting her from the semi pushing against my zipper.

I motion her to me with a flick of my fingers.

Eyes still on my hands, a blush spreads up her neck as she takes a step forward.

"Want me to show you how good I can be with my hands?" At her nod, I lay my hands on her shoulders, pushing the leather down, exposing more of that beautiful skin.

She shimmies, shrugging it all the way off, the movement making her breasts sway.

I go cross-eyed for a moment.

"Jackie—"

"No," she cuts me off, letting her jacket fall to the floor. "Call me darling. I don't quite feel like Jackie right now."

"Okay, darling." But her words confuse me. "Who *do* you feel like?"

"I feel like the kind of girl you'd actually take home."

I hear the words, but I'm not sure what she means. I guess it shows on my face, because she instantly starts backtracking.

"Never mind, you can call me Jackie, it's fine. Forget I said anything." She straightens her glasses and lifts up on her toes to kiss me, but in that moment my brain finally catches up. And I'm not too happy.

I raise my hands to capture her face, forcing her eyes to mine. "I want to make something perfectly clear."

"No really, it's fine. I promise I won't talk anymore. Just..." She takes a deep breath and I know what she says next costs her. "Just kiss me. Please."

I can't help but smile at her sweetness, the vulnerability she's showing me. But I don't want her to feel vulnerable. Not with me.

"Jackie. Listen." Involuntarily, one of my hands drifts down her body, settling at the dip in her waist, my thumb sweeping back and forth across her hip bone. "I don't know what kind of person you think I take home. But whatever you're picturing, stop. I've never brought a girl here before." I chuckle at the skeptical look she throws me. "Seriously." I lean in and brush my lips lightly over hers. "So if you're wondering what kind of girl I bring home, I'll tell you. She's gorgeous. Completely sexy. Which takes into account her wild, long hair and alluring, thick framed glasses. But what truly makes her the girl I take home is that every time she opens her mouth, it's like a goddamn revelation."

My hands drift up, thumbs grazing the sensitive skin under her breasts. "And that girl is you, Jackie. One hundred percent you."

When she licks her lips, I have to count to ten to regain control.

I close what little distance remains between us. "I swear, if I had had a teacher that looked and sounded like you when I was in school, I would have paid a shit ton more attention than I did." I laugh, which brushes my chest against hers. "That, and I'd proba-bly've injured myself walking around with a raging hard-on all the time."

"Really?"

"Mmm-hmm." I lower my head, skimming the tip of her nose with mine. "Never doubt that you are exactly the kind of girl I'd want to bring home. You're the girl I just never thought would say yes."

"Yes," she whispers, her breath tickling my neck.

We're so close, almost forehead to forehead. I'm trying to take my time, make sure she understands... whatever this is. Hell, maybe then she could explain it to me. All I know is, this isn't temporary. This isn't one night, and this means... something. Something I can't name, but it's there, hovering like the vapors off a burning engine.

This time when she moves to kiss me, I don't stop her.

TWELVE
LIFT OFF

Jackie

"Take me to the bedroom." It's my voice, but it doesn't sound like me. It's breathless but confident. A result of the words he spoke that were everything I hadn't realized I'd needed to hear.

My hands drift around to his back, hooking up under his arms, clutching his shoulders. He drags his mouth from my lips, teeth grazing my jaw and down my neck. My body presses up against his, but it isn't close enough. I grasp his hand, pulling him across the room, past the kitchen and down the hallway. I pause, not knowing which room is his. I'm hoping Flynn will take over and lead the way.

Instead, I'm caged against the wall by his strong arms, his shoulders bunching under his shirt, his eyes intent on mine. He takes my mouth.

It isn't slow. It isn't gentle. It's everything I want.

He grabs my ass and lifts me, my legs automatically wrapping around his waist. His hips thrust into mine, widening my thighs, rocking into my core.

Oh. My. God.

Flynn is dry humping me. And it's freaking fantastic. He kisses and thrusts and all I can do is react. Moaning, back arching, needing more friction, more everything.

"Wait." Breathing hard, Flynn lifts his head.

"Wait?" I can't wait. I've never felt so alive. I don't care that it's been forever since I've done this, or that our only date was over sub sandwiches. There will be no waiting.

"You're drunk."

"I'm not drunk." I sound indignant to my own ears. But seriously, if this is the reason he's stopped pressing against me, he deserves it.

"You might not realize you're drunk." He lets out a long breath. "I don't want you to regret this."

I stick my finger into his chest and jab. Hard. "First, I realize everything." Flynn opens his mouth to counter, but I forge on. "I've had four drinks tonight. Three of which I finished. And two glasses of water. The typical alcohol has, on average, about 80 proof per ounce or shot. With my body weight of 125..." I shrug. "Okay, more like 130, the alcohol has had a little over three hours to traverse my system, making my blood alcohol level between .06 and .09." I remove my finger from his chest and bring it up to straighten my glasses that have skewed during our make-out session.

Flynn growls.

I'm not sure what to make of that, so I continue. "So, although I should not drive, or operate heavy machinery, I am most definitely not drunk." Hair has escaped whatever clip Trish used, tickling my nose. I blow it out of my face. "Furthermore, the typical signs of drunken behavior are clumsiness and slurred speech. As proven by this interlude, I believe my elocution to be perfectly unimpaired. In addition, I would like to point out that I am wearing heels." I lift one leg out and point to my new boots. "I never wear heels. And as of yet, I have only stumbled once, on the dance floor, which I blame you for, as I told you I didn't know how to dance."

A smile creeps over Flynn's face. "Is that so?"

Sheesh, that smile does things to me. I shift, making him juggle my weight and push me harder against the wall. Maybe I should feel bad for making it difficult to hold me up, but then I feel his erection against me and I stop feeling guilty.

I clear my throat and fix my eyes on some point over his shoulder, gathering my thoughts. A burgeoning habit of mine, it would seem. "Yes. Because, as you see, alcohol affects several neurotransmitters including the cerebellum—"

"Jackie?"

"Hmm?" I blink, looking back at him.

"You're not drunk."

"Well. Yes." I tilt my head, not understanding the need for his statement. "Didn't I just explain that?"

"Oh yeah, darling. You explained it. You explained it *real* good." He emphasizes his words with a circle of his hips, making my mind blank, before he steps back, my legs drifting to the floor.

Once I'm steady, he kneels in front of me and begins tugging off my boots. My long hair falls forward like a curtain when I look down at him, closing us in.

Boots gone, his fingers trail upward, circling behind my knees.

"Now, where were we?" He dips his head to the hem of my dress. He nudges my center, inhaling a deep breath. Heat flames over my body.

"*Damn*, Jackie. You smell so good." His hands drift higher. "I love your pheromones."

"Um, Flynn, I should tell you—"

Cold air swirls around my hips. "Fuck, Jackie." He looks up at me. "No panties?"

I should be embarrassed, I should pull away. I should tell him my current underwear-less situation isn't because I typically go commando, but because thongs are the devil. But I say nothing, just nod, my glasses slipping down the bridge of my nose.

"Fuck." One hand palms my ass, while his other goes for the nucleus of my being, finding me wet and wanting. "Oh, Jackie. You naughty girl."

I jerk from that one touch, so unused to this kind of pleasure. This desire. There's so much feeling. Too much feeling. My legs start to shake.

He leans in and lightly kisses the small patch of curls before his hands leave me. I open my mouth to protest, but I'm up in his arms, being carried down the hall before I can speak.

I don't even get to look around before I'm tossed onto the center of the bed. But honestly, at this point, all my attention is on Flynn. The mattress dips as he kneels on the bed, looming over me on all fours. He stays there, bracketing me in, staring. It's like he's trying to memorize my features, although for the life of me I don't know what he finds so interesting.

Then one hand rises to remove my glasses. Sitting back on his haunches, he carefully folds the arms of the frames and stretches back over to lay them on the nightstand. I blink a few times, refocusing. Flynn makes it easier for my nearsighted eyes by leaning in, his weight on one arm, his other hand sweeping the contours of my cheek before sliding down my neck. He pauses there, squeezing for a moment. It's deliberate and though at first odd, I feel that dominant pressure reverberate through my body. His hand continues down, stroking the side of my breast before palming it. He pets and caresses until my nipple feels like it's cutting through the thin fabric of my dress. I squirm, raising my legs higher, trying to appease the ache he's building.

His thumb brushes over my budded nipple, lulling me further into the erotic daze I'm swimming in. The hard pinch and roll comes as a surprise and I buck, my dress now rucked up over my hips. Fully exposed, his attention leaves my breast, his hand cupping my sex.

I can't help it, I whimper. I need more. And if the smile on his face is anything to go by, he knows it.

Light pressure and whisper-like touches. It isn't enough, but it's everything. His fingers are slippery from my growing desire and they glide over my sex, making me crazy.

Slowly, he slides one finger inside. I moan. Once seated, he curls the tip of his finger, hitting that secret spot that not even my favorite vibrator can find with any consistency. My eyes roll back in my head.

His thumb circles my clit as he increases the pressure inside. He's tearing me down, breaking me apart with every stroke and touch. While his fingers continue their maddening pace and pressure, his mouth finds the pulse at my neck. His lips linger there, at first softly and then in pulls, sucking my tender flesh into his mouth. The rough shadow of his beard grates around the silken touch of his mouth and tongue—the opposing sensations making my body shudder.

Unsure of what to do and overcome with sensations, I run my fingers through his hair. He catches my eye, and we stare at each other. In that moment, I see with a startling clarity that has nothing to do with my eyesight. I see him, and in doing so, I know he sees me. All of me.

He pumps harder, his fingers continuing their dance on my sensitive flesh. He croons out sounds of encouragement when my hips lift in time to the rhythm he's set.

I close my eyes to concentrate on the looming explosion, but he pushes his forehead to mine whispering, "Open," fisting my hair in his other hand.

My eyes meet his. The green in his is more intense, though his beauty goes unappreciated in this moment as the solar flare under my skin builds, heat infusing my bones.

And then it hits, the sudden flash of brightness blinding me to everything but the feeling of energy ripping through my body, curling my spine.

I scream as I come apart, Flynn's soft kisses and easy touch milking the last of the tremors from my body. An unquantifiable amount of time passes before I come back to myself.

The reality of where I am and whom I'm with gradually invades my brain. Still, nothing makes sense. What just happened usually only happens to heroines in books, the damsels saved by cowboys, and to women other than myself.

My eyes focus on Flynn, to his soft gaze before he rubs his nose against my own. The simple, endearing move nearly brings me to tears.

I rarely do anything without analyzing the outcomes, studying the variables. Outlining the procedures.

But right then, looking into the unfathomable depths of Flynn's eyes, like the black holes they remind me of, I don't think. I simply push him to his back, straddle him at the waist and pull my dress up and over my head. He gave me an orgasm that rivaled the sudden flash of a solar flare.

It's only fair that he see stars.

———

Flynn

Holy freaking hell.

There's never been a more beautiful woman made. Jackie's hair falls around her naked body like a goddamn goddess emerging from the sea. I'm not a poet by any means, but when faced with Jackie's perfectly rounded breasts, bouncing lightly from her sudden sexual takeover, and tipped with delightfully tight, dusky rose nipples, I'd bet my prized Mustang that I could write the best damn sonnet since Shakespeare.

I'd been trying to be good. My plan had been to get her off and then let her sleep. She said she wasn't drunk, and I believe her. Even sober, who could come up with that adorable lecture on blood alcohol levels and the workings of the freaking cerebellum, for God's sake? But sex isn't my end game with Jackie. It never has been. So I thought that we should move slowly, take our time.

Hold off on sex until I'd at least gotten to take her out on an actual date.

But when staring the object of my desire in the face, or in this case, the chest, I find I'm rather lacking in the chivalry depart-ment. She's such a contradiction of assertive and shy it has my dick in knots. I just fucking *want* her.

Her fingers grasp the bottom of my shirt and I curl forward, helping her pull it off. The move brings me lip-level with her nipples and I'd be remiss if I didn't lavish a bit more attention on these beauties. They're perfection, just like Jackie.

I flick my tongue out in a quick tease before latching on like a man starved. She leans forward, her weight falling on her arms as she braces on either side of my head, pushing me back on the bed. I kiss, pull, and tug one breast with my mouth as I palm the weight of the other. Her hips started undulating over my jeans, the rough fabric moving against my cock, almost setting it off.

Her hands reach for my belt, fumbling with the buckle. I have one more thought of slowing her down, but when her hand wraps around my cock, my mind blanks and it's my turn to buck off the mattress. I give her breasts one last kiss each before rolling Jackie beneath me.

"Wait! I wanted to—"

I kiss her mouth hard before pushing up to my feet and step-ping over to the nightstand.

Jackie's glasses rest on top and the image burns itself into my brain as much as the picture she makes lying naked across my bed. The thick black frames make it even more clear who I'm with, and how much this particular woman has twisted me up, like the old beater she drives.

I grab a condom from the drawer and shuck off the rest of my clothes, standing naked by the bed. My cock juts out at her lustful stare. I'm so hard it's painful. Her eyes are riveted to my dick, and I swear I can almost hear her scientific mind gauging the anatomic fit. Her knees squeeze together, her breath coming in pants.

I reach out one hand to circle her ankle and pull it wide. With my other hand, I stroke myself. Which might be a mistake, as the move has Jackie licking her lips like she's about to consume a tasty treat.

Christ.

I know she wants to wrap those lips around me, just as she did that shot glass, but I can't let that happen yet. I won't last. And the first time I come, I need to be inside her.

Not looking away from her, I roll the condom on and climb back on the bed. She immediately wraps her legs around me, drawing me closer.

I pause, making sure to look into her eyes. "Is this okay?"

Her brow furrows. "Is this the drunk thing again? 'Cause I'll have you know that although alcohol can increase sexual desire, it can actually dampen sexual ability, especially in men. So if you're having trouble feeling *up* to it—"

I cut off her words by devouring her mouth, and this time I hear it; I do actually growl. Her fucking smarts and attitude are going to be the death of me.

I tilt her hips up, and in one motion, I'm there, gliding into her. Her walls squeeze my dick in the best, most painful pleasure I've ever experienced. That one thrust is like a trigger, and suddenly I'm unleashed. I bring her legs up high, hooking them under my arms as I begin to piston back and then forward. Our motions create an electric current that crackles like a welding torch across metal.

It's noisy sex, the best kind. Moans and grunts, all incoherent mumblings that only highlight how pleasurable everything is. Or maybe she's actually saying things, dirty things, but my mind is too drunk on sensation to comprehend.

Sweat glistens on her skin, and a flush spreads from the roots of her gorgeous hair to the tips of her hardened nipples.

I shift, moving my hands to grab her slim wrists, hauling them over her head. Then I plant my knees onto the mattress before I start to move again.

My eyes meet hers, my blood roaring in my ears, pulsating to the fast beat of my heart. Jackie's eyes widen, but she doesn't glance away at this sudden intimacy. It should unnerve me, letting someone look into my eyes, see me raw and exposed in this moment. But it doesn't. Instead, the way her pupils dilate fuels me on, and I pump harder and deeper. Each thrust pounds my pelvis into her clit, building more pressure. Soon there is nothing but the sounds of our breath, smacking skin and the thud of the headboard against the wall as we concentrate on the pleasure igniting between us.

And then it's there. Her back arches, her inner walls clamping around me. I thrust once, twice more before I still, drunk on pleasure, my eyes still staring down into hers while I moan.

"Darling."

THIRTEEN
METADATA

Jackie

MY MOUTH FEELS LIKE THE ARID SURFACE OF MARS, AND I ACHE in places that hadn't been touched by another in a long time.

Oh, sweet Neptune, what have I done?

Flynn. I did Flynn.

When my cerebral cortex comes back online, all the details of last night flash through my brain, causing a slow grin to spread over my face.

Holy moly, I did *Flynn.*

I told Flynn I wasn't drunk last night and I wasn't. But in the bright light of morning, I can say, with absolute certainty, that those shots had most assuredly lowered my inhibitions. Did I really...?

Yes. Yes, I did.

My smile stretches wider.

I'm on my stomach, one arm flung over the side of the bed. Awesome. *Super graceful, Jackie.* Gently, I pull my hand back toward my face and turn over.

The other half of the bed is empty. *Huh.*

On the downside, his vacancy sets off a little spark of panic in my chest. But on the upside, Flynn isn't there to witness my hangover face, which I'm pretty sure includes dried drool at the corner of my mouth and mascara smudges under my eyes.

I sit up, pleased to note that I don't feel sick. Just thirsty. Looking around, I notice what I hadn't last night. You know, since I'd been so busy getting busy.

A transom window above the bed lets in a lot of natural light. So either Flynn's an early riser or he can sleep through blinding sunlight. With his job as a mechanic, and the fact that he's not in bed right now, I'm thinking the former. Light blue walls, honey oak furniture and, of course, the massive king size bed I'm lying in.

His room feels like Earth to my space bedroom. I'm not going to think too hard about that.

Everything is a bit blurry and I scan the area for my glasses. They're right where Flynn placed them last night, folded nicely on the side table. I smile, thinking of the care he took with them, even in the heat of the moment. I put them on to continue my perusal with perfect clarity.

The closet door is open. It's a walk-in, so I can't see into its depths, but just inside there's a pile of laundry on the floor. The rest of the room is quite tidy. No clothes strewn about or dirty dishes or clutter.

My dress and jacket lie across a chair near what I assume is the bathroom door. In the light of day, I'm not too keen on putting that dress back on. Especially without liquid courage or girl posse peer pressure. I still, listening for Flynn, but don't hear anything. Slipping out of bed, I tiptoe toward the dresser. Surely after last night I'm entitled to steal a T-shirt and maybe some boxers.

I pause. Maybe not. I mean, Flynn hadn't been there to say good morning as I'd woken up. Plus, my clothes are laid out for me—maybe that's his way of telling me to get the hell out.

Holy crap. Is it happening again? Is he done now that we've had sex?

Panting, I sit back down on the bed and struggle to slow my breathing. Once I'm seventy-five percent I'm not going to hyper-ventilate, I begin to process reasons not to overreact.

One, I decided last night that Flynn was *not* Brian.

Two, I like Flynn. Getting over the fact that he's too hot for me by half, he's sweet. He's also a caring brother, a talented mechanic. And he likes my glasses.

Three, I'm a full-grown woman. I'm a NASA engineer and a freaking genius. I can handle this.

And four, if Flynn does turn out to be a douche, I'll just leave a scathing review of his shop on Yelp like the mature woman I am.

Feeling calmer, I push back onto my feet, snag my dress and head for the unopened door.

Yep, bathroom.

I catch my reflection in the full-length mirror. A whole lot of natural light helps illuminate the evidence from last night's activi-ties. Beard burn on my neck and oh, wow, on my thighs too. Sheesh, I have freaking hickeys on my collar bone.

I'm almost thirty and have hickeys.

Although, considering I've never had a hickey before, I'm sort of pleased with myself.

I shrug the dress on over my head and survey the rest of the damage. My hair is... big. No other way to describe it that doesn't involve words like rat's nest or tumbleweeds.

I find a bottle of mouthwash in the cabinet that I put to good use and scrub my face with water to get rid of any leftover makeup. My skin feels tight, but it's better than facing Flynn for the first time after a night of body-tingling sex with raccoon eyes.

Back in the bedroom I pull on my jacket. In a crowded, dimly lit bar, my dress looked okay. In the fresh, annoying light of day, I don't even think it could classify as a nightgown, let alone appropriate for public viewing.

I jump when my phone vibrates. Patting down the front of my body, I find it in my jacket pocket. Work email notifications. I can check those later. But what catches my eye are the many texts from last night.

Rose: *your blow job shot skills are legendary!*

Rose: *check the pantry: no glove, no love*

Trish: *ignore Rose. Have fun, sugar*

I click on a series of pictures Rose sent from last night. There are various selfies of us making silly faces, one picture of an unsuspecting Trish, a close up of my cleavage, and then one of Flynn and me dancing.

Against a background blur of twirling dancers, Flynn and I seem alone on the dance floor. In profile, my head is thrown back in laughter. This is the moment I realized I'd been dancing throughout my whole orbital resonance lecture. I appear happy, light, carefree..

But it isn't the freeze frame of me that captures my attention. It's Flynn.

His eyes are intent. Focused only on me. A smile plays on his lips as he holds me against him. He looks…captivated. Captivated by *me*.

You know that old saying about a picture being worth a thousand words? I'm not sure I could come up with a thousand to describe this candid shot, but the expression on Flynn's face makes me feel better about facing him this morning. I slide my phone back in my pocket, take a deep breath, and metaphorically pull up my big girl panties, seeing as I still don't have any, before making my way down the hallway and into the kitchen.

Holy Mercury.

Flynn's in a tight-fitting, long sleeve Henley, the sleeves pushed up, low riding gray sweatpants and bare feet. He's working a pan and spatula over the cooktop. And if that isn't enough to cause heart palpitations, his hair is all mussed and his lips are pursed to one side. The morning scruff gracing his chin reminds me of the beard burn between my legs. I feel my face flush just as he looks up at me, spatula in hand. His face is blank, as if I'd awakened him from a daydream. Then he blinks, a slow smile creeping up his face.

"Holy Mercury?"

Crapola. I said that out loud? I open my mouth to—

"Fuck!" Flynn slams down the pan and shakes his hand out. "Sorry." He glances up at me, looking a bit sheepish. "Burned myself. And breakfast too, by the looks of it." He runs his other hand through his hair, then places both on his hips. "But I make okay coffee." He pulls a mug out of a cabinet. "Or at least, Rose tells me I do."

"Is Rose here?" Please, don't let Rose be here.

"No. She texted me last night that she'd be staying with Trish."

"Really?" I walk over toward the stools pushed under the island.

"Yeah, but that's Rose for you." He shrugs. "Girl has a sweet-ass apartment downtown, but never uses it."

I pull out a stool and sit down. The large island separates us, and I'm grateful because when I sit, the dress inches up my legs again.

"Anything I can help you with?" I ask, looking over at the counter topped with cracked eggs, a bowl, whisk and open milk carton. There are splashes and spills everywhere.

He moves over to the coffee maker and pours a cup. "Nope. I was just making us breakfast. Or trying to. I usually just have cereal, but I thought I'd step it up today." He lifts the milk carton. "How do you like your coffee?"

"Oh, uh, I don't drink coffee." Shoot, I should've told him that before he poured it.

Flynn's eyebrows shoot up. "Seriously? How do you not drink coffee?" He sets the mug down on the island. "I'm not much use without at least one cup in the morning."

Embarrassed over something so trivial as not liking coffee, as well as the general situation of what to do after a night of hot loving, to my horror, I start to babble. "Well, during my first week of college, the study group I was assigned to took a coffee break. I'd never had coffee before and I didn't know what to order. Looking back, I should've asked one of my study group members, but I wanted to fit in. I could already tell they weren't happy getting stuck with the kid."

Flynn throws me a look.

"College at sixteen, remember?" He nods, and that sets me off rambling again. "Anyway, when it was my turn to order I just ordered the same as the guy in front of me. Turns out he drank a venti Americano. After I forced myself to drink it, I had to run back to my dorm to throw up. I had the shakes for the rest of the day. Never wanted to drink coffee again." I push my glasses up my nose and force myself to stop talking, focusing on tucking my hair behind my ears and folding my hands on the counter in front of me.

Flynn chuckles. "Yeah, I can see how that would spoil coffee for you."

It's silent for a beat, and I think it's no wonder I don't have more friends. Or date. I'm pretty sure sad, embarrassing child-hood memories aren't on the list of appropriate morning-after-sex topics. Especially if childhood memories happened in college.

"Okay then, no coffee for you. OJ? Water?" He places the full mug in the sink.

I give him a grateful smile. "Water would be great. Thank you."

Flynn opens another cabinet and grabs a bottle of water. "There you go. Unless you want ice and a glass?"

"No, this is fine." I take my time unscrewing the cap and placing it gently on the counter, studying the thin striations of gray in the white marble countertop.

"And now for breakfast."

He arranges two plates, putting one in front of me. Two eggs, both yolks broken, burnt toast and bacon. Flynn surveys the plates and blows out a hard breath. "I know this sounds weird, but I've never tried to fry an egg before. Rose or Holt always made breakfast." He looks back at the pan. "I made scrambled earlier, but I think I added too much milk. They were runny as shit."

Though it looks vastly unappealing, I pick up a piece of burnt toast and take a bite. I don't want Flynn to think I don't appreciate his effort. I make sure my face remains passive as I crunch the charred remnants of bread. I take a large gulp of water to help swallow it down. Determined, I go for the eggs next. They aren't bad exactly. I just never knew fried eggs could be this tough. When my fork doesn't cut it, I pick up a knife to saw through it.

Flynn busts out laughing. "Stop, please. I mean, I really appreciate you trying, but I just nearly cracked a tooth on this bacon. It's not worth it." The corner of his mouth kicks up in that sexy grin I love.

I mimic it with my own. "It isn't *that* bad."

"Yes, it is." He stands, grabbing both plates. After setting them in the sink next to the wasted mug of coffee, he turns to the cabinet and takes out two boxes. "So, Lucky Charms," he says, shaking one box, "or Apple Jacks?" he asks, shaking the other.

I giggle. Who knew I was a giggler? "That's not even a choice. Lucky Charms all the way."

He places the Lucky Charms box over his chest. "Girl after my own heart."

A weird feeling travels through me. Not embarrassment, but

warmth, almost like a physical manifestation of happiness, flows under my skin. Which is crazy. I'm being crazy.

Clearing my throat, I try to start a normal conversation and not randomly babble. "With your family owning a ranch, what made you want to become a mechanic?"

Great, now I am simultaneously picturing him in his mechanic overalls and a cowboy hat. I take a deep breath through my nose and let it out slowly through my mouth while Flynn pours the cereal and grabs the milk carton that's still on the counter.

"For a while I wasn't really sure what I wanted to do." He shakes his head. "No, that's not true. I guess I always loved cars, but I didn't have the guts to go after it until recently."

I can't imagine Flynn anything less than confident. Even the way he stood there making a breakfast he had no idea how to make, he looked sure of himself. He is so very fascinating to me.

I prop my elbow on the counter and my chin in my palm. "Tell me all about it."

FOURTEEN
EGRESS

Flynn

JACKIE LIKES LUCKY CHARMS.

Turns out she's a cereal girl who hates coffee. I love finding out these things about her. Small things. Intimate things. Like how she becomes quite the wild woman when she's mindless with pleasure.

"I wasn't always going to work with cars. Like I said before, I went to the standard four year."

"Where was that?"

"Baylor."

She nods. "That's a good school."

"Yeah, I guess."

"You didn't like it?"

"Honestly, I don't remember much. I passed, but not with flying colors. I was still messed up over my parents and acting like an asshole. I basically partied my way through."

"Oh."

My shoulders tighten, thinking of my past self: a stupid kid with too much money, a chip on my shoulder the size of Texas, and full of anger over my parents' deaths. But the hollow feeling that just hit my stomach comes from Jackie's soft-spoken disappointment.

"I majored in business, thinking I'd..." I trail off, not wanting to get into the oil business side of my family's ranch. Instead I wave my spoon in the air indifferently. "But thankfully I wised up and went to trade school."

"And do you love it?"

"Yep. Can't imagine being happy doing anything else."

"That really is the key, isn't it? Doing something you love."

"I guess it is."

"We are both very lucky that we can do what we love and make a living at it."

I don't bother telling her that I don't have to make a living at anything. That even if my shop made no money, I'd be okay. That I'm luckier than she even guesses. I'm not sure why. She told me about her mom, her odd relationship with her dad and the uncomfortable memories from being smarter than all her peers growing up. The guilt I feel is more than knowing I'm purposely omitting things, it's that I'm holding back from her by doing so. But I still don't share.

I try asking her about NASA, but she seems more interested in my shop and restoring vintage cars. Just as when I explained hot wiring, she soaks it all up. I have a feeling Jackie will be able to reiterate everything I tell her like an expert after just this one conversation.

"Do you know about the history between astronauts and Corvettes?" Jackie asks.

"No. What about it? Do a lot of astronauts drive them or something?"

"Well, they used to." She puts her spoon down and angles toward me.

I'm quite proud of myself when I stop myself from glancing down at her legs.

"See, Alan Shepard was a big sports car fan. A lot of them were." She pushes up the bridge of her glasses. "Astronauts, I mean." She looks off to the side. "I guess that makes sense, as in the early days astronauts really were the definition of adrenaline junkies. How else would you explain their drive to strap themselves into a shuttle built by the lowest bidder, attached to a rocket that literally creates explosions under them to propel them into the unknown?" She shakes her head, as if to clear it.

Adrenaline junkies. I know all about them, being raised by two of them.

"Sorry, where was I?" Jackie asks.

I clear my throat and focus on the present. "Corvettes?"

"Oh yeah." She shifts forward, her knees skimming the side of my thigh, and my fingers clench around the spoon. "So Alan Shepard was known to show up to his training driving a Corvette. And after he became the first American in space, GM gifted him with a Corvette that had a custom interior, complete with altimeter gauges, like a pilot would use."

Jackie could not be more perfect. She's teaching me something about cars, while giving me a hard-on just by breathing. I try to feign nonchalance. "Cool. That must have been, what, a '61?"

"'62," she says with a wave of her hand. "But that was just the start. After Shepard, no one was allowed to be given cars anymore, for fear that it might look like the government was endorsing General Motors. But some dealer in Florida got around that by offering all the astronauts a deal where they leased a Corvette for one dollar, and they could re-lease a new model every year for the same cost."

Her dress inches higher on her legs as she gestures.

I refocus on her eyes. "Dang. I guess it pays to be an astronaut."

"Unfortunately, the heyday of astronauts being treated like rock stars is over. Which I think is stupid. They are *so* much cooler than rock stars."

She has me chuckling at the pout on her face. It's rare a woman can get a guy rock hard and laughing at the same time.

I make a note to look into '62 'vettes.

She pushes around the cereal in her bowl. Only the non-marshmallows are left. She might not have a caffeine vice, but my girl definitely has a sweet tooth.

One more thing I like about her.

I can't ever remember wanting to know someone the way I want to know Jackie. And I want her to know me too.

The lies of omission that have been stacking up between us is getting to me. I want to—

The soundtrack from *Space Odyssey* reverberates across the great room.

Jackie jumps back and grabs her phone from her jacket pocket.

It probably isn't the best time to tell her I confiscated the thong I'd found in her other pocket. I'm musing over the fact that that means Jackie is still going commando, when I see her face as she checks the screen.

"What is it?"

Jackie spins around me and jogs over to her boots by the door, beginning to put them on. "I have to go."

Though momentarily stunned by the sight of her bare ass thrust up in the air as she tries shoving her feet into her boots, in a few long strides I'm beside her, cradling her face in my hand. "Hey. What just happened? You okay? Did I do something?"

She blinks once, her expression softening. "No, no, of course not. It isn't anything like that. I just forgot about Boondoggle's."

"Boondoggle's? The bar?"

She nods.

"I don't follow."

"The crew currently on the ISS is calling down today. I need to be there." She bends down again, trying without much success to jam her bare foot into a boot. "Jules is going to kill me."

"Wait." I have to close my eyes to think, so I don't just stare at her ass. "You have to go to a bar to talk to astronauts? And who is Jules?"

She seems to give up on her boots and straightens, lifting her arms to twist her hair into some sort of knot.

She must honestly not have a clue about what she's doing. Between bending over sans panties and pushing her no-bra breasts out while fixing her hair, my mind keeps stalling.

"It's something astronauts do sometimes to say thanks. They just completed a spacewalk a while ago, and though the results sucked, everything else went okay. NASA has a deal with Boondoggles where they can set up a video conference outside and everyone can gather and say hi to the crew and drink beer the astronauts paid for. Kind of like Face Timing from space. Or Skype." She shrugs. "It's a thing. It's been happening for years."

"And Jules?" I ask, trying to keep up.

"Jules is my friend. She's up in the station at the moment. She's the one who got me to go out that night when I met Rose." Jackie lowers her hands, giving up on her hair.

"She did, did she? I guess I'll have to thank her for that." I tuck a stray tendril behind her ear and straighten her glasses, loving how she seems to relax into my touch. "But why is she going to kill you?"

"Who? Oh, Jules. Long story involving her go-to blackmail move." She leans against the wall, trying once again to get her boots on. One finally jams on. "But bottom line—if I don't show up today she's going to tell Ian I want to, and I quote, 'bone him hard.'"

All thoughts of Jackie's bare ass, her sweet eyes and her sexy brain are overridden with one thought—*Oh, hell no.*

"I'm coming with you."

FIFTEEN
PIT STOP

Flynn

JACKIE'S HAIR IS A TORNADO IN THE WIND.

I love it.

She asked to put the windows down and now she's fighting to wrangle her hair with both hands.

"You sure you don't want me to put the windows up?"

"No, no. I got it." She finally seems to anchor it to the side of her head in one hand, her elbow propped on the car door. We speed by NASA on the way to her apartment, the breeze off of Clear Lake whipping through the car. "What kind of car does Ian drive, do you know?"

Her interest in her co-worker, even if it is about cars, dims my good mood. "A Tesla S P100D." I might not like Ian, but even I have to admit, the man has a sweet ride. Zero to sixty in two point five seconds.

"That's a mouthful," she says.

I snort, thinking about the mouthful I'd like to give her.

"What? What's so funny?"

Well, there's no way I'm telling her *that*. "Uh, I was thinking about orbital resonance."

"Really?" She does a little bounce on the seat, looking pleased.

I laugh, my mood restored. "Don't sound too excited—I don't really remember what it is. To me, though, orbital resonance is a mouthful. A Tesla S P100D is just a sweet-ass ride."

"I can see that." Her head tilts back, exposing the long and slender neck I love. She's so damn sexy, loose wisps of hair dancing around her face.

"How much does a car like that cost, you think?"

There goes my mood again. "Why do you ask?"

"I'm thinking it may be time to upgrade."

My jaw clenches for a moment before responding. "Ian's Tesla will run you about 135 grand."

"Seriously?" She sits up in her seat, one fist still locked around her hair. "Ian must be loaded."

I find myself wanting to snap, "Not as loaded as me," but I don't. One, because I'm not five years old. And two, I'd hate myself if I resorted to trying to win Jackie's affection with money. And then there's also the fact that if I did tell her I was a millionaire a few times over, she'd ask why I downplayed the ranch earlier. So I swallow it down, along with the unease I feel.

"You and Ian…?"

A gust of wind whips some of her hair into her face, and I can't see her expression. "What about us?"

Us. Thank fuck for the strength of my Boss's steering wheel, otherwise it would've snapped in my fists by the time I pull into her apartment complex. "He called you 'hon' the other day."

"He did, didn't he?" Jackie purses her lips. "I meant to ask him about that."

I park in Jackie's still vacant spot.

"I guess I should've driven my own car back. I didn't think of that," she says.

I try not to harp on the fact that she didn't answer my question about Ian. "All part of the plan. This way you have to come back to my place later."

She blushes, and I watch as shades of red travel down her neck and between her breasts. *Damn.*

Mood restored.

I lean over and kiss her neck, nibbling up to her ear. "You going to invite me in this time?" I ask.

"Hmm? Oh. Sure, of course. But I should warn you, the girls were over last night before we went out and they kind of exploded clothes all over the place." We exit the car and round the front. "It looks like my own personal gamma-ray burst," she grumbles.

I grab her hand as we head for the stairs, smiling. "Gamma-ray burst?"

"Extremely energetic explosions. They're the brightest electromagnetic events known to occur in the universe."

I let her go ahead of me on the stairs, 'cause I'm a gentleman, not because I get to look at her ass sway. "Extremely energetic explosions?" I ask, eyes glued to the bottom of her dress. "Yeah, that sounds like Rose."

My joke has her throwing a smile over her shoulder as we reach the top of the stairs. One leg on the landing, the other behind her on the last step, ass cheek slightly visible at the hem of her dress, sex hair thrown over one shoulder, glasses perched on her nose, and a wide smile — and I swear to God I almost throw her to the ground right there. Thankfully I'm just struck dumb, and Jackie continues on her way to the door, keys in hand.

Watching her at the door reminds me so much of that first ride home, where I wanted to do more than just kiss her cheek, but refrained, knowing then that this girl was more than just a hook-up. I lean forward and cage her, wanting to be closer to her. The lock clicks with the turn of her wrist, but instead of opening it, she rotates in my arms.

"I've never had a guy in here before." She adjusts her glasses, looking so damn innocent I have a hard time not feeling like the big bad wolf. I have a harder time not liking it.

"Is that so?" *Fuck you, Ian, I got here first.*

"Yeah. I don't really... I mean I haven't..."

"Jackie?" I lean in and lightly rub my nose against hers.

"Yes?"

"I'm going to kiss you now."

"Oh. Okay."

I dip my head lower, brushing her lips once before increasing the pressure. I take my time, savoring her, letting my tongue make small, leisurely strokes between kisses. I wait until her hands move away from her sides and bunch into my shirt before pulling away. While her eyes are still closed, I reach around her and turn the knob, swinging the door open.

"Let's get you inside and changed so we can get to Boondoggle's on time." And so Ian knows she most definitely does not want to bone him, 'cause she's boning me.

Her eyes flutter open with a smile. "Okay."

In the apartment, I immediately notice the couch and how it's ten times cooler than mine. And I could totally see that kitchen table in my breakfast nook.

Jackie walks across the small living space to another door, bringing my attention back to her. "I won't be long. Make yourself comfortable."

"Will do."

I take my time wandering around the apartment. With how small it is, it doesn't take long.

I hear water running and I have to take a few deep breaths after imagining Jackie wet and warm under the spray. Looking to distract myself, I walk over to look at several frames leaning against the wall. I flip one and then another forward, tilting my head sideways to read what turns out to be various degrees. Mostly from Stanford University, but there are also quite a few NASA certificates and awards.

These should be hung up. I look around at the limited wall space, angry that she doesn't have a spot for her accomplishments. They should be prominently displayed, a testament to all her hard work. I automatically think of the alcove in my foyer. It's a space the decorator said would be good for a small office.

Jesus, I'm already moving her in with me in my head. *Get a grip, man.*

Carefully, I lean the frames back against the wall and step away.

Besides the cool couch and kitchen table, everything looks like it came straight from a garage sale or college dorm. I'm about to park myself on the sofa when I hear voices from where Jackie had disappeared. Not too proud to snoop, I lean on the wall next to the door and listen in.

"So, I was thinking of my Converse, jeans and maybe one of the new tops you brought." There's a thud. "Sorry, I dropped the phone. Hold on, let me put you on speaker. I can't go through all these clothes with one hand," Jackie says.

There's some shuffling and then my sister's voice comes through. I mentally roll my eyes. Rose doesn't need to be put on speaker to be heard.

"What is it with you and Converse?" Rose asks.

"What do you mean?"

"I mean, you dress like a kid."

"Chucks are cool," Jackie insists.

"Chucks?"

"Yeah, that's what Converse All Stars are called—Chucks. After basketball player Charles Taylor, who wore and sold the shoes. A lot of basketball players wore them after that, as did athletes in the Olympics. Even soldiers sported them in basic training during World War II."

"Why do you know all that? Never mind, don't answer. You know everything."

I want to slap my sister for that remark, especially when Jackie remains silent.

"I'm sorry," Rose says. "I'm being a bitch. I'm just trying to figure out why you wear, despite their interesting history, what are now considered high school boy shoes all the time."

Jackie's voice sounds small at first. "They aren't high school boy shoes." Another pause. "Okay, maybe they are, but they're cool. There are photos all over NASA of John Glenn wearing Chucks during astronaut training."

"Sometimes I wonder how crowded your brain must be." Rose sighs. "Anyway. John Glenn's heyday was before you were born. Why this obsession? It's like you want to live and dress like a 1960s dude."

"I like NASA and its history. Nothing weird about that."

"You are crazy stupid smart. I don't get it. You could be designing an interstellar satellite, making millions in the private industry, or inventing a freaking time machine. Why this obsession with NASA?"

Jackie mumbles something and I press my ear to the door.

"What?" Rose asks.

"'Cause my mom loved it, okay?"

"Wait. What? I thought your mom..."

"Yeah, she died after I was born. My dad never really talks about her, but when I was little, I found all this NASA stuff she collected. News clippings from the time of the space race, astronomy books. Turns out she was a big space nerd. She would chart stars and once even went to Florida to watch a launch. She was a real NASA geek."

"Oh."

"So, when I got older I started reading about the Mercury 7 and all the Apollo missions. I loved the idea of space being the last uncharted territory." There's more shuffling. "It was the one topic my dad would talk to me about that wasn't about his research or my grades. And... I don't know, I guess I think my mom would have thought me working at NASA was cool too."

"Yeah, Jackie. I'm sure she would've."

I had to strain to hear my sister. For once she's speaking at a normal decibel level.

Jackie sniffs, and that's all I can take. I stride into the room.

"Flynn!" Jackie's hands go to her towel, which is precariously wrapped around her breasts.

"Is that my brother?" Rose shouts in her normal pitch.

"Yes, Rose." I speak to the phone lying on the bed. "May I ask why you are screaming at Jackie on the phone?"

"I'm not screaming. I'm just helping a sister out with some clothing options."

I step behind Jackie and wrap my arms around her middle, loving how it shifts her towel a bit lower. I nuzzle her neck, working my way down to her shoulder. She giggles.

"Ew. Gross, dude." Rose makes gagging sounds. "Ugh. That's my cue to hang up. I'll see you in a few." The screen goes blank.

"See you in a few?" I ask.

"Yeah. I called for clothing advice, and Rose thought a NASA work get-together complete with astronauts sounded like a bomb-ass good time."

"Bomb-ass good time?" I move my hands down her sides and up under the towel.

"Rose's words." Her voice sounds slightly strangled.

"Hmmm." I hum against her neck, tugging the towel to the floor.

Naked and damp from the shower, Jackie's skin feels like liquid fire. Up and down, soft and hard, I drag my hands across her body. When I cup her breasts, she arches against me, grinding her ass into my crotch. My eyes roll back as my dick throbs against my jeans.

One hand plucks her nipple, while my other moves between her thighs, dipping into wetness.

"You okay?" I murmur.

"Hmm?"

I dip again. "Are you sore?"

"No. I... I'm okay." Her arms reach back and grab my ass, showing me just how okay she is.

My chest rumbles in pleasure and I add a finger, stretching her, while my thumb circles her clit. Pressing up and grinding, Jackie starts making wild, desperate sounds.

I love this. Jackie undone.

"That's right, darling. Let me hear you." I pinch harder on her nipple and she jolts in my hold before stiffening. A deep moan wrenches from her throat.

After the final tremors leave, I slip my fingers from her and turn her body in my arms. Her eyes are half closed and she lays her head on my shoulder.

"Where are your glasses?"

"Nightstand." Her voice breathless. "Why?"

I walk her back a step until her legs meet the bed. I lean her back, her damp hair spreading out on her white comforter, the sheen from the shower now a sheen of sweat from her orgasm. She looks like a pornographic angel and I fucking love it. "Don't move."

I grab her glasses from a stack of books that acts as a night stand and move back in front of her, hovering over her. Propping my weight on one fist, I place her glasses on her with the other. Then I push back up, admiring the view.

My genius, pornographic angel.

I rip off my clothes, pulling a condom from my pocket before kicking my jeans out of the way. Jackie starts to shift up on her elbows, but I stop her, repeating, "Don't move."

She licks her lips at my command and settles down on the mattress again.

I can feel my dick pulsating as I roll the condom on. No one has ever gotten me hard like this before. I bend down and grab her legs, one in each hand, pulling her until her ass meets the edge of the bed. I rest her ankles on my shoulders. The view only gets better.

I grunt as my first thrust hits deep inside her. I have to bite down hard on my lip to keep from coming as I watch myself slide in and out of her, my cock slick from her wetness. I glance at Jackie, her eyes framed by her glasses, hands fisting in the comforter, and I'm overcome with an urge to dominate.

"Touch yourself."

And she does. My beautiful genius palms her breasts while they bounce from my pounding.

"Pinch your nipples."

She does.

"Harder."

She moans in response, whether from my command or the act, I don't know. But it's so fucking hot.

I reach down and lift her ass with my hands so I can hit deeper. After a few driving strokes Jackie's head thrashes while her hands leave her breasts to pound on the mattress.

"Flynn!"

The sound of my name echoing in the room has me losing the rhythm, my thrusts slow then fast, then slow again until the chaos of the moment shatters with my orgasm and I grind my hips against hers until she follows me across the finish line.

———

Jackie

Flynn drops to his knees, my legs still perched on his shoulders. Sliding one hand from under my bottom, he glides it over my stomach and between my legs, where I can still feel the friction from him pounding into me.

"I've dirtied you up again." One side of his mouth kicks up. "Sorry."

I smile back. "No, you're not."

"No. I'm not." He chuckles and reaches out his hands.

I put my hands in his and he pulls me up. My breasts bounce lightly in his face. He leans in and softly kisses each peak before standing and redressing.

I watch as he shifts his weight to tug up his pants, his muscles bunching and contracting with his movements.

Good God, the man is the living embodiment of one of the heroes on my romance novel covers. I chance a quick glance at the shelf where my collection rests. *Please, don't let him look over there.*

I walk in the opposite direction over to my dresser and pull out some underwear and socks. There are new thongs on the floor from Rose's shopping spree, but I'm not about to endure that torture again.

I try to avoid the mirror. Lord knows the state of my hair. I chance a glance and sigh. Definite sex hair. I pull it up and try to twist it into some kind of order. Fail.

At least I'm not wearing that sorry excuse for a dress. I'm not sure my co-workers would even recognize me if I'd shown up looking like a bed-headed prostitute.

"What's with all the new clothes?" Flynn picks up a silk blouse from the floor, wrinkled from our recent exertion.

"Rose bought me a bunch of stuff yesterday." I tug on my

plain black cotton panties, trying not to be fazed by Flynn watching me dress.

"Rose bought all this?" A funny look passes over his face as he takes in the pile of clothes strewn about the room, all with the tags still on them. I'm too busy trying to situate my breasts in the cups of my bra while not looking like a complete idiot to analyze it.

"Yeah."

Flynn sighs, tilting his head back at the ceiling. He stills. "Fuck, Jackie." He looks at me and points up. "You do that?"

I'd almost forgotten about my personal galaxy. "Oh. Yeah." My face heats. He must think I'm such a nerd.

"That's awesome."

I let out a breath. "Really?"

"Yeah. Really." He shakes his head and smiles, the look from earlier gone.

Something comes over me at his look, making me want to share with him something no one else knows. "I… I want to be an astronaut."

His eyebrows arch. "Really?"

I try tucking my wild hair behind my ears. "Um… yeah. I haven't told anyone yet, but I've made it past the initial round of resumes and interviews."

"That's… wow, Jackie, that's great."

Though he sounds a bit stiff, relief courses through me. I don't know why his opinion means so much, but it does.

"But isn't it really dangerous? Being an astronaut?"

I pick up a jean skirt off the floor. I don't think I'd be comfortable in a lot of what Rose bought me, especially in front of my co-workers, but a jean skirt seems like a nice, safe step up from my usual jean pants. "Statistically, being an astronaut isn't that dangerous. Loggers, truckers and even farmers have higher fatality rates than astronauts."

I shimmy the skirt up, pausing once I snap the top button when I realize how short it is. Hmmmm. I'm thinking of asking Flynn his opinion, but one look at his eyes and I can see he's in favor of the skirt. "Plus NASA has come a long way since its cowboy days."

Trying not to think of all the skin currently exposed on my legs, I grab my Converse off the floor at the end of the bed. They've seen better days, I guess. The soles are still attached, but they're worn smooth from use, and the white isn't really white anymore. Maybe Rose is right. Maybe I do dress like a high school boy. I grab my boots from last night and start to slip them on. It's a lot easier when I have socks on.

"Why don't you wear your Chucks?" Flynn asks.

I jerk my head up. "You call them Chucks?"

"Of course. Who doesn't?"

I think my face breaks with the expanse of my smile. "You really don't mind if I wear sneakers?"

"Why would I mind? You look sexy as hell in your Chucks."

Honestly, I feel my face crack.

"Plus I get to keep looking at those mile-long legs I just had propped up on my shoulders."

"Oh."

I stand there blinking until Flynn reaches over and pulls me in for a quick kiss.

"If I stay here and watch you shake your way into more clothes, we are never leaving this apartment." Then he touches his nose to mine once before leaving me to get dressed. In a daze, I simply scan the room trying to sort out what new shirt I should wear when I see the clock on the nightstand.

Crap!

I'm late. And I'm never late.

But as I grab my Chucks off the floor, I just keep smiling.

SIXTEEN

YELLOW FLAG

Flynn

BOONDOGGLE'S PORCH IS PACKED. APPARENTLY, NASA THROWS a mean happy hour. Even if their happy hour is more like brunch. I took hold of Jackie's hand while walking across the parking lot, and I squeeze it before stepping up the stairs, but she seems too distracted to take much notice.

It occurs to me that Jackie spends a lot of her time distracted. When she lectures on a topic she has laser focus, but the rest of the time her mind seems to be racing in a million different directions. That's probably why she never notices all the attention men give her.

Like now.

"Jackie!" Ian weaves through the crowd to get to her. He's wearing a pressed dress shirt and slacks, for fuck's sake. To a bar. "Didn't think you'd be here," he says once he reaches us. "You usually don't come out to these things."

She mumbles something about interfering, blackmailing astronauts, but I don't think Ian's paying much attention. The man's eyes are looking at the tight black tank top stretched over Jackie's chest and the skirt that rides low on her hips, revealing an inch of midriff. To give the guy credit, his checkout is subtle, so maybe that's another reason why Jackie's so clueless.

Jackie tugs her skirt down with her free hand, which only widens the expanse of skin shown at her waist. A sigh escapes me.

I know I shouldn't be mad at my sister. I mean, when she put the thing on, I certainly appreciated how Jackie looked in the skirt. But damn, I had not factored in that the clothes Jackie would be choosing from are ones which Rose, with her less than ladylike taste, had bought. So not only is the skirt short, but the top is tight. Now I'll have to fight off everyone else's bad intentions as well as calm my own.

Ian's gaze travels to me, then down to our clasped hands. *That's right, buddy. She's here with me.*

Jackie tries to loosen my grip, but I squeeze tighter. It has been a long fucking time since I've felt this way about anyone, and I'm not above caveman-like maneuvers to scare off the competition.

"Ian, you remember Flynn. Flynn, Ian." She gestures between us with her free hand.

I nod at Ian.

"Yes, I remember Flynn." Ian looks somewhat amused as he motions us to follow him through the crowd. "Better take a seat while you can. The crew should call down any minute," he says when we reach an open table.

"Thanks." Jackie moves to sit down, but hesitates. The tables are picnic style, with attached benches. There's no way she can straddle a seat in that skirt without flashing someone.

My lips twitch. "Problem, darling?" I let her hand go and wait to see what she'll do.

Jackie stares hard at the bench. "No. I just need…" She tilts her head to one side, surveying the bench. "…to think a moment."

Then she sits down and spins on her butt with her legs straight out, in one smooth motion. She did it so quickly there's no way anyone got a glimpse of anything.

And I should know. I'd been looking.

I swing just one leg over, straddling the bench so I can bracket Jackie with my body. I rest one hand across her lower back.

Ian seems to have gotten the message, but I might as well let the rest of her co-workers understand she's taken. Speaking of co-workers, she seems determined to avoid their eyes, despite their attempts to catch hers.

If I think about it, she hadn't actually invited me. Is she embarrassed of me? When it comes right down to it, I *am* just a mechanic. True, I might be able to buy and sell these people twice over, but they don't know that. Hell, *Jackie* doesn't know that. At least, I hope she doesn't. I lift my hand from her back, about to ask her if she'd like me to go when someone shouts out to her.

"Yoo-hoo! Jackie? We're here!" Trish stands on the steps of the bar's porch, waving her arm like a beauty queen on steroids. Rose is next to her trying to steer clear of getting clobbered. I see her eyes cut to the corner of the room, but before I can follow my sister's line of sight, I see my brother behind her.

My whole body tenses. It's been a while since Holt and I have been in the same room. In fact, the last time we were in the same room, he'd been busy plowing Beth.

Rose brings her attention back to Trish. "Yoo-hoo?" She rolls her eyes and makes her way to our table. "Jesus, Trish, between you and Jackie, I swear I'm hanging with the Bobbsey Twins. Why don't you just start saying 'Hi-dee-ho there, neighbor' for fuck's sake?"

"Rose. Language," Holt's familiar strong voice admonishes.

I smile despite the awkward situation. I'd forgotten about Holt's life mission to get our sister to talk and act more like a lady.

Trish reaches the table and gets in Rose's face. "Yeah, well the fact that you know who the Bobbsey Twins are negates any point you were trying to make."

"Hey, my Gramps read those books to me. So suck it. And negate? Who are you, Jackie now? One genius is enough."

That wipes the smile from my face and I look to see if my sister's careless words have hurt Jackie. But she surprises me by laughing. Slowly, she stands, careful to tug down her skirt before waving to the rest of the crowd. "Everyone, these are my friends Rose, Trish and Flynn."

Trish does the big wave again and Rose just smiles, throwing her shoulders back and putting one hand on her hip. Everyone on the porch seems transfixed with the newcomers, and I'm just happy to be included, even if she called me a friend.

I see Ian throwing a particularly intense look in Trish's direction.

"Holt, is it?" Jackie asks, turning toward my brother.

Holt has been glaring at Rose, but looks to Jackie at the sound of his name.

"Yes, ma'am." He tips his cowboy hat toward her and sticks out his hand. Jackie seems to melt a bit at the whole cowboy schtick Holt has always been good at, and a flare of jealousy hits me hard and fast. I stand before Jackie can take Holt's hand, ready to plant a fist in his smiling face. But before I can even raise my arm, I'm interrupted.

"Holy shit, Jackie. You do *not* mess around."

Everyone, including me, turns toward the bar at the back of the porch where a screen has been set up. On the screen, a cute brunette with tight spiral curls winks. I glance at Jackie to see her roll her eyes at the woman. "Nice to see you too, Jules."

"You going to introduce me to these fine-looking men?" Jules asks.

Jackie sighs. "This is Flynn, he's my—"

"Date," I supply. "I'm her date." I wrap one arm around Jackie's waist.

"I see. Well, hello there, Jackie's date." She winks again. "I'm Jules." Her eyes track beside me to my brother. "And what's your name, cowboy?"

"Holt West, ma'am." He tips his hat again, this time toward the camera.

"Mmmm… me likey." Jules blows a kiss and I'm shocked as shit to see my brother's cheeks turn red. Jules' eyes move back to Jackie. "Well done, hooker, well done."

Everyone at the bar laughs while muscles I didn't realize were tense relax a bit.

Jackie blushes and narrows her eyes at the screen. "I'm going to kill her so hard when she gets back to Earth," she mumbles.

"Sweet Jehoshaphat." Trish's wide eyes meet Jackie's. "Can astronauts say hooker?"

"This is a private feed, it isn't broadcasted or anything. They can basically say what they want," Ian says, stepping up to the table, still staring at Trish.

Jackie leans into me. "Which Jules definitely takes advantage of."

I smell her hair while my fingers glide over the exposed skin at her waist. "So that's the blackmailer, huh?"

The camera zooms out and the rest of the crew, floating in air, comes into view. There's one woman besides Jules, and three men. They all wear polo shirts with NASA patches and cargo pants. Cheers go up, people shouting hello while raising their glasses.

"Hopefully that will be me someday," Jackie whispers, throwing a shy smile my way.

I make myself nod, though I can't help but hope it doesn't happen. Jackie may have her statistics and be able to brush off concerns for safety, but I remember the Challenger and Columbia tragedies.

I try to shake off the doom and gloom when we sit back down, and Rose, Trish, Ian and Holt follow. Everyone starts grabbing glasses, pouring beer from the pitchers on the center of the tables and talking. Only in Texas are beer pitchers a staple of brunch. But in the midst of all the activity, I catch Rose's eyes bouncing back and forth between Holt and me, like she's waiting for a throw-down. Even Jackie's brow furrows as if she, too, realizes something doesn't feel right.

I wait for old anger and resentment to surge through me. And it does, no surprise, since Holt never even fucking apologized. But what does surprise me is the realization that the pain has dulled. No longer a sharp spike to the chest, but more like the ache of scar tissue being prodded. I'm really too preoccupied with Jackie. With this new feeling of contentment that I haven't had since, well, ever. It's a little disconcerting how much impact this blond genius already has over my life after just one week.

But Jackie wants to be an astronaut. I mean, she sure as shit is smart enough. How many people have a doctorate at twenty-nine? And all those awards stacked up against the wall at her place. But... space?

My dad, being a race car driver, always put himself in danger. It didn't help that my mom insisted on drag racing with him in the underground circuit. They were the ultimate thrill seekers. Leaving Holt, Rose and me behind to chase whatever adrenaline rush they could find. They didn't need to. They were filthy rich oil barons. Apparently that wasn't enough for them. Hell, being parents wasn't enough for them. And now the girl whose hand I'm holding wants to strap herself to a rocket. A shudder races down my spine and I try to play it off by shrugging my shoulders and reaching for my beer.

It was a long time ago, but I remember when our parents died.

Racing with a bunch of other adrenaline junkie motorheads, taking risks they had no right to take with three kids at home. It was an underground street race, so all it took was one pothole at high speed, and the car my dad had lovingly restored spun out and flipped until it resembled nothing more than a crushed beer can.

My mother had been a gold-digger. There's no getting around that. But the one thing my mom and dad had in common, besides a love of money, was their love of racing. My dad loved the cars and my mom loved the thrill. And the expense of the sport, no doubt. They weren't the most stable parental presence, but they were our parents and they had died doing something selfish and dangerous.

I may not know much about aerospace engineering, but I know if a simple pothole can kill so easily, riding a rocket to the Space Station has to be a hell of a lot more dangerous.

All the talking and laughing around us distracts me, which is good, because as Gramps would say, worrying about the future is as effective as pissing in the wind.

Jackie blushes her way through the NASA group chit-chat, using a weird mix of acronyms and engineering terms like a second language. I don't understand most of it, but I do understand passion, and Jackie has it in spades when it comes to NASA. I'm not about to ruin this for her with my own insecurities or my family's shit.

I ignore the anxiety building in my chest at the thought of Jackie in space, and I ignore my brother. Maybe Jackie won't get offered the astronaut position. And maybe it's time for Holt and me to move beyond the past.

Maybe.

———

Jackie

I have a hot auto mechanic wrapped around me while sitting in a bar on a Sunday. I've spent the last half hour introducing my co-workers to my friends and Flynn. A girl from work actually high-fived me when I introduced her to Flynn. Jules even got them all to stand in front of the camera so she could 'get a better look.'

I thought it especially interesting how much Jules relished making Holt blush. I don't question everyone's interest. The Wests are one good-looking bunch of siblings. Flynn with his blue-green eyes and light brown hair. Rose's ironic sweet country beauty. And now Holt, all tall, dark and handsome complete with a Southern twang and a cowboy hat.

Flynn nuzzles my neck and I see Rebecca from Payloads sigh. I can't get over that this is my life now. Operation Social Life is working. Mental fist pump.

"Earth to Jackie?" Rose calls from across the table.

I blink, refocusing. "Mmm?"

"Trish has decided that Holt is not her type." Holt sputters into his beer glass while Trish sends him an apologetic shrug. "Where be all the hot man astronauts?" Rose jerks her thumb to the screen. "You know, the ones currently on land who are more easily doable."

"Christ, Rose," Flynn mutters. His breath tickles my neck, sending shivers down my spine. My glasses slip down my nose, but before I can adjust them, Flynn's index finger pushes the frames back into place. He's been staring at Rose, shaking his head in exasperation when he adjusted my glasses. I know I'm making more of it than I should. But it's just that the movement was so fluid, so second nature, that it made me feel... I don't know, important to him somehow.

Annnnnd, I need to stop thinking like this. Emotional rationale is not a thing, no matter how much I want it to be. Flynn probably has good reflexes or something.

"Holt, we're out of beer. Go get us a new pitcher." Rose pushes the empty one toward her brother.

I jump up, ready to change my train of thought. "I'll get it!" Flynn starts to object, but I cut him off. "No, really. The astronauts are buying, remember? I just need to show them my badge." I pull my lanyard out from my pocket and slip it over my head.

"Geek chic, girl." Rose nods at my badge.

"Oh yeah. We're real fashion conscious at NASA." I swing my leg over the bench.

Rose clucks. "So you decided not to go for the thong, huh?"

I freeze mid-step. *Dang it.*

"Rose!" Trish smacks Rose's arm.

"What? I was just saying..."

The surface of Mars has nothing on the current shade my face is turning, I'm sure. I make to hustle off and get the beer when Flynn pulls on my arm, bringing my face level to his. The first kiss is light. The second, not so much.

"Get it, girl!" someone shouts.

At the end, I can't dredge up any embarrassment over having flashed my underwear. In fact, I would probably strip down to my bra and panties for another kiss.

Instead, I rein in my newly raging hormones and head toward the porch bar. It's jam-packed so I decide to try my luck inside.

The rush of air conditioning chills my sweaty skin. People say you get used to the Texas heat.

They lie.

I lean forward on the less crowded bar, badge in hand. NASA throws a lot of business Boondoggle's way, so even though it's kind of shameless, I wave my badge around in order to get faster service.

I have a hot auto mechanic to get back to. A hot mechanic who likes *me*.

Lost in daydreams, I don't realize someone's stepped into the space next to me until they speak.

"Well, aren't *you* cute!"

I glance over my shoulder to see a woman worthy of a Victoria's Secret commercial standing a few inches away, leaning on the bar like she owns it. Sleek, shiny blond hair falls in a precise, angled bob. She reminds me of a Barbie doll, especially with the insanely high stiletto heels. And her dress is reminiscent of the outfit I wore to Big Texas, except hers is actually shorter and tighter and she isn't wearing a jacket. Thinking in Flynn terms, I'd describe it as not exactly street legal.

Not a single freckle mars this woman's deeply tanned skin. Her left brow arches over a heavily made-up eye as she returns my study of her person with her own of mine. All I can think is—who'd wear *that* to lunch at a family restaurant/bar?

I look around, thinking she's talking to someone else. But I don't think she was calling the pot-bellied, long-bearded man on my other side cute.

"Excuse me?" I ask, turning back to her.

"I said, 'aren't *you* cute?'" Her smile looks stiff and mean while the tanned skin of her forehead and around her eyes is tight and unnaturally smooth.

"Thank you?" I search for something nice to say back, as I'm pretty sure that's correct social protocol, but I definitely don't think she's cute, nor do I think comparing her to a Barbie doll will go over too well. I settle for, "You must have exceptionally toned legs to walk in such high heels."

Her lips twist, as if she can't tell if I'm being a smartass or not. Honestly, I don't know myself. I just know I'm extremely uncomfortable talking to her. And for someone who is usually uncomfortable in social situations, that's saying something.

"You must be his flavor of the month." She pouts, her thick lip gloss melding her lips together.

Huh?

"Flynn," she continues, when it's obvious I'm not grasping her insinuation. "I can see how a woman of your...style?... might attract him for a bit." She flashes her teeth. "He always did like unique models. But after he fixes them up and drives them for a while, he gets bored and trades them in. Looks like he got himself a real fixer-upper this time." She gives me another once-over. "Oh, darling, are those sneakers?" She laughs. Not kindly.

My hands bunch into fists at 'darling.' I don't think I've ever wanted to hit someone in my entire life, but I desperately want to take a swing at her overly plumped lips. "Who *are* you?"

"Me? I'm Beth." She pauses, like I'm supposed to know what that means.

"Beth who?"

Her expression falls for a moment, but she recovers quickly. "I'm the girl Flynn West wants to marry."

My mouth drops open and it's enough to bring that smug look back to her face.

"Marry?"

"That's right, little girl." She waves her pointy, polished talons at me. "You might interest him enough for him to want to pop your hood and figure out how you tick, but I'm the classic he'll keep coming back to." She runs both of her hands down the sides of her body, then looks pointedly at my shoes and laughs again. It's soft and deep and sexy. And mean.

Mean enough that I don't correct her on her faulty metaphor. Cars don't tick, clocks do.

"Flynn is just slumming, sweetie. He'll come around and realize his place is with me. He always does."

The bar tunnels around me and suddenly I'm back in college, listening to the guy I liked joke with his friends about me, about how he finally bagged the nerd. Only now Brian's face is Flynn's and the laughter sounds like a woman's high-pitched giggle.

"Here's your pitcher." The bartender sets it down, the noise making me jump. He looks to Beth, smiling. "And what can I get *you?*"

Beth licks her lips and angles forward, effectively turning her back on me.

And just like that, I'm forgotten.

Looking at the weirdly symmetrical everything on this woman, I wonder how long it will take Flynn to forget me too.

I pick up the pitcher and make my way outside. I stand there for a moment taking in the scene. Trish is talking to Ian. Holt watches the screen while Jules shows off, doing flips in zero gravity. Flynn sits facing away from his brother but smiling at Rose. It's a scene that a moment ago would've made me feel like I was living the dream.

Someone bumps me hard from behind and half the pitcher of beer spills, soaking my Chucks.

"Oops. Sorry." Beth has her hand over her mouth, but she can't quite hide the smile behind it. She brushes past me and struts toward the steps.

I wiggle my toes in my sopping shoes, tears burning behind my eyes.

"Jackie?" Rose stands, looking at me. Her attention snaps over to where Beth is grouped next to another blonde. "What. The. Fuck." Gone is the usual affable, sweet smile. Rose looks frightening, and with how the blonde next to Beth straightens and backs up, I'm sure she thinks the same.

Rose is up and over the bench, striding toward the two women before I can take a deep breath and collect myself.

Flynn stands as well, looking at the women Rose just charged up to. "What the hell, Holt? Isn't it enough you fucked my ex, now you invite her out? What the hell is wrong with you?"

All of my co-workers' heads swivel around the bar, taking in the new drama I've brought to their door.

Holt opens his mouth, but never gets a chance to speak.

Because right then, all hell breaks loose on the ISS.

Sirens wail from the speakers by the bar. Everyone flinches and covers their ears. The small LED emergency lights flash yellow across the white station on the screen.

I forget about Beth and my squishy shoes. I put the pitcher down and run over to the camera.

"Jules!" I shout into the microphone.

The astronauts have started pulling themselves in different directions, zooming across the TV, and Jules grabs onto one of the wall handles to steady herself, looking into the camera. "Gotta go, hooker. But if you'd get yourself to MCC to sort this shit out, I'd appreciate it." Her head turns for a moment as she talks to Bodie off screen. "Yeah, got it." She turns to me. "Looks like the second EXT isn't syncing like we hoped." Her words sound like her, but her tone makes the back of my neck itch. She blows me a kiss, reaches past the camera and then the feed goes dead.

I spin and scan the crowd of people now fumbling for their phones or making for the parking lot. I see Ian on his cell near the stairs. He catches my eye and waves me over. I maneuver through the chaos, but Trish waylays me halfway there.

She grabs hold of my shoulders in her hands. "Jackie. What's happening? You okay?"

"Something's wrong on the station. I have to go."

She looks down to my wet shoes for a beat before looking me in the eye and squeezing my shoulders briefly. "Okay, good luck, sweetie." She pulls me in for a quick hug and steps out of my way.

"Thanks," I say, already on the move to Ian. When I get there we both jog down the stairs to his car. I glance over my shoulder and see Flynn shoving Holt while Rose is rolling on the porch floor with Beth and the other blonde.

"Jackie, you coming?" Ian asks.

I pull my gaze from Flynn and back to Ian. He's holding the passenger door open.

"Yeah. I'm coming."

I REFUSE TO FOCUS ON BETH. MY TUNNEL VISION IS ALL FOR Holt and the desire to punch his face in. It was bad enough he showed up today, but then dragging my past in with him? In front of Jackie and her co-workers? I'm not letting that slide.

"I can't even believe you, man," I say, stepping into Holt's face.

He steps back, hands up. "Get a hold of yourself, Flynn. I didn't fucking invite her."

Holt saying 'fuck' makes me pause mid-shove. My brother hates cursing.

"I haven't seen her since I tossed her out of my bed," he continues.

I can see and hear people milling about, in more of a hurry than usual, but my mind isn't processing it. I'm having a hard time understanding Holt right now. "What the hell are you talking about?"

"I slept with her one time, Flynn. *One time*. I haven't seen her since."

He looks so fucking earnest I can't help but believe him, which oddly makes me more mad, as I'd been looking forward to releasing some of this pent-up anger.

A small hand rests on my arm and I turn, expecting Jackie. Instead, Trish is there, eyes wide.

"Rose. I need help with Rose." She tugs me back toward the stairs where Rose is currently rolling around on the ground, beating on both Beth and Pam. If she'd had a rope I have no doubt my sister would've had them hog-tied by now.

"Jesus," I mutter, striding over and lifting Rose off the pile by her armpits.

"Let me go! I'm not finished with these bitches yet." Rose twists in my grasp, wrenching my shoulder.

"Calm down, Rose." I glance down at the torn dress and bloody nose on Beth and the swollen eye on Pam. "Relax, sis. You won."

Rose's breath is coming fast and her eyes are still glued to Beth. "Damn straight I did."

"Like fuck." Beth scrambles to get up. When she finally manages, she's listing—one of her heels has snapped off in the fight. "Your sister needs her head examined."

Rose lunges again. "I'm going—"

I pivot, turning my back on Beth. This creates a barrier for Rose, and also keeps me from giving Beth a moment more of my time. Rose wipes her nose on her arm, leaving a smear of blood.

"What the heck, Rose?" Holt joins the group, stepping up to our sister.

"Don't start with me. Someone needs to take a stand against this waste of a human, and I'm not real keen on your way of doing it," Rose snaps at Holt, who visibly flinches. "This one," Rose continues, jerking her thumb over my shoulder at Pam, "thought she'd get payback for Flynn rejecting her ass at my party. She called the bitch from hell over there and told her where he was. Once they got a glance at Jackie they decided to have a little fun with her."

"Wait, what?" I glance at Pam, who has the decency to flush and look at her feet, embarrassed. A glance at Beth shows her looking far too pleased with herself for having just had her ass handed to her. "Jackie?"

"Oh, is that her name? The unfortunate one with the glasses?" Beth snickers. "You used to have standards, Flynn."

A band tightens across my chest at the thought of this venomous woman spreading her poison on Jackie. "Yeah, and they were a lot fucking lower than they are now, Beth." The smile leaves her face fast, but the pull in my chest remains.

"She cornered Jackie," Rose whispers to me. "At the bar."

"What? What do you mean?" The band tightens.

Rose's usual cheerful demeanor is gone, in its place a serious, intense girl I'm not used to dealing with. "I saw her, Flynn. I saw Jackie when she came out with the beer. Beth was right behind her." She tries stepping closer to Beth, who shrinks back. Louder, she asks, "What'd you say? I swear to God I'll hit you so hard I'll knock the Botox right out of you if you don't tell me what you said to Jackie. Stop messing with my family."

"Family?" Beth snorts. "Please, that girl will never be a West." She smirks. "Besides, I didn't say *much*."

Rose lunges, and I let her go, too dazed to be much help.

But both Holt and Trish step in front of Rose, Trish drawing everyone's attention by saying, "She left. Jackie left."

"What?" Rose spins, scanning the much thinned-out crowd.

"Didn't you guys hear the sirens? The bar just turned off the speakers, along with the astronaut Skype session." We all turn to the now blank screen, the feed dead. "Something happened on the station." Trish addresses me. "She looked for you, but you were, uh… occupied."

The weight sinks heavier on my chest. I look at the few faces left in the crowd, hoping to see Jackie's. But it's clear Trish is right; Jackie isn't there. In fact, no one from NASA remains on the bar's porch. Just my messed-up family and two unholy bitches.

"Where'd she go?" I ask Trish.

"Mission Control, I think." Trish frowns and looks out to the parking lot. "She left with Ian."

Beth's laugh hits my ears, but is immediately cut off when Rose's fist connects with her face.

———

Jackie

The lead Flight Director, Sean, waves at the projection screen lit up with pictures of the station's damaged panels and exposed wires. "Okay, people, this is where we stand. Earlier, while most of you were cheersing and beersing with the crew, a failure alarm sounded." He scans the room. "The second EXT computer has been having syncing problems since early this morning. At first they were minor things like being non-responsive to basic commands. But during the video chat session at Boons the EXT suddenly stopped responding to thruster commands. If it gets worse, this threatens the whole station as well as the astronauts inside."

It's a mess of an emergency meeting. People are sweaty, smell of beer and probably one or two of the team is too intoxicated to be productive—but it's all hands on deck.

"We can't power-cycle the second EXT without the first being operational," one of the CHRONUS members says.

"No shit." Sean glares at the person. "The question is how do we fix it?"

There's a pause before Gary from the International Space Station Program dares to come forward. "We have the astronauts working on building a new EXT on the station, but it isn't operational without the materials from the Progress, and that isn't scheduled to dock until after the beta period."

One of the interns pushes through the door. "We have confirmed debris heading toward the station."

"Jesus," Sean mutters.

"How close is the debris you're tracking?" I ask, my mind running through various scenarios and outcomes.

"Estimated impact in ten hours," the intern says.

I nod. "Do we have a read on where it will impact?"

"It's aimed dead center in the pizza box."

The "pizza box" is an imaginary container NASA created. It's about a mile deep by thirty miles across and thirty miles long, with the vehicle in the center. When predictions indicate that debris will pass close enough for concern, Mission Control centers in Houston and Moscow work together to develop a prudent course of action-- usually an evasive maneuver, or moving the onboard crew to the Soyuz spacecraft in case of impact or the need to evacuate.

Ian speaks up. "Can we move up the Progress launch?"

"Negative," Gary says. "Due to the beta angle, the Progress can't dock until next week."

The beta angle determines the percentage of time the ISS spends in direct sunlight, absorbing solar energy. The beta angle of the space station's orbit is a crucial consideration when deter-mining when a shuttle can be safely launched to the ISS.

Everyone's quiet.

My mind sharpens on the task ahead. "Start closing the hatch-es," I tell Sean.

When faced with possible impact, closing the hatches between the different sections of the station helps preserve pressure and function to those sections not hit by whatever space junk is headed their way.

"Why start now?" Sean asks. "The EXT is our priority."

"No, the crew is our priority."

Sean looks like he might argue, then changes his mind and inclines his head for me to continue.

"I saw the crew when the alarm sounded. They've already been on alert since the EXT-1 went down. They're on edge. Give them something to do other than wait around to build a computer that can never be built. Make them useful by starting emergency evac procedures a little early." I look around the room. "Meanwhile, we work on the EXT failure from here."

"You're right. Crew first," Sean says. "But why not try and maneuver the ISS away from the debris first? Then start emergency procedures."

"Because we can't trust the EXT-2 to take our commands anymore. We don't know if it will maneuver the station in time, but we can at least minimize damage of any impact and get the crew to safety."

"When the hatches are closed, do you think they should hunker down in the Soyuz?" someone asks.

If the hatches are closed, the crew will be able to enter the Soyuz, the essential lifeboat of the station, and wait out the collision. If, after the collision, the pressure and life support are damaged, they can return to earth. Or if the EXT-2 fails completely.

"Maybe. But hopefully by then we have a plan in place to get the station back to functioning again," I answer, my mind already moving on to solving that very problem.

"I'll get the flight director on console to give the command to start closing the hatches. Meanwhile, you all have thirty minutes to clean the fuck up and start brainstorming a work-around or a fix for this shit storm we're in." Sean looks at the clock. "The countdown to evacuation starts now." He picks up the phone to relay the information to those working in Mission Control.

———

I'M BEING RIDICULOUS. And unprofessional. My usual focus has been damaged by a mean, life-size Barbie.

Nothing Flynn has said or done should make me believe anything Beth said. I mean, yeah, she obviously knows him somehow. And yeah, the thought that she is indeed his ex kinda makes my insides feel small and hollow. But I should at least give him the benefit of the doubt. It isn't like I told him about my exes. Or ex, rather.

So when I text Trish and ask if everything's all right and she replies that the police are at Boondoggle's arresting Rose, I use the mandatory half-hour break Sean ordered to steal Ian's car.

Technically, I don't steal it. I leave a note. A note that may have been hidden under a pile of papers I accidentally shuffled across his desk when I grabbed his keys from his drawer. But whatever.

And as an aside—Teslas are sweet. I mean, I've been thinking of buying something with a vintage restoration vibe, à la my heroes of the Mercury Seven, but this car could make me switch to commercial.

I pull into Boondoggle's parking lot and slip out of the car. I'm berating myself for taking time away from work during an emergency, time that I'm pretty sure Sean wanted us to use to shower and dress appropriately. But that all stops when I see Rose sitting on the steps talking to a police officer. I say talking, but really it's more like flirting. She's smiling and seems completely unconcerned.

"You gonna use those cuffs, officer? Or are they just for show?" Rose leans back on her elbows and looks up at the officer standing over her.

"Uh, ma'am, I don't think you're taking the situation seriously." He's young and good looking, and I bet the redness in his cheeks isn't from the heat.

"Oh, I'm taking it seriously. My attorney is on his way."

"You have an attorney?" I ask.

Rose's head snaps in my direction and she's off her feet and hugging me before I can get the last syllable out.

"Jackie, you okay? What did Beth say to you? Is NASA like, exploding or something?"

"I'm fine. I'm on a break. NASA isn't exploding, but I don't have much time. Trish texted me about the cops." I ignore the Beth question and glance back at Officer Good Looking, who I now see from his name tag is T. Harrington. "What happened?"

"Nothing to worry about," Rose cuts in.

"Ma'am, you're being brought up on assault charges from two different women," Officer Harrington states.

Rose shoots him a look and he suddenly gets really interested in his shoes.

"It's just a misunderstanding," Rose tells me.

"I see." I look over her shoulder and see Holt sitting at one of the picnic tables talking to another officer, with a blond woman I sort of remember seeing earlier. The blond looks a little roughed up. "Where's Flynn?"

"Um, he's—"

"Miss West?" A short, pudgy man, probably on the higher side of thirty, addresses Rose. "I'm John Watson from Myers, Simon and Schwartz."

"Watson? For all the money my family pays, the firm sends an intern? Where's Myers? I usually deal with him," Rose demands.

"Sorry, Miss West. Myers and the other partners were indisposed, as it is a Sunday. I, a *junior partner*, was the closest to you at the time." He glances at Officer Harrington. "And I was told timing was important."

"Ah, yes. I guess so." She claps him on the back. "All right, Johnny, let's get to the precinct and take care of this business." She holds out her hands to the officer. "Cuff me."

"Um..." Harrington rubs the back of his neck with his hand. "I don't think that's necessary, even though you're technically under arrest."

"Spoil sport." Rose turns back to me. "Okay, I've got to take care of this nonsense. We should get together later for drinks."

"Okaaaaay. But I probably won't be able to, what with NASA and all."

"Oh, yeah." She frowns, then immediately perks up. "Dinner tomorrow?"

I laugh. "We'll see, Rose. I've got to go, but I was hoping to talk to Flynn before I left."

Rose's expression shutters. "He left. Don't worry about Flynn. He's fine. You should probably go so the cops don't hold you up from work."

Her demeanor changes so quickly, I don't have time to process it or ask her what's wrong before she puts her arm around me and leads me back toward the parking lot.

"How did you get here?" She looks around the lot.

"I took Ian's car." I gesture to the Tesla.

"Took?"

"I, uh, borrowed it," I say, pointedly not looking at Officer Thomas.

Rose chuckles. "I've been a bad influence, I see," she says, checking out Ian's shiny silver car. "Okay, girlie. I'll see you later. I'll have Flynn call you." Then she waves like she's going on vacation rather than dipping her head into the back seat of a police car. Her lawyer shuffles over to his car and follows them out.

"Jackie."

I jump, turning to see Trish poking her head around the corner.

"Trish? You okay?" Her hands are twisted in front of her and she keeps glancing at the other police officers getting statements from people still at the bar.

"Uh, yeah." She looks over my shoulder to where Rose had left in the squad car. "Do you think Rose will be all right?"

"Rose? She'll be fine. I mean, she's Rose, right?" I do my best to assure her, since Trish looks genuinely freaked out.

"Okay, I'm going back to wait inside. Holt said he'd give me a ride when he's done talking to the cops."

"I'm sorry, Trish. I'd give you one now, but I'm already cutting it close—"

"Don't worry about it. Really." She points to the wine bar next door. "I'll go take care of a bottle of wine, and you go take care of NASA, sugar." Although she is saying and doing normal Trish things, it feels forced. A quick glance at my watch tells me I'll have to figure out all that happened here at a later time.

I jog back to the parking lot, my shoes squishing with each step. I'm about to get in Ian's car when I see Flynn's Ford Mustang Boss still parked in the same spot from earlier. I turn back to the porch but don't see him. I'm about to call out to Holt when I spot Flynn by the side of the building.

My breath leaves me so fast I feel like I've been launched into the vacuum of space.

Beth, albeit a more disheveled and bruised Beth, is leaning against the wall. And Flynn has her caged between his arms, just like he'd had me, twice, outside my apartment door. His shoulder muscles strain from pressing in close and his forearms flex from bearing his weight. The movement lifts up his T-shirt in the back, showing a sliver of skin where his narrow hips meet his jeans. From this angle, I can't see his face, but I can see Beth's and she's quite pleased.

Her laugh this time is deep and throaty when she brings her hands up to cup Flynn's face.

Before they can kiss, I spin on my soggy Chucks and slide into the Tesla.

It really does reach 60 mph in 2.5 seconds.

EIGHTEEN
FAIL SAFE

Flynn

I FLEX MY ARMS AGAINST THE WALL. IT'S EITHER TRY TO CRUMBLE brick with my bare hands or strangle the woman in front of me. Sweat drips down my neck. Not from the heat, but rather the exertion of all the willpower it takes to remain in her presence and not commit violence.

Beth continues to ramble on about how much she misses me and how obvious it is that I'm not over her blah, blah, blah. Sweet Jesus, how in the world had I ever thought I loved this person? I've never been so grateful to my brother than I am right now for lighting a fire under my ass to get out of town. Even if he lit that fire by fucking my ex-girlfriend.

"It was just a misunderstanding, Flynn."

I'm not sure if she is talking about whatever she said to Jackie or if she honestly is trying to say she misunderstood Holt's dick in her? I surprise myself by laughing, but I stop by taking a deep breath and letting it out slowly. Who would've thought I'd ever find humor in this situation? I'm feeling pretty far removed from it now.

I have Jackie to thank for that.

"It was only ever you, Flynn." Beth pouts, trailing her death talons across my chest.

I try not to roll my eyes and fail.

"Hey!" She stomps her foot, forgetting the broken heel and swaying to the side. "You know I'm right. You and me, we're meant to be together." She takes a deep breath, pushing her doctor-made breasts in my face. She's gone up a size or two since we were together. "It's been over long enough, sweetie. Let's move on." She rolls her eyes, like me not getting over the fact that she used me for my wallet then fucked my brother is somehow annoying. "And don't worry, baby, I'm not mad about that girl. I know you had to get this out of your system."

She needs to shut up for her own safety. And not just from me. If Rose hears her spouting this shit I'll have another brawl on my hands. It's only for my sister's sake that I hauled Beth away. All so Rose doesn't get in any more trouble with the cops. Before they'd arrived, Rose mentioned it wasn't her first time tangling with Beth. Lord knew what happened last time, but a second offense with the same person would not be good for Rose.

"I know you miss me, Flynn." Beth raises her hands to cradle my face.

"Don't fucking touch me," I snap, done with playing mediator.

Beth's hands freeze and slowly drop back down to her sides.

Tires squeal as someone peels out of the lot. I turn to catch a glimpse of a silver car turning onto the road.

"Flynn! Pay attention to me." She tries stomping her foot again, but only manages to wobble on her broken heel. "Or I'll go talk to the cops," she sing-songs.

The look I give her makes her eyes go wide.

"I—"

"How did you think this would work, Beth? You come back

and mess with our lives again and one of the West brothers would take you back? Let me guess—your latest sugar daddy get tired of your drama? Looking for another rich man to whore yourself out to for the high-end lifestyle?"

Beth pales.

I know I'm being harsh, but I just don't care. "I'm with Jackie now."

At Jackie's name, Beth's eyes light up. "You can't honestly think *that* girl would fit in where we're from. She's not in our league, Flynn. Get real."

"Jackie is so far beyond your league it isn't even funny. She's got a goddamn doctorate. She's a genius NASA engineer. How the hell you thought you'd compete with that, I'm not sure."

This time Beth rolls her eyes. "You think just because someone has a few degrees that makes them any less interested in your money?"

The band around my chest snaps. "You don't know what you're talking about."

She laughs, like a hyena going in for the kill. "Don't I? I know exactly what I'm talking about. How many student loans did she have to take out to pay for all those genius degrees? She can't even afford decent clothes. Those ridiculous sneakers, for God's sake. And yet she surrounds herself with people with money." The side of her mouth tilts up. "Who was that fine man she left with? The one with the Rolex and the Tesla?"

"Leave it to you to price out every man in the room, Beth. Not everyone needs five-hundred-dollar shoes."

She pats my arm like a small child and my already tense muscles turn to stone. "What was she going to say, that she's stringing her co-worker along until she decides who can offer her the better life? That she likes wearing cheap clothes?" Beth scoffs. "Please. I saw her looking over my outfit when we talked. She practically drooled."

I remain silent, but it doesn't stop Beth.

"All I had to do was mention a few of the gifts you'd given me when we were together." —she pulls back her hair to expose the diamond studs I'd given her for her birthday one year—"and her eyes lit up. I could practically see the wheels turning in her head, wondering how long she'd have to wait, and what to do to speed up the process."

"You're lying." And I *know* she is. Jackie honestly doesn't care about material things. But a sick feeling settles when I think of the huge amount of school debt she must have. I'm such a privileged ass for not thinking about it. My degree was simply paid for out of pocket, not even a drop in the bucket to the West fortune.

"Am I? Or is that just what you want to believe, Flynn? You said yourself she's a big shot NASA engineer. What could someone like that want with a *mechanic*?" She spat the word. "But an heir to the West Oil fortune? Oh yeah, I can see that."

"Not everyone is a money-grubbing social climber, Beth."

Beth laughs so loud, my jaw ticks. "Oh, you poor, sweet, delusional man. So much like your father."

The mention of my father has me pushing back away from the wall.

"You drive her around in your half-a-million-dollar car, take her to your top-of-the-line house and you think she didn't notice? You did say she was smart, didn't you? Have you ever Googled your name? 'Cause I'm pretty sure she has."

Images of Jackie's face when sitting in my car and when she'd looked over my house shuffle through my mind. I shake them off.

"Flynn West, the joke of the oil elite everywhere," Beth says on a satisfied sigh.

I push back into her space.

"News flash, Beth—you're the one they laugh at." I look her up and down, making sure not to hide even an ounce of my contempt. "You think the people back home like you? You're the goddamn entertainment. Walking around like you're mightier than everyone, working off your shopping habit on your back."

It's Beth's turn to stiffen.

"You already messed with my family once, Beth. You mess with them or Jackie again, I will end your social climbing."

"What are you talking about?"

"You think I don't have connections just because I dirtied my hands with my 'stupid cars'? Think again. You'll be blacklisted from every event in Houston. You'll be lucky if you get invited to some backwoods hoedown when I'm done."

"You think you've got that much pull? You're just a mechanic these days, Flynn."

"But *I'm* not."

I turn to find Holt beside me.

Beth crosses her arms over her chest. "What are you going to do, Holt? Fuck me again?"

"God, no. Once was enough to get my brother out of your gold-digging clutches. You couldn't pay me to touch you again. I don't even like being this close to you."

Beth's mouth drops open. Mine too.

"Don't think for one minute that Flynn can't follow through on his threat. Or me. I know all about your activities these last few years. I know your debts, and I know your suppliers."

Beth's shoulders drop against the wall.

"Still like a little blow when you party, Beth?" Holt asks, crossing his arms over his chest.

"I don't know what you're talking about." Her voice is shrill.

"No? 'Cause I have a video that proves otherwise."

"What—?"

"Leave." Holt steps forward and Beth tries to shrink further back. "You don't know us. You don't talk to us or about us. You don't so much as look at us. And it goes without saying that you don't press charges against Rose and you convince Pam to do the same."

Beth scowls at both of them. "Whatever. You Wests think you're so great, well think again. Y'all are nothing but trash," she shoots back before hurrying away.

Holt and I stand in silence, watching as Beth speaks to one of the cops, then pulls Pam away to her car and leaves.

"Do you really have a video of her buying drugs?" I ask my brother.

"No."

I bark out a laugh, causing Holt to smile.

"Did you really just fuck her so I'd dump her?"

"Yeah," he admits, smile fading.

I shake my head. "That's messed up, Holt."

"I know." He lifts his hat, runs his hand through his hair and settles the hat back on his head. "But think back to what you were like on the ranch, Flynn. You got in with that society crowd—going to parties, thinking your shit didn't stink. You had passion before Beth, dreams of owning your own shop. I tried to talk to you about it, bring up the stupid shit she was getting you into. All the bills she ran up. You wouldn't listen." He rubs the back of his neck. "You stopped working on cars. You even let her talk you into working the corporate side of West oil. A desk job of all things. Then she started talking about engagement rings and penthouses. You hate that stuff, man. That was going to be your life and I knew you'd be just as miserable as—"

"Dad?"

"Yeah." Holt sighs. "I just couldn't take it if you choose someone like Mom. You deserve better."

"Then you should've talked to me. For God's sake, Holt. I'd figured out what she was a whole month before I saw her in your bed."

"But you were still home. And she was still hanging around,

waiting. I wanted more for you, so I made sure you left. And if making you hate me is what it took to make you leave, it was worth it." He looks me square in the eyes when he says, "I know it was a crappy thing to do, but I'm not sorry. I'm not sorry because it worked. You left. You're doing what you love. And if that girl here today is any indication, you've found someone worthy of you for a change."

We're quiet for a while, watching the boats sail by on the lake on the opposite side of the lot, listening to people drinking on the porch, now that the cops have gone. Beth's words about Jackie echo in my head. I'm about to ask Holt what he thinks when Trish interrupts.

"Yoo hoo?" She's leaning around the corner of the building. "The cops are gone, but did you guys forget about your sister at the police station?"

"Shoot."

"Shit."

Holt and I say in unison.

————

Jackie

Hours later, I find myself in Mission Control's back room, in the middle of a think tank. The crew onboard the ISS is busy closing off module hatches, following space debris protocol. No one at NASA can figure out a way to get EXT-2 synced without first having EXT-1 operational. Though the station can fully function with only one EXT, there's no way to fix the failed EXT-1 without EXT-2 in full working order.

"Beyond the debris scheduled to hit in five hours, astronauts can't stay on the station long-term without the EXT computers maintaining and regulating the ISS's heat and power. Especially now, right before we enter a beta period. The station will turn into a barbecue where the sun hits and a deep freezer where it's in shadow," Sean says to the room.

"What about using the Soyuz to maneuver the station?" I ask.

Ian shakes his head. "We thought of that during the break, but after a data analysis we recalled the long rendezvous to the station after its launch. The extra eighteen hours of approach to the station burned a lot of propellant. There isn't enough gas to maneuver the station out of the debris path *and* get the astronauts back home safely, should they need to make an emergency evacuation."

"What kind of shit storm *is* this?" Sean yells, making most of the people in the meeting jump. "How did we get two EXT failures, low fuel and possible space junk all at once?"

No one answers.

I shift in my seat, much more comfortable since I changed out of my bar outfit. Ian caught me returning his keys to his desk. The look on my face must've tipped him off that I'd been on the verge of a breakdown, 'cause all he did was hand me his gym bag and tell me I was welcome to anything in it.

I'm currently sitting around a high-level meeting with various suits in a large Harvard T-shirt and men's basketball shorts cinched tight. My feet are big, but Ian's running shoes still hang off a few inches past my toes. I don't care. They're better than the beer-soaked Chucks I'd sadly tossed in the trash.

For a minute, I worry about what Flynn would think, me wearing another guy's clothes. Especially Ian's, after that whole proprietary scene when he'd dropped me off at NASA's gate and kissed me. But then I do a mental eye roll. I may be smart, but I've been played. *Again.*

Flynn isn't serious about me. I mean, what did I expect? He teaches me how to hotwire a car, I have sex with him and then we live happily ever after?

I still.

Flynn. Car. Wires.

Sweet Neptune.

I surge forward in my seat. "Bring up the schematics." I may have shouted, because all eyes turn to me, startled.

"Of the Russian vehicle? They're right there." Ian points to the screen.

"No, forget the gyroscopes. The EXT-1—I need the schematics of the external wires running outside the station to the box."

Sean nods, and interns run out of the room, presumably to get the schematics. I barely register the chaos, my mind on the wires. It's a much more complicated vehicle, but the fix should be just as simple...

Ian rests a hand on my arm, bringing me back to the room. "Okay, schematics should be up in a minute."

"Good." I look to Sean. "Get Jules and Bodie suited up."

Vance Bodaway, a.k.a. "Bodie," is a Flight Engineer astronaut currently onboard the ISS with Jules. He's as much of a badass as she is, so what I have planned will be entertaining, if nothing else.

Sean raises both hands. "Wait a minute. What exactly are you thinking? I need more information before I tell some of the crew to stop emergency hatch procedures and take an hour to suit up in EVA gear."

"We don't have a minute. As you said, it'll take them an hour to suit up, then another for the spacewalk I'm planning. And if what I tell them to do doesn't pan out, they'll still have two hours to get back into the station, de-gear and make their way to the Soyuz with the rest of the crew."

"I don't—" Sean starts.

"Come on, Sean. This is Jackie. You *know* that if she's this confident about an idea, it's got to be good," Ian says.

I nod at Ian in thanks.

"Worst case scenario, Jules and Bodie waste a bit of time messing around with their suits," Ian finishes.

Sean looks from Ian to me. "Fine." He picks up the phone and gives the order to the Flight Director on console. When he puts down the phone he sits back and stares me down. "So, Dr. Jackie Darling Lee. Just what exactly *do* you have planned?"

I take a deep breath. "We're going to hotwire the station."

NINETEEN

FINAL COUNTDOWN

Flynn

MY SISTER HUMS WHILE RIFLING THROUGH MY KITCHEN PANTRY. Not at all like she's just been arrested and almost jailed.

"I can't believe this wasn't the first time you've been arrested for beating up Beth," I say to Rose. "Do I even want to know when that happened?"

Rose pokes her head out of the pantry, looking me in the eye. "You know when." She disappears again for a moment, coming out with a bag of cookies. "That's why I have my own lawyers." She tosses the bag on the counter. "And why I paid Beth off the first time and made her sign papers saying she could never sue me. I knew she wasn't done causing trouble." She yanks open the fridge door, mumbling, "I'm not stupid."

"That's yet to be proven," I say, but laugh softly, remembering the look on Holt's face at the police station. "I thought Holt was going to have a conniption." For an hour, Holt sequestered himself with Rose's lawyer after he'd discovered Rose's previous run-ins with Beth. Holt had been even more pissed when Rose's lawyer wouldn't tell him anything due to client confidentiality.

Rose retrieves the gallon of milk and clears her throat. "Speaking of Holt, you two seem to be getting along better." Her voice is hopeful.

After our manly little heart-to-heart after dealing with Beth, my brother and I *have* gotten along better. Or at least a lot of the tension and resentment has lifted. Holt still moseyed back to the ranch after the police station. I think we're both going to take this new reunion of sorts one day at a time.

I amble over to her, pushing her out of the way. "Yeah." I grin, then grab myself a soda from the fridge. I realized today how much my anger had been controlling me. I'd been so consumed by it, I'd let it blind me to what's important—family. And now, Jackie. So I'm letting the anger go. It's easier than I thought it'd be. My brother is an idiot, but at least he was trying to help.

"That's good." She pours a large glass of milk and takes a healthy swig. "I was getting tired of playing go-between for you two asshats."

"Nice mustache, dude," I say, ruffling her hair.

"Hey! Watch it," Rose ducks her head and wipes her milk mustache off with the back of her hand. "I still have that just-been-arrested look. It's hard to fake. Gotta make the most out of the real thing." She smirks before ripping open the bag of cookies.

"Whatever, Rose," I say, rolling my eyes.

"Don't forget to call Jackie," she says, mouth full of cookie. "We had a near miss earlier."

"What do you mean? When Beth and Jackie talked at the bar?" I take a sip of soda. "Beth told me what they talked about." I shrug. "Or at least Beth's version of it."

"Uh, yeah. I wouldn't go believing anything that bitch says." She shakes her head. "I was talking about when Jackie came back after the cops arrived."

I set the can carefully on the island. "She came back?"

"Yeah. She was all set to go look for you but I knew you were with Beth, so I steered her back out to her car." She shoves another cookie in her mouth. "Good thing I got her out of there. The last thing Jackie needed was to see you and your crazy-ass ex huddled together inside at the bar. Beth may be batshit crazy and the devil besides, but she's hot. No girl wants to think their man hit that."

I stand very still. "We weren't at the bar, Rose."

"What are you talking about?" Rose mumbles around the cookie. "That's where you went when the cops came."

"Until the manager asked us to take it outside because Beth was being too loud. We were in the parking lot."

We stare at each other. Rose gulps.

"Jackie would've said something if she saw you. Right?" Rose asks, eyes watering as she chokes down the cookie. She picks up her glass of milk, trying to wash it down.

I replay that part of the day, back to caging Beth against the wall just to keep her from running her mouth off to the cops. From the parking lot that would not have looked good. I check my phone. "She hasn't answered my text or calls from earlier."

"She's at work. Big NASA emergency, remember?" Rose's voice sounds unsure, which is when I know I'm in trouble.

Again, I mentally run through my interaction with Beth. No one called out my name, I didn't so much as glimpse wild blond hair walking up the porch steps from where I'd been standing. But then it hits me. My mind stalls on the one thing that had distracted me from isolating Beth.

That silver car.

"Wait, how did she even get to the bar? Her car is in my garage," I say, praying I'm wrong.

"Ian's Tesla."

"Fuck."

———

I'VE NEVER BEEN SO glad for my astronomic cable bill. I have to pay for a huge number of channels to get all the specialty channels that deal with vintage restorations and racing. But along with that expensive bundle is NASA TV. There was no way I could get on site with all the security and no badge. I'm pretty sure making a scene at the gate would not endear me to Jackie. But Jackie had mentioned NASA TV once, so I flip through until I find it.

Apparently, NASA TV provides live coverage of launches, spacewalks and other mission events, as well as the latest news briefings and video files. What I'm interested in at the moment is the live footage from Mission Control. The channel shows a bunch of desks with multiple computers stacked on top. Each long desk is manned by two or three people. Then there are the people standing in the center of the room.

There are three of them. One of them is Jackie.

Beside her are two men, one in a suit and one in khakis and a polo. For some reason, Jackie is in an oversized T-shirt and gym shorts. She also has a headset on and is gesturing to one of the men. There isn't much sound. A bunch of murmurs, and typing sounds, but that's it.

It feels really weird being able to see her, what she is doing, and her not know I'm watching.

Rose perches on the edge of my couch with her laptop on her knees, following the current news feeds as well as NASA TV. Turns out while I was busy having a white trash family brawl, Jackie had been trying to save the International Space Station and its crew. Talk about perspective.

I don't think she has her phone on her, but I pull mine out and text her good luck anyway. Just in case.

I'm surprised when I see Jackie's head swivel to one of the desks. She picks up a cell phone, looking at the screen. A frown mars her face before she slaps the phone back on the table, screen side down. Her expression clears when Ian waves her over to another desk. She walks over to him, leaving her phone and my text behind.

Not good.

———

Jackie

I focus on the schematics projected on the screen in front of me. Sitting at a table, along with most of the higher-ups at NASA, I'm surprised I'm not nervous. I don't even adjust my glasses. Instead, I take charge.

"You can see the damaged wires in the shots Astronaut Starr took of EXT-1 after it was hit. What we need to check on are the wires that continue running under the exterior panel." I look at the electrical engineering team assembled to one side of the room. "What do the plans tell you?"

"According to the electrical drawing, the wires continue under the panel, and even coil for slack. You should have enough give to cut and reconnect," one of them answers. "If that fails, we can banana clip around the damaged section."

I address the EVA division. "What's our timeline? How fast can Jules and Bodie be out the door?"

Astronauts always go on spacewalks in twos—the classic buddy system. Though Jules will run the show, Bodie will be her backup.

"They're suited up. They just need to connect their helmets and get to the airlock."

I pace back and forth in what feel like clown shoes on my feet. Anyone going on a spacewalk needs to depressurize to avoid decompression sickness, or 'the bends,' which happens when someone is exposed to a rapid drop in external pressure and expanding nitrogen gas bubbles in the bloodstream escape too quickly. To prevent this, an hour before the spacewalk an astronaut dons the full space suit and breathes pure oxygen inside the sealed airlock while the pressure gradually decreases. Once the area reaches the appropriate pressure, the astronaut pulls himself through the airlock hatch and into space.

"They'll have both the tether and the SAFER jetpack, since we don't know how long this could take," an EVA engineer continues.

EVAs usually take weeks to plan. Not hours. There's a detailed list of procedures, which are followed to the letter. In comparison, what I have planned is like giving a toddler paints and a brush and expecting a Rembrandt.

All those movies about astronauts jumping into their suits and then diving into space to save the day? Yeah, not so much. Even this hastily put together spacewalk is bending protocol almost to the breaking point.

"Okay. Make sure Jules has her tool belt fully stocked with clippers, cables—the lot. We don't want a failure simply because she forgot to properly pack her purse," Sean says.

Ian barks out a laugh. "Jesus, Sean. You should be glad this is an emergency. Otherwise you'd have your ass handed to you by Human Resources for that remark."

Sean dismisses him with a wave and an eye roll, mumbling something about millennial safe zone bullshit. Everyone pretends they can't hear, but the chuckles continue.

I move to the door, my nervousness flaring up with a stiff smile. "Let's go get the EXTs back online."

———

THE LARGE SCREENS in Mission Control show various images of the interior and exterior of the ISS, and now include a countdown to the estimated impact of debris. Jules and Bodie have had time to properly depressurize. I catch something flashing out of the corner of my eye. My phone screen is lit up with a text message notification.

"You guys are good to move to the hatch," Sean instructs the astronauts, speaking into his head set.

"Houston, on our way," Jules replies.

Jules might be a space cowgirl, but when it comes to the job, she's all focus. She almost doesn't sound like herself over the airwaves. Which is probably a good thing, as calling a flight director 'hooker' on national television isn't the kind of PR NASA is going for these days.

All the eyes in the room are glued to the screen as Jules and Bodie work together to open the hatch and spin it back against the interior wall. I take the moment to pick up my phone.

Flynn: *Good Luck, darling.*

Seriously? He goes from making out with his Barbie doll ex to sending boyfriend-like texts to me in the span of a few hours. Maybe he has multiple personality disorder. Or maybe Rose is wrong—he *is* just like Brian and I *can* actually draw the conclusion that men don't want the nerdy girls.

"EVA hatch is open and stowed." Bodie's deep voice comes through the speakers. "Switching suit power to battery mode."

I put my phone down with more force than required and take a deep breath. *Focus.*

"Jackie?"

Ian waves me over to the EVA console.

I put blinders on my feelings about Flynn and home in on Ian. "Yes?"

"Just wanted to show you the suit specs, and the battery and oxygen levels, so you have that in the back of your mind as we cowboy this spacewalk."

"Cowboy?" I laugh softly, thinking of my romance novels and how Jules would love the comparison. "Thanks, Ian."

He smiles and gives the command to close the depress valves.

"Depress valves closed," Jules replies.

"Station, visors down," an EVA flight controller instructs. Spacesuit visors are coated with a thin layer of gold. It helps filter out the sun's harmful rays, which in June, at a beta period, is extremely important. The visor also protects the astronaut from extreme temperatures.

Jules and Bodie begin maneuvering to the Starboard Zero truss—on the space-facing side of the U.S. Destiny lab. It's the centerpiece of the station's truss where solar rays, radiators and cooling loops are housed, as well as the EXT-MDMs. Luckily the airlock is right below it, so they don't have far to go.

A camera is attached to Bodie's helmet, giving everyone in Mission Control a hands-on view. Next to the screen that feeds from Bodie's camera is the countdown. Four hours. It seems like a lot of time, but in space everything takes a lot longer, and when you have to factor in the extra hour needed after the spacewalk for decompression, every minute counts.

Jules and Bodie take their time, moving in tandem, making sure to lock the safety hooks on their tethers to the station as they go. Astronauts always look like they're moving in slow motion in the lack of gravity, but in reality, attached to the space station, they're traveling at 17,150 miles per hour. That's 1.76 miles per second.

What I'm asking Jules and Bodie to attempt is akin to having a surgeon perform open heart surgery wearing winter gloves while riding a roller coaster.

No pressure or anything.

By the time they've made their way to the Starboard Zero

truss, I'm sitting down. The adrenaline that's been pumping through my system since the sirens at Boondoggles is wearing off. Jules' voice comes through the head set, forcing me to my feet again.

"Houston, EXTs are in reach."

Bodie unhooks one of his tethers and pulls himself forward to tether it next to EXT-1.

Jules comes from the opposite side of the ISS truss and tethers between EXT-1 and EXT-2.

"Houston, we are in position," Bodie relays.

"Station. Okay, guys, you need to look at the cable feeds following out away from EXT-1 and 2, the ones hit by the meteorite a few weeks ago," I advise into the headset. "The exposed cable bundles were hit, but we need you to unscrew the panel that hides the rest of the cables."

"Houston. Will do. Unloading pack now," Jules says, starting the spacewalk procedure I wrote just an hour ago.

This part of a spacewalk is somewhat tedious. Every time an astronaut makes a move they have to verbally announce it back to MCC, even though we can see them on screen from the cameras housed on their helmets. And though they memorize each EVA's unique procedure before suiting up, we send verbal commands to the astronauts for each step through their coms. It's redundant, but protocol. And since protocol has saved lives multiple times throughout NASA's long and illustrious history, we don't mess with it.

On the monitor, Jules retrieves the battery-operated drill from her pack and tethers it to her suit and slowly, so slowly, unscrews the panel next to the cable with charred and broken wires. The drill tip is magnetic, helping Jules maintain control. Even so, I see one screw float away.

"Shit." Apparently, Jules forgot about the public broadcasting.

Ian and I both glance at each other, fighting smiles.

"Station. What was that, astronaut Starr? We couldn't hear you down here."

"Um, nothing, Houston. Just lost a screw. I have backups in my bag."

Seth covers his mic and looks at Ian. "And that is why I always make sure astronauts pack their purse."

A soft ripple of laughter flows through Mission Control, breaking the tension that has been ratcheting up since Jules and Bodie left the airlock.

"Houston, panel removed," Jules narrates as she hands Bodie the large panel. Unable to tether the panel to their suits, Bodie braces his feet into the handrails of the truss of the station and uses his hands to hold the panel so it doesn't fly away.

His light illuminates the wires under the panel. "Houston, the cable bundles are clean and intact."

Thank heavens. I lose a shaky breath. "Station. Excellent. We are good to go with the hotwire." I skim the schematics spread out over the table. "Station, I need you to de-mate the blind-mate connector on the back end of EXT-1, at the J1/P1 interface. Do you see them?"

"That's a positive, Houston. I see them, and they are in reach," Jules says.

"Okay, Station. Grab the P1 capped cable coming from RPC 4. There should be an open cavity to the right, where no box is connected. That is the connection you're going to be using."

"Houston, I see it."

"You're going to have to traverse above. Behind the open face there should be three cables. De-mate and uncap the J1/P1 connection there," I instruct.

MCC is dead quiet as we all wait while Jules follows the commands. When she reaches the area, I ask, "Do you have enough length to move the uncapped cable to the EXT J1 connection?"

There's a long pause. "No. It's too tight," Jules replies.

This time Sean curses.

Bodie turns his head toward the wires on the truss, lighting up the monitors with the image. "Wait, Houston, there are zip ties routing the cable bundle along the station, including the cable we need. If Jules cuts the zip ties, she'll have enough slack to bring the cable to the proper connection."

One thing a lot of people don't know— NASA likes to hold things together with duct tape and zip ties. For real.

Sean speaks into his headset. "Station. Hold," then gets up from his desk and comes over to where I'm standing. He reeks of body odor and coffee. But then again, who doesn't in MCC right now? "If we loosen those wires, will it cause any potential damage or malfunction to the ones still operating?"

I call over one of the engineers and repeat the question.

"That's a negative," he says. "That group holds scars four through six. All are unused and capped." Scars are what we call infrastructure that is viable but unused, specifically for future needs.

Sean gives me the go-ahead with a nod.

"Station, that's a go to cut the zip tie," I say. "But careful with the cutters. We don't need any more challenges."

"Houston. You got it."

Jules' tone does more to ease my mind than a Xanax would've in this moment. I can tell she's firmly in control of the situation. That woman is a legend in the making. I only wish I could be up there with her.

"Bodie, move your fat head. I need more light."

"I'm a glorified street lamp out here, aren't I?"

God, I love these guys.

A few minutes later, cutters tethered and in hand, Jules cuts the zip ties along the four-foot stretch of truss.

"Station, did that give you enough room?" If not we're back

to square one and evacuating. In a true hotwire, you can cut wires, strip the coating and connect them, just like Flynn taught me. But live wires in the hands of astronauts are not a good thing. One singe and their space suits could depressurize. We need the scars intact to make this work.

"Oh yeah, Houston. We're good to go," Bodie drawls into his mic.

I allow myself a small smile. But my body is still tight with tension. Even though reaching the proper connection is a significant part of the plan, plenty of other failures can occur before we're finished.

"Station, extend the cable to the J1 interface."

For the next fifteen minutes, we watch as Bodie turns his head this way and that while Jules tugs the new cable and maneuvers around the truss to get to EXT-1's connection panel. Eventually I have to sit down again. I'm exhausted from waiting.

Everyone watches as Jules tries and fails to connect the cable. She tries again. No go.

"Houston, the third time, as they say, is the charm. Cable connected."

"Excellent, Station. Jules, I need you to re-secure the external panel. Bodie, check to make sure all connections are secure."

Once done, Sean addresses the CRONUS console. "Send the command to send EXT-2 into a diagnostic state."

A diagnostic state will initiate FDIR, a software program that detects faults, isolates them and tries for recovery. Once completed, we can get EXT-1 back to functioning order if the hotwire works.

Waiting is excruciating. Each line of data that FDIR brings up on the monitors makes my heart thump louder. Luckily, each piece of data continues cycling without failures.

"FDIR completed successfully. Connection is viable. EXT-1

powered up in primary state, healthy, and taking commands," the CHRONUS console announces.

Applause hits the room, people shouting, clapping and hugging each other. Ian leaves his console to pick me up in a spinning hug, both of us laughing.

"You're a damn genius, Jackie," he says, setting me back down. The spin jostled my glasses, and I freeze as Ian pushes them back up into position. He doesn't notice my statue-like stance, moving on to pump Sean's hand and congratulate the rest of the team. With shaky fingers, I readjust my frames myself, thinking of Flynn and wondering if he's with Beth at this exact moment.

Though I'm so overwhelmingly happy at the outcome of the space walk, my smile is forced when I speak to Jules and Bodie through my headset. "Station, we have two fully functioning EXTs up and running. You are good to maneuver back inside."

Disregarding proper public loop protocol, Jules simply replies, "That'll do, hooker. That'll do."

TWENTY

DIAGNOSTICS

Jackie

IAN'S SHOES WILL NEVER BE THE SAME. I HAVEN'T BEEN ABLE TO fully pick up my feet while walking home, my exhaustion like an extra dose of gravity on my limbs. Drag, clump. Drag, clump. It's been my theme song since I finally left Mission Control a little while ago, making my way to my apartment.

I should've caught a ride with someone at work, but most of my co-workers were heading out to celebrate, picking up where we'd left off at Boondoggles. Not me. I don't think I've ever been so tired. Physically, yes. I didn't have much sleep last night and I've mostly been standing and pacing since the alarms sounded in the ISS. Mentally exhausted? Check. If I close my eyes I still see electrical and structural blueprints as well as command codes flitting beneath my eyelids.

I've been both mentally and physically exhausted before. Not usually at the same time, but still. Nothing new. The real kicker is my emotional state. I've never truly understood what people meant by emotionally exhausted until the adrenaline crashed when Jules called me hooker after the EXT booted back up. After that I could've slithered to the floor and crashed. But I kept my feet under me, even with the many congratulatory slaps on my back, until Sean called it and sent us home, the next MCC shift taking over.

Thankfully, we won't debrief until tomorrow. And I have a feeling I'm going to need all the recovery time I can get. As exhausting and stressful as the spacewalk was, it did one thing for me. It kept my mind off Flynn.

I finally make the turn into my apartment complex. No need to put in a code, as the gate's still broken. Mental eyeroll. I need to add "scroll through real estate listings" to my to-do list, along with a new—

I pull up short in the parking lot and blink. My car is sitting in my assigned parking space. I push my fingers under my glasses and rub my eyes, straighten the frames and check the parking spot number again. It's still there. Not that anyone else would have the same POS as me, but still, I had to check. Because if it's here that means…

I haul in a deep breath.

Don't do it. Don't you dare do it, Jackie. You will not cry.

My nostrils flare as I take several deep breaths, closing my eyes until I feel the sting behind my eyelids cool. Once I'm sure I'm under control, I continue walking toward the stairs, pointedly not looking at the reminder that Flynn and I are over. Not remembering how he hadn't wanted to give me my car as it ensured I'd come see him again. Because if I remember, then I have to face the logical conclusion that he simply doesn't want me to come see him again. That what I saw in the parking lot of Boondoggles was more than just my skewed perspective, that it was real and true.

My foot catches the front of the treads a few times as I climb to the third floor. Step by step I concentrate on my feet, willing myself to make it to my bed. If I can just collapse into my safe space, I'll be okay. I can sort everything out tomorrow. I just need to shut down and sleep. Reboot, like I rebooted the ISS tonight.

Maybe if I'm lucky, tomorrow I can figure out a way to hotwire my mind, jumpstart the synapses in my brain. I crest the final landing. Just a few more feet and I'll be there.

"Jackie?"

Flynn? Why is Flynn sitting in front of my apartment door? I blink a few times, but just as with my car, the image doesn't change. I stare, taking in his arms resting across his knees, his long, booted legs pulled up toward his chest. His eyes seem heavy and his hair is a mess. He looks so *good*.

"Jackie? You okay?"

I guess he's asking me that since I didn't respond the first time. I can't find it in me to respond this time either. Maybe I started the mental reboot too soon.

Slowly, he pulls his legs in further, pushes off against the door and rises.

"I watched you," he says. "On NASA TV, I mean." He tilts his head down, staring into my eyes. Like he is trying to get a read on me. "I'm so glad everything worked out, that your friend Jules is safe."

Still I continue to just stare, not really processing what is happening. I wonder if I'm having a mental breakdown. That seems like a logical conclusion to the day I've had.

He takes one step toward me and stops. "I'm sorry, Jackie. So sorry. About earlier. About Beth."

At that, I can feel myself flinch, that woman's name landing like a blow to my chest. He sees it and takes another step forward, hands out.

"I'm sorry, Jackie. I should've ignored that whole messed-up situation and been there for you when all that stuff at NASA happened." He runs his hand through his hair and takes a deep breath. "I was just shocked. I never thought I'd see her again. Hell, I never *wanted* to see her again."

Something must be getting through, because I feel myself tilting my head, drawing my brows together, trying to concentrate on that last part, and what it means.

Flynn must read my confusion because he closes the distance between us, his arms clutching my biceps. "I don't want Beth, Jackie. Please say you know that. Please say you know I'd never do that to you."

I open my mouth, but something catches in my throat. I try to clear it, but still my voice is rough when I speak. "You don't want Beth." I'm not sure if I'm asking or just trying to repeat what he said so it sinks in.

"God no." He wraps me in his arms. "You, Jackie. I just want you."

It could be his words. Or the feel of his arms around me. Or even the fact that he's taken on most of my body weight in his strong embrace, relieving my exhausted muscles from the epic strain of keeping myself upright.

Whatever it is, it sparks something inside me. But instead of jumpstarting my brain, I'm pretty sure Flynn just hotwired my heart.

And I cry.

————

Flynn

Jackie's hair is tickling my nose. I will the itch away and concentrate on the silkiness of her bare skin under my fingertips as I move them up and down her back.

After she cried against my chest outside her apartment, I picked her up, carried her inside and set her down on the edge of the bed. While I locked up the place, I heard her shuffle into the bathroom. A few minutes later she padded out barefoot, still in oversized mesh shorts and T-shirt. I stripped her down, pulled back the covers on her monstrous, cloud-like bed and tucked her in. She looked so young, her freckles more prominent against the white bedding, her long lashes resting on her cheeks.

It took effort, but I moved to walk away. The couch had my name all over it, and I was fine sleeping there. Fine with just being someone she could lean on, count on, without any strings. I'd only taken one step, when, quicker than I would think someone so exhausted could, Jackie grasped my hand and tugged me toward her.

Newscasters are saying Jackie's a hero, that her idea to "hotwire" the computers saved the International Space Station. And she is, but she is also just a person. A person who had one of the most stressful days of her life, not at all helped by the bullshit drama I dropped on her doorstep. There is only so much a person can take, and Jackie has well exceeded that limit today.

She was more than half asleep, eyes closed, body cocooned in her cloud, but she still had a grip of steel. It wasn't until I murmured I needed take off my shoes before getting into bed that she let go of my hand. But she opened one eye, keeping me in her sights while I shucked off my shoes, jeans and shirt and climbed into the bed.

Even as tired as she was, it wasn't until I was fully settled behind her, spooning her tightly against me, that I felt her body finally relax into sleep.

I wasn't there for Jackie earlier, but I damn well will be here for her now. I can't just show up at her door after the fact. Jackie's smart, strong and capable without me. But in this moment, with her hair tickling my nose, my arm asleep from holding her tight, and rocking a painful hard-on, I know that I'm right where I need to be. Making sure she's safe.

TWENTY-ONE
BLACK FLAG

Flynn

I STILL HAVEN'T MANAGED TO SCRAMBLE AN EGG.

Which is probably the first lesson in 'fending for yourself 101,' aka 'adulting.' Even so, I have realized I will never earn that badge, insomuch that if my survival is one day dependent on me cooking eggs, I'm a certified dead man.

Grilled cheese, however, is a different story. I dominate the grilled cheese game.

I'm cooking for Jackie tonight. To be fair, grilled cheese is what I cook most nights we don't eat out or get take-out, but she doesn't seem to mind. In fact, she was so overcome with gratitude when I made it for her after work last week, I swear she almost cried.

Personally, I think she's set the bar too low. Though, after she'd told me about her dickhead ex, it makes sense. Even in my more douchebag school years I'd never made bets on a girl putting out. That's a whole new kind of low. And knowing that dickface is just forty-five minutes away in Houston, playing for *my* city's baseball team, chafes. Chafes hard. But part of the reason Jackie opened up to me, apart from wanting to explain why she'd been so quick to assume the worst when she saw me with Beth, was promising I said I wouldn't do anything about the close proximity of her ex. Which was an easy promise to make before I heard the whole story. Now? I want to pummel his ass with his own bat. Although I now regret that promise, Jackie and I have come a long way since then.

It's been two weeks since the emergency spacewalk, since the night I took Jackie home and held her as she slept, exhausted from stress and worry. The morning after, we talked. I explained the what-the-fuck fallout from Beth showing up at Boondoggles, complete with the incestuous backstory of Holt and her having slept together. We'd verbally committed to our relationship, so there'd be no further confusing anomalies (Jackie's words). And then we talked some more. We've talked about our childhoods, our aspirations, and how our past relationships influenced our present. And we kept talking. We've even talked about the small stuff, like how Jackie thinks avocado toast is overrated and how I think self-driving cars will be the first step toward Armageddon. I now know she was scared out of her mind for her friend Jules during the spacewalk, but she set aside her fear and worked on a solution, like the badass she is. And I know she wants a dog and two kids, just like me. Well, if I had my way it'd be more like four kids and two dogs. But, you know, close enough.

Our talks have continued every night after work when she comes to my house in her piece of shit Honda. We've gone out a few times, meeting up with Rose and Trish, but mostly we order in take-out or I show off my culinary grilled cheese skills. I try a new cheese each time. I'm awesome like that.

It's been a great two weeks.

I'm trying hard not to lose my man-card over how happy she makes me, but it's a near thing.

Smart, beautiful and funny. Jackie's the trifecta, for sure.

I hear the garage door opening, which gives me a few minutes to set the table.

And by set the table, I mean scooping the sandwiches onto paper plates and plopping them down on the counter. Two bottles of water, an apple each, and I'm set. Gourmet at its finest.

The laundry room door opens and closes. "Flynn?"

Yeah, that's right, not only did I give Jackie my extra garage remote, but she has a house key too. This shit is serious.

"Hey, babe, in the kitchen," I call out across the great room, ripping two paper towels off for napkins.

Jackie comes bounding into the room in that special way that she does when she's excited. It's not quite skipping, but it's damn close.

She bounces to a stop in front of me, smiling wide. "Hey."

I lean down and kiss her, my favorite part of the day. Well, if you don't count bedroom time.

I pull back and rub my nose lightly against hers. "Okay, spill."

She leans in, placing her hands on my chest. "How did you know I have something to tell you?" She pouts and it's adorable.

I touch her nose with mine again. "Never mind how. Tell me. What has you so happy?" I gesture to the paper plates. "Besides my awesome dinner, of course."

Jackie looks over at the dinner set-up and lets out a happy sigh. I love how she loves the small things.

And then she snaps back to attention, full of energy again. "You'll never believe who called me today."

"Well, if I'll never guess, you better tell me." I reach for her hips and draw her in closer. Which I regret when she bounces on her toes again, nearly slamming her forehead into my nose.

"The astronaut office! They called to set up my final interview, Flynn." She is full-out jumping up and down now and I'm momentarily distracted from her words due to the wonderful things her exuberance is doing for her boobs.

She stops bouncing, much to my disappointment, and holds her thumb and index finger up, only an inch apart. "I'm *this* close to becoming an astronaut! Can you believe it?" And then she's bouncing again while my legs become rooted to the spot, as if they are weighed down with lead.

"Wait. What?" I put my hands on her shoulders, holding her still. I catch her eyes. "What are you talking about?"

My tone must surprise her, either that or the intensity of my stare, because she gives me a funny look before shaking it off. "The final step in the astronaut hiring process. You know, the one I've been going through, that I told you about?"

My ears are buzzing and the heaviness in my legs has spread to my chest. "You told me you got through the first round, but I thought becoming an astronaut was a really fucking long process, and crazy hard or something. Isn't it basically impossible?"

"Well, yeah, but—"

"And why are you so excited? I mean, I held you as you cried not two weeks ago. And you told me a big part of that was how scared you'd been for Jules. I thought that alone would cure you of this ridiculous scheme."

Jackie steps away from my grasp, my hands sliding off her shoulders. "Ridiculous?"

Part of my brain knows I'm spiraling. That I need to take a step back and a couple deep breaths and not say something I'm going to regret. But the larger part smells the burning engines, hears the metal crumpling, chokes on the devastation from the inevitable crash. I can't seem to separate my parents' end from the history of space shuttle crashes, ISS safety alarms and the gut-wrenching feeling of Jackie being in constant danger.

"It's too dangerous."

Jackie lets out a nervous laugh. "You're kidding, right?"

I just continue to look at her.

"You realize that statistically speaking, mechanics and those who drive vintage cars without all the modern safety features are more likely to injure themselves than astronauts, right?"

I still don't say anything. I can't. All I see is twisted metal and fire.

She lays a hand on my arm. "I'm sure if I give you all the—"

"No," I hear myself saying.

I can't see Jackie's face anymore. She's a blur, even though she's just a foot away. But I hear her, her voice timid and shaky.

"What do you mean, 'no'?"

I blink repeatedly, bringing her beautiful face back into focus. "I mean no, you can't be an astronaut." She flinches. "Not if you want to be with me."

TWENTY-TWO
REAL TIME

Jackie

HE GAVE ME AN ULTIMATUM. CHOOSE BETWEEN FLYNN AND becoming an astronaut. Choose between the dream I've chased my entire life and the man I've come to love.

Love. It's almost as unbelievable as the ultimatum. Both no less true the more I repeat the words in my head.

I haven't seen Flynn in a week. Not since I looked at him, stunned, eyes probably as wide as those flying saucers people think the government hides in the desert of New Mexico. When he remained stoic, jaw set, fists clenched at his side, immovable, I simply stepped back and walked away. To my crappy car. Drove to my crappy apartment and picked up where I'd left off in my crappy life before Flynn.

And that's the kicker. As smart as everyone tells me I am, I'd never realized just how crappy my life was, until it wasn't.

Oddly enough, as my love life has been imploding, my occupational life is taking off like the proverbial rocket. I'm back at my console in Mission Control, my personal problems crammed into their own little compartment in the back of my mind. Sean is currently on his seventh cup of coffee of the day. Jules and Bodie are safe, with the ISS back in full working order.

I even had my astronaut interview yesterday. I was able to break free from the haze that Flynn's conditional demands had thrown me into long enough to answer the questions Roger McAllister, the Chief of the Astronaut Office and Jorge Salazar, the Director of Flight Operations Directorate threw my way with a modicum of intelligence.

And though it's been two weeks since the NASA EXT emergency, news outlets and reporters are still camped out at NASA. I've done all the sound bites HR has required of me, and that's it. But my reticence hasn't prevented reporters from referring to Jules, Bodie and me as the *saviors* of the ISS. I gave myself a headache when I eyerolled after I heard that one. Whoever came up with that headline should have their journalistic credentials stripped.

But I'm sure that's not what the PR team I just spent a few hours with wants me to say in my upcoming interview on Fox News. The one NASA insists I do.

Deep breath.

I'm going to ignore everything in my life that doesn't involve this moment in Mission Control. I'll pretend everything is back to normal. Normal, everyday real-time decisions with the crew and the station's technology. No imminent space junk, no hotwiring, no car honking text notifications and most assuredly, no more tears. Just my normal, everyday life, crappy or not.

"Jackie?"

I swivel in my chair to hush whoever's calling my name only to have the words stick in my throat.

"It *is* you!" Walking toward me is Brian Hampson, the new shortstop for the Houston Astros and the man who popped my cherry.

This is so *not* normal. But still very crappy.

He's with a group of four very tall, very large men. To round out their group is a woman with a camera and a press badge around her neck. Brian pulls me to my feet and engulfs me in a hard hug before I have a chance to respond. A camera flashes.

"No flash photography!" Sean whisper yells. The journalist shrugs, but adjusts her camera.

Brian leans back, looking me over, all while keeping a perfect angle for the photographer. "How've you been?"

"Um, great?" A quick glance around MCC has me wishing I called in sick, or took that vacation everyone said I deserved. I try to will away the blush that's threatening and clear my throat. "You?"

He turns us so that we're facing the photographer, with the Mission Control sign behind us. "Fine, thanks," he says, talking to me but posing for the camera.

And he is. Fine, that is. He's always been, but the past few years have broadened his shoulders and sculpted his arms into steel bands. Steel bands that are still around me.

I adjust my glasses and step back. "What are you doing here?"

He gestures to the men in front of us. "I've been signed to the Houston Astros, so they wanted me to see the sights." He poses again, slightly shifting his weight, and I think… yes, he's flexing his arm. His hair is longer. Gone is the buzz cut from college, replaced by a man-bun. He has more hair styling ability than I do. "A few of the boys on the team are taking me on a tour of NASA. Good PR, what with the recent news coverage." He scans around the room, much like a socialite probably does at banquets, trying to find more important, wealthier people. Brian seems resigned that I'm all he has to talk to at the moment.

"I see."

"You're the big hero at NASA! It's all over the news," Brian says, drawing a lot of attention from my co-workers.

Before I can shush him and maneuver back to my console, the

photographer jumps in, corralling me over until I'm in the middle of all the baseball players, and takes more pictures.

"As much as I love all this bullshit reunion crap—this is Mission Control, and you guys need to shut your traps. Some of us are working here," Sean says from his console.

"Sorry, Sean," I say.

"Can't get too mad at the *hero,* now can we?" Sean winks and I feel my face heat. "Besides, your shift's over." He motions all of us toward the door. "Go take your celebrity friends out to eat, Jackie."

"I really don't think—"

"That sounds great," Brain says. "Thanks for the idea, big man."

It's nearly worth seeing Brian again just to witness the look of pure outrage on Sean's face from being called "big man."

Nearly.

————

I'M SITTING across from Brian, the crusher of my virgin heart, at a table for two.

In a sushi restaurant, that, according to Brian, is *the* place to get lunch. Of course Brian would want to eat at a high-profile restaurant.

I don't even like sushi.

When we left NASA, Brian steered me to his two-seater Audi. The other ballplayers took off to get BBQ. They hadn't even said good-bye, which I thought was rude until I remembered…Brian. I'm sure he's pissed people off on his new team already.

When the waiter comes over, Brian orders for both of us without even consulting me.

"So, what have you been up to all these years?" Brian asks. "Besides saving the Space Station and all."

I would've been shocked at his interest if his tone hadn't been so obviously derisive. I'm suddenly thrown back ten years, sitting in the library, tutoring him in basic math while his buddies snicker from a few shelves down. As if from muscle memory, my shoulders start to roll forward and my eyes dart down to the table top.

"Nothing much," I say, pissed at myself for being so weak.

"Yeah, I guess in between all that geeky stuff you were always into, there isn't a lot of time left over for anything fun." He picks up some sort of bean pod a waiter brought over and starts straining the beans out with his teeth. He continues to talk around his food. "That's part of why I came. Give you a good time, take you to a few things coming up around town." He's gesturing a lot with his hand. The one holding an empty bean pod husk. The green slimy sliver flops back and forth with each motion. "Maybe treat you to some publicity events for the Astros."

I look at him blankly. He can't seriously be asking me out. Not after what he did in college. Not without even acknowledging it or apologizing for being such a.... What had Rose called him? Oh. A "legit dick."

"Figured I'd do you a favor. Take you out of nerd central, let you see how the other half lives. There are a few banquets I should have a date for, and you'd be perfect with all the publicity you've been getting lately."

Wow. He *is* serious.

In the past few days I've been bombarded with requests from the higher-ups at NASA. From public relations people. From reporters. From Rose and Trish via text. And studiously ignored from the one person I've ever loved. All of which I've felt completely ill-equipped to deal with. Being ill-equipped does not sit well with me. I'm so very tired of being ill-equipped.

I roll my shoulders back and look Brian square in his pretty, obnoxious face. "No."

He drops the limp bean pod to pick up his chopsticks. "Yeah, there's some big shindig in River Oaks later this week, plus a charity ball next weekend. Figured the whole Astro-Astronaut angle will go viral." He chuckles, apparently amused at his own cleverness. And apparently not listening to me.

"No," I repeat louder.

Brian's hand pauses halfway to his mouth, a piece of raw fish falling from his chopsticks. "No?"

"That's right. No."

He looks equal parts shocked and confused. Confused, probably because no one has ever turned him down before. Shocked, probably because *I'm* the one turning him down.

"Oh. My. Gosh." A teenage girl comes up to our table, practically bouncing on her toes.

Brian smooths his furrowed brow and leans back in his seat, looking her over. Probably assessing whether or not she's of legal age. "Let me guess, Astro fan?" He sets his chopsticks down. "You want an autograph, right?" He reaches into his pocket and retrieves a Sharpie.

The girl glances at Brian. "Huh?" She looks at me. "You're Dr. Jackie Darling Lee, aren't you?"

I blink. Brian's brow creases again.

I can't understand why she'd know my name. "Yes." I draw the word out, unsure of where this is going.

"You are? That is *so* cool." I blink in surprise as she turns to her family at a table a couple down from ours. "It *is* her!"

Brian speaks up. "Look, kid, you want a selfie with me or what? We're kinda busy here."

The girl jumps at his tone and I roll my eyes. I reach out and touch her arm, redirecting her attention. "I'm sorry, what were you saying?" I ask.

She narrows her eyes at Brian in one of the best annoyed teenager looks I've ever seen before answering me. "You basically *saved* NASA. I want to work there too. Maybe I could work in the payload division. I've read that they help organize all the experiments that astronauts conduct in space. I've been getting really good grades in all my science classes, and I read that you did too. I'm not so great at math, but my parents said they'd get me a tutor so I can take some AP classes. I've also been going to Space Camp every summer at Space Center Houston and I'm hoping to go to the more in-depth one in Alabama next year. I'm even thinking of going into the Air Force so that I can be a pilot. NASA loves military experience, don't they?" She's slightly out of breath after speaking.

My smile is wide and genuine for the first time since leaving Flynn's place. It always makes me happy seeing young women interested in space exploration. "That's really great. NASA performs some pretty amazing experiments in space. We're always looking for new things to test and people to test them. And it's true that in the past most all astronauts had a military background, but that isn't always the case now. Engineers, scientists and even teachers have become astronauts." I glance back at her family, who are all smiling in our direction. "What's your name?"

"*My* name?" The girl's eyes widen, and for a moment I think she's forgotten her own name. "Megan!" she shouts, winces, then repeats herself more softly. She yanks Brian's Sharpie from his hand and thrusts it and a napkin at me. "Can you sign this?"

"Hey!" Brian protests.

"Of course." I speak over him and scribble on the napkin.

Megan reads it aloud, "What would you attempt to accomplish if you knew you could not fail? Jackie Darling Lee."

I smile. "I'm not quite that philosophical. The quote is usually attributed to Robert Schuller, an American pastor who used it in inspirational sermons and books. Somehow NASA acquired it, and I must say it *does* fit."

"Awesome." Megan holds the napkin with both hands. "Thanks, Dr. Lee."

I slide the marker over the table toward Brian. "Call me Jackie. I'm sure you will sooner or later when you're working at NASA alongside me."

I'm not prepared when she launches herself at me, but my arms automatically go around her and tighten a moment before she straightens, waves and heads back to her table. An older woman, probably her mother, nods at me with a smile.

"Can you believe that loser?" Brian laughs, jerking a thumb in her direction. "Isn't she going to feel like a dumbass when she realizes she missed the opportunity to get my autograph? I mean, seriously, what could *your* signature be worth?" He tosses some food in his mouth with his chopsticks while I contemplate taking them from his hand and stabbing him in the throat.

Unaware of my homicidal thoughts, Brian continues, "But this could work to our advantage. When you go with me to these things, you can get the nerd vote and I can get the cool vote. People love that shit. We'll be at the top of Houston's high society in no time. Probably Hollywood too." He swallows. "Doesn't hurt that you know people like Rose West, either."

"Wait. How do you know that I know Rose?"

"You're in a lot of her Instagram shots lately. That's how I figured out you were here." He stabs another piece of fish with his chopsticks. "Couldn't believe *you* knew a West." The fish falls off the wooden spear. Honestly, he should just use a fork.

"What do you mean, 'a West'?" And why is he following Rose's Instagram?

The waiter interrupts before he can answer, asking if everything is okay. Ignoring, or simply not caring, that I haven't touched my plate, Brian nods and waves the guy away. He keeps talking, even as he shovels in the food. About how the Wests are a well-known, old family name in Houston. Then he's rambling on about publicity photos, endorsements and how the two of us could garner thousands just for making appearances at parties. I don't bother telling him that as a government employee I can't accept money for those sorts of things. Or ask him any of the many follow-up questions I have about his interest in the Wests. I don't bother saying anything. I figure the more I talk or ask, the longer this will take.

Instead, I wonder at my eighteen-year-old self. Had I been that naïve? Had I not known what kind of douchebag he was? Maybe it was because he'd been the first guy who showed me that kind of attention. But that train of thought dies as I flip through my memories like a slide show. Brian was the first guy I'd *let* show me that kind of attention. I might not have been popular, being the youngest kid in high school and college, but if I'm honest with myself, I'd had other opportunities. I'd just been more interested in school than boys. Brian had probably gotten through to me because he'd been driven by a bet, an ulterior motive making him unwilling to back down. But Flynn...

Flynn had gotten through because he'd been the first man whom I'd deemed worthy of my brain time. Instead of my head always being full of cosmos, probabilities and mathematical angles, I'd taken time to think of him. Of his smile, his laugh, his hands. The way he seemed to love my glasses, my body, but best of all, my mind. He's the one guy I hadn't resented for taking up space in my thought process. Thoughts of him make me just as happy as thoughts of science. Happier, even.

It's quite a jolt to my senses when I come back in focus and see Brian on the other side of the table. Why am I even here? I'm so beyond this, beyond *him* and the feelings of inadequacy I used to let him fill me with. I rise from my seat, intent on leaving, when Brian's hand grips my arm.

"Whoa, where are you going? Didn't you hear what I said? We could make some serious money if we—"

"Stop talking." I try to shake off his arm.

"Excuse me?" His hand tightens and I wince.

"I said stop talking." I yank on my arm, not caring about the bruises that are sure to appear later. "And let go of me." But his hand just clamps down harder and he uses brute strength to shove me back in the chair.

"I wasn't done talking. And no one tells me to shut up." He's pointing a finger in my face. I don't like that. I don't like any of this.

In a few seconds I calculate the probable angles and necessary torque needed.

"Jesus, you're not even listening to me, are you? I've always hated when you space out. I'd hoped you'd outgrown such sh—"

I grab his finger and apply the correct amount of pressure at a forward angle, which immobilizes Brian while not actually breaking bone. Although I've calculated for that too, if he tries anything. His mouth drops open and his complexion pales.

Slowly, I rise from my seat, making sure to keep the necessary angle to ensure Brian's physical cooperation. When he tries to swing his other arm in my direction, I simply apply more pressure. He yelps.

"Don't even try it," I tell him.

He lowers his free arm while I pivot away from the table. To keep his finger from breaking he has to drop to his knees.

"You'll break my fucking finger. I'm a baseball player, you bitch. I need my fingers to play. I'll fucking sue." Now that the shock has worn off, his face is red and beads of sweat are forming on his forehead.

And people think math is for weaklings. With just a few calculations, a lowly nerd like myself has brought a Neanderthal to his knees.

"And I need you to. Stop. Talking." I step toward him, his head jerking back to look at me. "You are never to talk to me again. *You* were lucky I ever decided to talk to *you*. *You* are not good enough for *me*. Understand?" I utilize an infinitesimal extra amount of force on his finger, which results in a satisfactory whimper from Brian. "I do not care about making money on appearances with you. I do not care about being part of society's elite or maximizing your social media exposure. And I sure as crap do not care about you or your baseball fingers. You sue me and everyone will know you got your butt handed to you by a girl. And not just any girl, a nerd." I let his finger go and step back out of reach. "And now this nerd has better stuff to do and more important people to talk to."

People clap as I spin on my heel and make for the door before Brian can recover. When I cross the threshold, the heat slams into me. I take a moment to let my lungs adjust before stomping in the humidity toward my apartment.

TWENTY-THREE
STALL

Flynn

"WHAT THE *HELL* ARE YOU DOING HERE?"

I look up from under the hood of a 1975 Barracuda to see Rose barreling through the garage.

I've been at the shop since the crack of dawn this morning after another sleepless night. When the rest of my crew arrived, one look at my face was enough for them to give me a wide berth. They've learned that lesson the hard way the past couple of days. Apparently, though, my anger doesn't faze Rose.

"I don't want to hear it," I tell her.

"Hear what?" She makes it to my side, hands on hips, cowboy boot tapping.

"Whatever it is that you're going to say." I lean back over the motor. The guy who dropped the 'cuda off yesterday said it needed a new carburetor. But after checking the spark plugs, I'd reassessed. Often an electrical problem will appear similar to a fuel problem. That's something I like about fixing cars—identify the problem, fix it and move on. It's one of the things I love about Jackie. We both analyze and fix shit.

My hand tightens on the wrench.

"You're supposed to be lying in bed with Jackie right now, doing unspeakably dirty things to her while apologizing for being such a dick. And that's *after* you beat the shit out of her douchebag ex-boyfriend."

"Excuse me?"

"You heard me." Rose pivots on her foot and leans under the hood, getting into my face.

"What the hell are you talking about, Rose?" I hunch forward, bracing my arm on the fender. "Jackie's the one who hasn't called me. She knows where I stand. The ball's in her court."

"You. Are. A. Moron." Rose punctuates each word with a stab in my sternum. "I let you spew that shit about Jackie choosing a dangerous job over you 'cause I just thought you needed to hear how much of a selfish prick you were being. Or maybe you needed some time to get your head out of your ass. Obviously, you're not as smart as I'd given you credit for."

I find myself twisting my lips, holding back angry retorts, because I know Rose is right. But she still doesn't get it. She'd been too young to remember when Gramps broke his neck riding that stallion, and then away at boarding school when Holt took the call about Mom and Dad's car crash. But I was old enough to feel the pain of all those losses. I've been falling in love with Jackie since the first time she slid those glasses up her nose in front of me. And I can't take losing anyone else I love.

Rose crosses her arms over her chest, looking at me hunched under the hood. "So you're saying you don't care that her ex got physical with her and pushed her around in public?"

The clink and clang of my wrench pinballing down through the motor echoes through the otherwise quiet garage. I straighten and turn toward my sister. "What. The. Fuck?"

My anger might not usually faze her, but whatever I'm putting out there now sure freaks Rose out. She takes a step back. But it still doesn't stop her snarky attitude. "Some NASA fan was taking a video of Jackie when it happened. She caught the whole thing. She posted it and tagged NASA's twitter account. Viral in an instant." Rose snaps her fingers. "Lucky for you, Jackie seems well versed in self-defense." Rose looks down her nose at me, which is impressive as I'm nearly a foot taller than her.

"Jesus, Rose... I..." I run my hand through my hair. "Self-defense? Is she okay? Did someone call the cops? Maybe I should—"

"No, jackass. The time to act has well fucking passed. I told you she wasn't going to wait around forever for your apology."

"I—"

"I mean, she thinks you're a fucking mechanic, Flynn. For God's sake, she doesn't even know what being a West *means*. And yet the girl still loves you." She sneers at me. "And yet you, the person she came to first with the news that she was one step away from her dream job, wants her to turn it down." She taps her finger on her chin. "Wow, does this seem like déjà vu to anyone else? Like when a little privileged douche bag gave up the oil business to open his own mechanic shop because it was *his* dream? And what did his girlfriend at the time do? Gave him an ultimatum, if I remember correctly. Isn't that right, Flynn?"

I open my mouth but nothing comes out.

She blows out a slow breath, her eyes shiny. "You might care about her, but you sure as shit don't deserve her."

Fuck. She's right.

Jackie

Big and Rich are singing about saving a horse and riding a cowboy while I lie on my bed in my underwear, trying to cool down from my drive home from work. The air conditioning in my car conked out. Of course it did.

So I came home and took a cold shower, trying to both stop sweating and relax after the long day I've just had. A day of dealing with the aftermath of Brian frigging Hampson's male chauvinist antics and the video of the subsequent butt kicking I gave him. Or finger bending. However, though not as accurate, butt kicking sounds better than finger bending.

I need a plan. A procedure to get me through this mess. *Hmmm.* Seeing as Operation Social Life hasn't panned out all that well, maybe just a to-do list.

Step one, buy a new car. This should be fun. A new car involves research. I love research. But now, thinking about cars makes me think of Flynn. And that makes me sad. I guess I'll just buy the same make and model as I have now, but new. It won't be as badass as one of Flynn's vintage cars, but hopefully it will last me another ten years. I blow out a sigh, wondering how many things that would normally bring me joy won't, because they'll remind me of Flynn.

Step two, deal with the publicity nightmare of the video of Brian's butt kicking. By itself, I don't think the video would've been too bad, even with Brian's celebrity. However, when you factor in the fact that the media is still trying to call me one of the saviors of NASA, and the leaked news that I'm in the top running for the new astronaut class, NASA's public relations team has me on speed dial.

Big and Rich stop singing, only to start up not ten seconds later. Rose is tenacious, I'll give her that. Unless I turn my phone off, which I've been expressly told not to do in case PR needs to go over something with me for the upcoming interview they've demanded I do, I'm going to hear Rose's ringtone all night. A ringtone which she personally selected. I'm all for Big and Rich, but this is killing my newfound love of country music.

On the next ring, I take a deep breath and pick up the phone.

"Don't say anything," I demand.

"I—"

"No. It's my turn to talk. Okay?" She's silent, so I figure she gets the message. "You and I are good. I'm sorry I've been dodging your calls. First there was the ISS failure, then the Flynn and Beth thing, then everything seemed fine. More than fine, it was… well, it was amazing. And then just as quickly, it wasn't. And now the stupid video." I take a deep breath, angry that my eyes are stinging. "I just feel so drained. I'm not used to all this *stuff.*" I gesture in the air with my free hand, even though Rose isn't there to see me. "I don't think I'm equipped to deal with roller coaster emotions."

She's still silent.

"Right now, I just do not have the head space to deal with whatever happened between Flynn and me. And I know he is your brother and you want to defend him." Rose makes a sound, but quickly quiets. "But I just can't hear it right now." I clear my throat. "Okay?"

"Okay, Jackie."

"So you and I are good. Just no Flynn talk, okay?"

"If that's what you want."

I blow out a long breath and blink a few times, trying to get my emotions under control. Goosebumps spread over my legs as my body temperature finally starts to cool down.

"So, Jackie?" Rose asks after a bit more silence.

"Yes, Rose?"

"I just need to say two things that involve Flynn. But only so you aren't blindsided later."

"I—"

"I promise I'm not defending him, it is just information you need."

"Fine," I say on a sigh.

"One, I told Flynn about the video and what happened at the restaurant. And two, I will not defend my brother. In fact, I recently told him he was an asshole and didn't deserve you."

I heard what she said. I even think, subconsciously, that I've computed what it means. But all I can manage is a very un-me, "Rose. What the fuck?"

"Wow," Rose breathes. "You said fuck."

A giggle shoots out. "Uh, yeah. I guess I did."

"That's okay. Sometimes you need a fuck."

After a small pause, both of us start laughing, me curled up on the bed until tears do fall from my eyes.

"Jackie?" Rose asks.

I close my eyes, trying to draw up some strength. I'm not sure I can handle any more announcements from Rose. "Yes?"

"Could you teach me that self-defense finger thing? I have a feeling that might come in handy the next time I throw down."

"Yeah, Rose. Of course I will. That's what friends are for."

———

STILL LYING IN MY UNDERWEAR, though the shadows on the wall have moved and darkened with time, my phone rings again. For once, it is the standard shrill ringtone it came originally programed with.

I glance at the screen, annoyed when I see the Houston area code. I should probably pick it up and see what whoever it is wants, instead of lying here like a lump for the foreseeable future like I'd planned.

"Hello?"

"Dr. Lee? This is Roger McAllister here."

I sit up quickly, nearly losing my grip on the phone.

"Yes, uh…" I clear my throat. "Evening, Mr. McAllister. How can I help you?"

"You can start by taking the position of astronaut."

"Holy Mercury."

"Dr. Lee?"

"Sorry, sorry. I, well, it's just a shock."

He chuckles. "It shouldn't be. Not after your final interview, as well as you coming up with the solution for the EXT failure as well as spearheading the emergency spacewalk."

"I—"

"So, what do you say? Are you going to give me an answer, or do you need to talk to your family and loved ones first?"

Family and loved ones? I suck in a deep breath, thinking of Flynn. Of what my next words will mean for him. For us. But then I think of my dad, of how supportive he's been of me my whole life, if a little unorthodox in showing he cares. And then I think of my mother and her NASA scrapbooks and love of space.

"No need to wait. I have my answer." And really there is no other answer. Not because I want this more than Flynn and the life I thought we were making. But because by him making me choose, he left me no choice at all. "It's affirmative, sir. I'll take the position."

TWENTY-FOUR

ASCENSION

Flynn

I'VE FUCKED UP. BIG TIME.

I thought about going back to Jackie's place, but what the hell would I say? What does a guy say who's basically let his girl get shoved around by another guy because he was too fucked up over his past to man-up and say he was wrong?

Fuck, it's so much worse when I say it out loud in my head.

Instead, I begged Rose for help, and when begging wasn't enough I promised her a real sit-down family dinner with her and Holt if she'd give me Brian Hampson's downtown address. Which she somehow had, and was willing to share since it didn't directly relate to Jackie or 'breaking girl code.' Whatever that means.

Then I floored it into Houston and used my last name to grease the palm of the condo's building manager to get access to the damn garage. Sometimes it's nice to be a West in Houston.

Thankfully, I don't have to wait long for Hampson to drive in. The asshole steps out of his Audi dressed head to toe in designer workout gear, wearing sunglasses in an underground garage, one finger trussed up in a splint. The guy has a freaking man-bun for fuck's sake. He needs to be set straight for that alone.

But the man-bun isn't why I'm here.

"Yo," I call out, getting the guy's attention.

He smiles when he sees me pushing off the side of my car to walk toward him. He actually pulls a Sharpie out from his pocket. "Always have time for my fans," he says.

I hate him on so many levels right now.

I stop about a foot away, letting all the rage I have boil to the surface. "I'm not a fan."

"What—"

My fist connects with his face, snapping his head back before he crumples to the ground. The man-bun cushions his fall.

Honestly, for a shortstop, his reaction time is for shit.

When he just lays there in a puddle, I nudge him with my boot, which gets a low moan out of him.

What a pussy.

I crouch down to make sure this douche bag hears every word. "You ever lay a hand on Jackie again, you even speak her mother-fucking name, and I will end you. Physically. Financially. Socially. *End* you."

I rise and step over the groaning ballplayer and slide into my Mustang Boss. I flex my slightly swollen fist, then grip the steering wheel hard.

First, I need to hit the shop. I have some work to do.

But then? Then it's time to get drunk.

———

"TURN ON THE TV!" Rose flies through the side door and runs over to the TV.

I wince at her booming voice, lifting my head from the couch. "Rose?" Six p.m. and I'm still nursing my hangover from the night before, after I finally finished my project at the shop. It has taken a full week of nonstop work, but it was worth it.

"Where is it?" She turns one way, then the other before she starts ripping cushions off the couch. Cushions I'm currently lying on. "Where's the fucking remote?"

"Damn it, Rose. Hold up." I get off the couch, squinting as my head pounds. "Calm down, it's right here." I pick up the controller from the side table and hand it to her.

Rose whirls to the TV, clicks it on and starts channel surfing like a champ. "Fox News! What channel is Fox News?"

"Rose, you're going to break the—"

"Ah ha!" Rose triumphantly gestures toward the TV. "There she is."

Sitting on a red chair in a newsroom studio is Jackie. Well, it *looks* like Jackie, but not. This Jackie is infinitely more polished. Her hair is up in some sort of twist thing I usually see on older women driving Mercedes four-door sedans. Instead of her usual uniform of jeans and Converse she's wearing an actual pantsuit with heels. She looks about as comfortable as a 1978 Corvette off-roading across the desert. At least she's still wearing her glasses.

Those sexy fucking glasses.

The screen splits, showing her friend Jules and another guy floating around in the International Space Station. Holt walks around the couch and sits down. Rose takes the chair.

"Dr. Lee, astronauts Julie Starr and Vance Bodaway, thank you for being with us today," the newscaster says, then chuckles. "Well maybe not *here*, in your case, Miss Starr and Mr. Bodaway, but thank you for taking time to call down to us from the station."

"No problem, Vanessa. I can call you Vanessa, can't I? And I sure hope you'll call me Jules. Miss Starr sounds like a beauty pageant contestant."

"Just Bodie for me, ma'am," Vance says.

"And I'm pretty sure Jackie is cool dropping all her titles, aren't you, Jackie? Dr. Lee is her father." Jules winks into the camera. Jackie starts rolling her eyes but stops halfway, glancing at the camera and blushing.

"Of course." Vanessa adjusts the tilt of her head away from Jules to address Jackie. "Let's get down to it, shall we?" At Jackie's blank stare, she continues. "As a NASA Flight Operator, you have many different tasks associated with keeping the astronauts safe and the station up and running. But out of all that you do, what gave you the idea to essentially hotwire the International Space Station?"

"A mechanic." Another blush.

"A mechanic?" The reporter's eyebrows rise, hinting at her to elaborate. Jules smirks from the monitor and motions Jackie to continue.

"Yes. He is, ah, was a friend." Jackie clears her throat and shifts in her seat, rubbing the palms of her hands on her pants. "He showed me how to hotwire a car recently."

"Hotwiring a car? You wouldn't happen to be a car thief on the side, now, would you?" Vanessa leans forward like she's having a private moment with Jackie. Like they're just two women having a conversation and not being filmed on a national news show. Jackie turns a deeper shade of red.

"I was told it wasn't illegal if it was your own car."

The reporter laughs along with Jules and Bodie, which seems to surprise Jackie. She relaxes a bit in her chair.

"So, how did you end up hotwiring a car?" Vanessa asks.

"My friend was going to give me a ride home from work. But I accidentally knocked his keys down a storm drain." Jackie pushes her glasses up her nose. "He had to hotwire his car to start it."

"That's some friend."

"Yes. He was."

I cringe at the past tense, the pounding in my head escalating. Rose glares at me. The phrase 'if looks could kill' takes on new meaning.

"Anyway," Jackie says, "as he was hotwiring his car, he took me through the procedural sequence. And later, when we were in the emergency briefing about the computer failures on the ISS, it suddenly hit me that we were thinking too complex. All the station really needed was a work-around from the damage sustained by the debris. Bypass the corroded wires and we could jump-start the EXT-1 externally."

"I see," the reporter says, but her facial expression says otherwise.

"That would give us the ability to then power-cycle EXT-2, which was behaving erratically due to a software update. Two birds, one stone, so to speak. It was simple, really. Anyone would've thought of it, I'm sure."

"Jackie's being modest," Jules jumps in, bringing everyone's attention to the monitor on set. "Truth is, she's the smartest flight operator we have at NASA. Did you know she holds not one, but two masters and a PhD? And she's only 29 years old."

"She can talk circles around any of us floating around up here," Bodie adds.

Jackie turns red again.

"Especially those who are no more than glorified streetlights, right, Bodie?" Jules smirks.

Bodie simply laughs and pushes her off frame. She climbs back up in front of the camera using the hand rails along the wall of the station, laughing back. They both seem relaxed, happy even. Not in imminent danger. And I wanted Jackie to give that up? I'm such a dick.

"Yes, you do have quite an impressive background, Jackie." The newscaster glances down at the notepad on her lap. "Jules mentioned your father earlier. Dr. Gerald Howard Lee is a renowned scientist with several patents in the chemical field. I guess the apple didn't fall too far from the tree then?"

"My father and I have different interests, but he's always encouraged me in mine." Jackie's answer seems rehearsed. She reaches up, as if to run her hand through her hair, then stops when she encounters the twist thing. She jerks her hand back down, and a few strands fall to the side of her face.

"You might not have any patents that I'm aware of, but as a child prodigy you were given a full academic scholarship to Stanford after winning the Siemens Math, Science and Technology Award at just sixteen years of age. You have two masters, one in physics with a focus in astronomy, and the other in aeronautics and astronautics, which you later followed up with a PhD."

Jackie nods then adjusts her glasses when they slide down.

"But most impressive, besides saving the International Space Station"—Vanessa pauses to smile at the camera—"is that you were also the recipient of the MacArthur Fellowship."

"I was very fortunate." She rubs her palms on her pants again.

"That's why they call her NASA's Darling," Jules says with a smirk.

Jackie cringes, mumbling, "At least I'm not NASA's Starr," making everyone laugh.

"I'm feeling a little left out here. I think I need a nickname too," Bodie says.

"Bodie, any nickname that would suit you wouldn't be suitable for a public audience," Jules quips.

Jules and Bodie continue their back-and-forth camaraderie for the camera, while Jackie looks relieved to have the focus off of her.

They talk a bit more before promising a special announcement after the commercial break.

"Holy. Fucking. Shit," Rose says, her fingers flying over her phone.

"What?" I ask, my eyes barely leaving the TV.

"That Siemens thing?" she asks while reading her phone screen. She chuckles. "Sounds like semen."

I put my hands on either side of my head, trying to ease the pounding. "Rose. Focus."

She looks up at me, thumbs hovering over the screen.

"What about her award?" I prompt.

"Oh, yeah. Jackie won, like, a hundred grand," Rose says.

"What?"

"Yeah." Rose's head dips back to her phone. "And the MacArthur Fellowship? That's over a half million."

"*What*?"

Rose gives me an odd look when she sees the expression on my face. "Why are you so surprised? Didn't you know?"

I think back to all those times Jackie and I could've talked about money, instances that it would've been such a natural segue to explain my family's background, and in turn she could've shared this with me. But every time money came up, I'd shied away or just plain shut down the conversation. 'Cause I was afraid money would change her view of me. Like Beth. Like Mom with Dad.

Nausea that has nothing to do with the remaining alcohol in my system rises in my throat.

"You didn't know?" Rose asks when I don't reply. She looks down for a moment. "Wait. You did tell her about us though, right? I mean, you two got pretty serious before you fucked it up. You had to have told her about the oil and the ranch."

"I—"

"Flynn?"

"Um, no. I didn't."

Rose shakes her head. "No wonder she jammed all that cash in my purse on the sly after I bought those clothes for her." She laughs. "Although knowing Jackie, she would've done that anyway." She gives me a pointed look. "You know, you and Holt made me go to a therapist after Mom and Dad died. But I'm starting to think it was you two who needed the help. You guys are both trying so hard to not repeat their mistakes, you keep making other, more idiotic ones."

"What do you mean?"

"Um, Holt sleeping with your ex and spending all his time on the ranch. Determined to keep the West Ranch legacy alive. You, worried every woman is a gold digger like Mom and pushing Jackie away when her dream job doesn't include some safe little cubicle behind security access doors."

Huh.

Commercials over, Rose turns back to the TV.

The news comes back with a close-up of Vanessa.

"Hello and welcome back. I'm Vanessa Hughes. Today's segment touched on the recent emergency spacewalk at NASA and the men and women being called the saviors of the International Space Station." She turns to look at a different camera. "The first United States astronauts were elected in 1959. Men from military service, mostly pilots. Over the years, NASA's group of highly selective individuals chosen for space flight has evolved. Now both men and women from all different back-grounds have proudly flown into space under the American flag." The camera moves out, panning to the side, where seven men and women are lined up in blue NASA jumpsuits.

Jackie's in the middle.

"Today that selection process continues. Here stand the seven men and women chosen for the next class of astronauts." She turns to the group, applauding softly. "Congratulations."

"Holy shit," Rose breathes. "She did it."

The newscaster goes down the line, introducing the new astro-nauts. A man from the Air Force Academy with a masters degree from MIT. A woman from the Naval Academy who's a Gates

Cambridge Scholar. A Colorado native who earned his doctorate in geology from UCLA.

When all the credentials have been established and the formal announcements made, Vanessa asks about family and personal hobbies. Down the line each astronaut talks about their husband, wife, fiancé, kids. When she gets to Jackie, Jackie simply says 'single' and moves on to her love of the stars.

That one word is a punch to my gut and it takes me a moment to breathe normally again.

"You're my brother. And I love you," Rose says, still looking at the screen. "But sometimes you can be such a fucking dick."

I say nothing. What *can* I say? I'm such a fucking dick.

TWENTY-FIVE

DEBRIEF

Jackie

"HOLY MERCURY!" ROSE WHOOPS AND HOLLERS, LAUGHING AT my expense. "I mean really, girl, *that's* what you say after you find out you're going to be an astronaut?" More laughter.

Rose and I are sitting at the bar in Big Texas, on either side of the corner, while Trish serves drinks from the other side. Rose has an honest-to-God newspaper laid out on the bar in front of us. And not just any paper, the paper with the headline "Holy Mercury" splashed on the front page in big old letters.

Journalists are killing me right now. Just killing me.

And I'm not too fond of McAllister, who gave them that quote. I'd been prepared to take that to the grave. Stupid Astronaut Chief.

"I didn't mean to say it out loud, you know," I mumble around my straw. Rose just keeps laughing.

"It's okay, sugar. It just seems to have endeared you more to the public." Trish pats my arm like a child. Seeing as how she is not tall by any means, the fact that she can so easily reach me means she has to be rocking some seriously high heels in order to see and serve over the bar. I'm grateful for my height, as I don't really need heels.

The wide heels of my cowboy boots seem to be all I can handle. And as much as I love them, the memory of Flynn kneeling before me to strip the boots off before we made love made me toss them into the back corner of my closet.

So I'm wearing a new set of Chucks to the bar tonight. Rose gave them to me. I don't know how she managed it, but she'd gotten someone to decorate over the Converse patch on the side with a sequined NASA symbol. I'm pretty sure you aren't supposed to use the NASA symbol like this without permission, but they're too freaking cool for me not to wear them.

Trish has just served me my third drink, so I'm feeling slightly more awesome than I usually feel about myself. I think drinking may have something in common with G-Force. After the initial shock to the system everything starts to feel pretty good.

I'm back in jeans too. Rose argued that jeans were not for going out unless they had rhinestones, but the look I gave her must have shut her up, 'cause she didn't push me. Especially when I agreed to let her burn my old jeans in favor of me wearing the new fitted ones she bought me. I may be wearing shoes with rhinestones, but I draw the line at a bedazzled butt.

Trish finishes filling drink orders and props an elbow up on her side of the bar.

"What'd I miss?" she asks.

"I think it is time for a debriefing," I declare, drink in hand.

Trish leans forward to hear. "A what?"

"Is that when you pants someone?" Rose asks.

She's stone cold serious, and I love her for it.

"No, you nut," I say, shoving her shoulder. "It's after an operation or mission has been conducted. The people involved sit down and discuss the purpose of the experiment and the positives or negatives of its outcome."

"Wait, what experiment?" Rose asks. "Was I drunk when this happened? The last time I experimented when drunk I nearly woke up married to a woman." She smiles and sighs. "Ahh, Vegas."

Trish's mouth falls open. "Oh. My. Gosh. No, just no."

Rose and I laugh at Trish's shocked expression.

"Wait!" Trish says, recovering and waving her perfectly manicured hands. "I remember—Operation Social Life." She winks at me. "Always knew you'd be my most interesting customer, sugar."

Rose straightens on her bar stool. "How did I not know this?"

"Probably because you were crumpled on the floor drunk," Trish replies with a smirk.

"Oh. Yes. Well. That makes sense." Rose stops pouting and salutes us with her drink.

I take a sip of my own. "After each operation, it's good to review what happened so that future operations can be more successful."

"I'm in on the next operation. I don't want to miss out again," Rose says.

"You were a pretty big part of this one," I tell her. "Even if you didn't know it."

"Damn straight." She nods.

"Well, you met us," Trish starts. "So that's a success." She raises her beer bottle toward us.

"Hear, hear!" Rose shouts and we all clink glasses before knocking them back. "And you stood up to that douche-hat Hampson," she continues after we lower our glasses.

"Yes, there was that. Don't think I ever would've had the confidence to do that if it weren't for you guys and Fly—" My breath catches. I cough and take another sip of my drink, trying to play it off.

Seeing the look Trish and Rose give each other, I have a feeling I'm not fooling anyone.

But surprisingly, Rose doesn't jump on my Flynn slip-up. Instead she squeals and shouts, "And now you're an ASTRO-NAUT!" She throws her head back on the last word, her voice ringing out over the music. People stop and stare. Rose stares right back, then balances her heels on the last rung of her stool, standing up.

Hurriedly I grab her hips, steadying her.

"Did you hear that, Big Texas? My girl here is a freaking astronaut!"

People cheer and raise their glasses in my direction. A couple of young men catcall Rose and she blows them a kiss.

Laughter ensues, and Trish grabs Rose's drink out of her hand before she spills it as she retakes her seat. Well, spill it any more than she already has, at least.

Then we drink to the success of Operation Social Life the rest of the night. Every time our glasses clink I feel triumphant.

I don't count the time I spend scanning the crowd for Flynn. I pretend my heart doesn't lurch each time I see a couple revolving on the dance floor. And I refuse to acknowledge how often I glance at my phone.

Roughly eighty percent of the mass of the universe is made up of material that scientists can not directly observe, which they call dark matter. It does not emit light or energy. Though the concept is pretty much accepted, there's no solid evidence to support dark matter's existence. Flynn is my dark matter. Therefore, I feel no guilt not including Flynn in my operation success chart.

I search the faces in the bar once more. Nope, no guilt at all.

———

I WAKE up with a hard length pressed up against my back. For a moment, I smile thinking of Flynn. But when the rest of my body spasms in pain, I realize it's the metal bar from the pull-out couch.

Hazy memories of line dancing to David Bowie's Space Oddity and saying the lift-off countdown to each shot we did come to mind as I smack my lips together, trying to find moisture. I've been hungover more this month than I have in my entire life.

I hear someone moving around and open my eyes a millimeter. Long, dark hair. Trish.

"Please tell me you don't sleep on this thing with any regularity," I mumble.

"Hey, that couch was free, I'll have you know," she chirps, far too awake-sounding after the night we had. "Found it on the side of the road."

"What?" I jack-knife off the mattress, whacking my head on something above me.

Trish laughs so hard I barely hear her gulp out the word 'kidding.'

"That was seriously a horrible thing to do to a friend," I admonish.

"I don't know, that was pretty freaking funny," she says, wiping her eyes.

"If I had known what a cruel person you were I never would have agreed to crash here." I rub my head and search for my glasses. "Why did I agree to crash here again?"

"When Rose found out you'd never been to a slumber party, she felt we needed to correct that childhood slight." Trish leans against her galley kitchen counter and takes a sip of coffee. "I guess she forgot that my home is a trailer."

Rose flings open the narrow bathroom door, adjacent to the kitchen. "Don't go in there," she says, closing the door behind her. "For at least five to ten minutes."

"Gross," Trish says, scrunching her nose.

"Hey, I grew up with two boys," Rose says. "Blame them for my ladylike ways."

I find my glasses on the floor next to me and slide them on, blinking as things come into focus. The couch is against one side of the trailer with a mounted TV across from me, the kitchen and dining area to the left and a bathroom and bedroom to the right. There's a twin-sized Murphy bed pulled down over the couch I slept on, essentially making bunk beds. That explains the large egg-shaped bump I'm now sporting on my forehead.

I see Trish glance my way. She's biting her lip and I realize she's nervous about what I think of her place.

"This is really cool," I say to her, noting the rounded shape of the ceiling. "Is this one of those silver Airstreams?"

"Yep."

"That's so awesome. They look like spaceships."

Trish smiles into her mug.

"Can you just pick up and go whenever you want?" I ask.

"That's the idea." Trish fills another mug from the coffee pot. "Beats having to apartment hunt whenever I move, I guess."

"Wait, you move a lot?" Rose asks. "'Cause that doesn't fit into my plans. You're just going to have to hang around Clear Lake, honey."

"Your plans, huh?" Trish smirks at Rose and then holds out the mug to me.

"Oh, I don't drink coffee. Sorry."

"That's okay, hon." Trish puts the mug on the counter. "I have juice if you want." She waves at a dorm-size fridge.

I start to get up, but Rose waves me back down. "I love you, but I don't need your boobs in my back as we all stand in the kitchen." She bends and opens the fridge. "I'll get you some juice."

I stay seated on the pull-out, as there really isn't room to maneuver around two people to get to the small dinette set at the other end of the trailer. Thankfully Trish walks over the few steps to me and pushes the top bunk back up against the wall so I can sit up straight.

Rose pours a glass of orange juice and hands it to Trish, who hands it to me. After putting the bottle away, she glances into Trish's mug. "Only weirdos drink black coffee, Trish." Rose takes the mug I refused off the counter. "You don't even put sugar in it. That's not right."

"When you grow up without money for sugar or milk, you get used to it," Trish says with a shrug.

We're quiet for a beat. It suddenly hits me that that is the most personal thing Trish has ever volunteered about herself.

"Well, that put me in my place," Rose mumbles.

Trish sticks her tongue out at Rose and the tension passes.

"Okay, so I'm the pampered pussy who puts both milk and sugar in her coffee," Rose says, proceeding to pour a generous helping of milk into her mug. In fact, she has to pour some coffee out into the sink to make room for all her milk. "Jackie makes do without and Trish, the apparent badass of the group, takes it black." She finishes preparing her coffee with a spoonful of sugar and takes a sip. "Who knew coffee could be so fucking metaphorical?"

Trish snorts. "I don't know whether to laugh at the fact that you're the pussy of the group or be in awe that you know what metaphorical means."

"Hey—I know shit."

"Yes, you know... shit," I say. "That sounds about right."

Rose's mouth hangs open for a second. "Was that a non-science related joke?" She looks at Trish, then back to me. "And did you curse?" She salutes me with her cup. "I knew I'd be a good influence on you."

"Good Lord." Trish rolls her eyes.

"Hey!" I get up from the couch, carefully this time and

squeeze past Rose and Trish to an open shelf on the other side of the kitchen. "Are these Audrey Cole's books?" I pull one down to confirm it.

"Uh, yeah." Trish blushes.

"This is great," I say. "Now I have at least one friend who can't make fun of me for my romance collection." I turn the book for Rose to see. "I love Audrey Cole. She's one of my favorites."

"Holy shit. No wonder," Rose says, looking over the cover. "If the book is as hot as that model I need to start reading bodice rippers too."

"They aren't bodice rippers. They're romance," Trish says, pouting.

"Whatever. That cowboy has a twelve pack." Rose gestures to the guy on the cover who's straddling a horse and holding a thick length of rope. "I'd like to know what else he's packing."

"You find out on page fifty-six," I say.

"Get out!" Rose yanks the book out of my hand and starts flipping through the pages. "You dirty, dirty bitches. I knew there was a reason I liked you two."

TWENTY-SIX

FUEL INJECTION

Jackie

WE READ THROUGH ALL OF AUDREY COLE'S SEX SCENES. IN ALL eight of her books. By the time we're done, I feel flushed and need to take a cold shower.

"Audrey Cole is a genius," Rose declares, fanning herself.

I nod. "Agreed."

Trish shakes her head with a smile and pours herself another cup of coffee. She'd been suspiciously quiet as Rose and I made our way through all of Cole's novels, but had looked pleased all the same.

When the coffee is gone and the books put away, Trish takes Rose and me home in her pickup truck.

"This is a pretty cool truck," Rose says, appreciating the classic Ford model. "I like the older trucks. Before they got all boxy and boring." She's perched on my lap in the passenger seat. Though the truck has a bench seat, the long-handled stick shift makes it impossible to sit in the middle. Rose had insisted, since she's shorter than me, that she had to be on top. I'd tried explaining how mass density and weight don't have anything to do with height, but it had been a lost cause.

"You should take it to Flynn's shop. He could fix it up like new. He'd love to get his hands on a vintage truck."

I still at the mention of Flynn. I see Trish cut her eyes to me as she shifts gears.

"Uh, I mean..."

I awkwardly pat Rose's shoulder. "It's okay." I clear my throat. "Trish *should* take it to West Auto. I've seen what he can do with vintage cars. It's amazing."

There's a beat of silence before Trish speaks. "Maybe I will, but I'm kind of used to it all rusted."

Rose snorts. "Why do my new besties think driving rust buckets is cool? You guys are just weird."

A few minutes later we pull into my apartment complex.

The first thing I notice is the car in my spot.

It is not mine.

My first thought is that someone stole my car. But, seeing as that's improbable, my second, more logical thought is that my car finally imploded with rust and my landlord hadn't wasted any time selling my parking space to someone else.

But then I *really* look at the car.

"Stop. Stop the truck," I yell.

"Sweetie, we *are* stopped," Trish says to me.

"Oh."

Rose murmurs under her breath, "About time, you fucker."

"What? About time, what?" I glance back and forth between the back of her strawberry blond head and the shiny white 1962 Corvette parked in my space. "Did you do this?"

"Me? Oh, no." She laughs. "But I may have to quit giving my brother the cold shoulder. First, he decks that prick and now—"

"Wait. What prick?" I ask.

"Uh..."

"Sweetie, don't you want to go see your new car?" Trish interrupts. Without waiting for my answer, she opens her door. Rose quickly wiggles off my lap, crawls over the stick and follows Trish out. I sit in the truck for a few more seconds trying to comprehend this new turn of events while also waiting for my legs to regain feeling.

Once circulation in my thighs resumes, though still without an answer to the car's presence, I get out of the truck.

"There you are, *chica*. Finally."

I turn to see Paulie leaning against the carport, his usual wife beater and low slung pants in place.

"What? Were you waiting for me, Paulie?"

He nods and tosses something at me. Without much thought I catch it. I open my fist to see a car key attached to a NASA emblem keychain resting in my palm.

Paulie gives me a two-finger wave. "And thanks for the clunker, *chica*. Amy will be able to get to more classes without having to use the bus."

"Wait, I—"

"Two guys dropped it off last night. Your guy said he'd already fixed it up so I wouldn't have to. Plus, he gave me a job." He looks at the ground, shaking his head in disbelief.

"Flynn hired you?" I look back at the keychain. "That's great, Paulie."

"Thanks, *chica*." He turns to go, but stops. "Not sure what kind of name Flynn is, but any man who gives a car like this to his woman and a man like me a chance can't be all bad." Paulie walks away but calls over his shoulder, "But if he turns out to be a *pendejo*, you let Paulie know. Boss or not, I'll fuck him up."

Rose laughs.

"Um, yes. I will. Thanks, Paulie," I call out. But he's already turned the corner out of sight.

"Dude, you know some interesting people," Rose says, stepping up beside me, staring off to where Paulie disappeared.

Slowly, I maneuver around Rose and walk to the front of the Corvette. I realize now why it looks so familiar. It's an exact replica of the car General Motors gave Alan Shepard after he'd become the first American in space. It even has altimeter gauges.

Flynn built me an astronaut car.

"Holy Mercury," I breathe, still looking at the car. I reach out to touch it, but stop just short of the hood, afraid to mar the shiny paint. I glance at Rose, then back to the car. "I don't understand."

"What's there to understand?" She shrugs. "My brother loves cars. He loves you. Figured he'd get around to getting his head out of his ass and both his loves together sooner or later."

"Wait— what?" I spin to face her. "He doesn't love me... he said he couldn't be with me if I became an astronaut."

Rose's eyes narrow. "I'd like it on record that I do think my brother can be a bit of a dick."

"Uh, okay," Trish says, giggling at the end.

"However, seeing as our parents died in a car crash, I can see where he would freak out over you going into space."

"Statistically speaking, flying into space is much safer than driving a car."

"Sugar, I know you're super smart, and we all love that about you," Trish says.

"Especially Flynn," Rose adds.

Trish nods and continues, "But sometimes statistics and logic aren't enough to overcome fears and emotions. At least not at first."

"Oh." Suddenly, Flynn's pathos-based reaction to my interview makes more sense.

"Plus Flynn took the time to punch out a famous baseball-playing asshat who happened to try and manhandle his lady love."

"Rose, sweetie. You can't make fun of Jackie and me for our

romance novels anymore if you're going to use phrases like 'lady love.'"

"Please. I bet it's because we just read all those romances that I'm talking like an eighteenth century lord."

"Wait, hold up," I say. "Flynn punched Brian?"

Rose rocks back on her heels. "Yeppers."

"When? Why?"

"I think it was the day after he tried pushing you around in that restaurant." She gives me a look. "And I think you know why."

"But... he said..." I trail off, lost in my thoughts, and my reflection in the high gloss paint.

"Well, whatever my stupid-ass brother said, he did manage to drop Brian with one punch," Rose says with disgust. "You'd think a professional athlete would be tougher than that."

Trish walks up to me and places her hand on my arm, giving me a gentle squeeze. "Maybe you should go talk to him, sugar."

I blink and look away from the car. "I'm an astronaut. He said—"

"Okay." Rose butts in, hands out. "I think we can all agree that my brother has said a lot of stupid shit. But he *did* start working on this car before making his stupid line in the sand, and he did keep working on it after." She shrugs. "So actions speak louder than words and all that, right?"

"Wait. You *knew* about this?" I ask, pointing to the car, my voice high-pitched and squeaky.

Trish stomps her foot. "And you didn't tell *me*?"

"Shit." Rose shoots a pleading look to both of us. "I, ah, well it was supposed to be a surprise." She steps back toward the truck.

Trish follows after her, mumbling, "*I* didn't need to be surprised."

"Okay, I'll make it up to you, Trish-the-Dish." Rose hops into the truck, smiling at Trish's scowl. "Come on, let's go to Cavender's and I'll get you some new boots."

"Hold on. Now we're going to Cavender's?" I ask.

Rose shakes her head, blond hair bouncing. "Not you, honey. You have to stay here and figure out what to do about my idiot brother. Lord knows I don't need to be around if you guys start going at it." She mimes gagging. "And if you knee him in the nuts, I don't want to feel obligated to step between you guys to keep the peace." She nods to herself. "Yep, you two are on your own." She leans out the window and thumbs over in Trish's direction. "But apparently I owe this girl a new pair of boots. Buy back her friendship and all that."

Trish scoffs and opens the driver side door. "You don't *buy back* friendship, Rose. And you don't have to buy me boots."

"Oh yeah? So you haven't been drooling over those ridiculous red-fringed boots? Or was that some other Southern midget?"

"Ooo, you mean the Liberty Black ones—" Trish cuts herself off. "Hey, wait a minute. I am not a midget!"

"Well you aren't—"

"Where's Flynn?" I yell, bringing their attention back to me.

Rose smiles one of her devious grins and I have a feeling my life is going to be a lot of fun with her in it. Exhausting, but fun.

"He's having a big old manly cry fest at the ranch."

"Ranch?"

"Yep. Holt texted me last night." She gestures for Trish to get in.

With a smile Trish hops in the truck, turns over the engine and turns around in the small lot. Before she takes off, she rolls down her window and Rose leans across her lap.

"The West Ranch is on the northwest side of town." She rattles off the address, then blows me a kiss.

"Good luck, sugar," Trish sings before she and Rose drive off.

I stand there watching the truck disappear down NASA Road

1, not blinking. Slowly, everything starts sinking in. Making sense. Giving me hope. Jumpstarting my legs.

I run back to the Corvette, unlock the door, and jump behind the wheel. Flynn had rebuilt this car with love, that much is obvious. Everything looks right off the assembly line, but I know he must've had to overhaul it. The altimeter gauges alone are custom made. This took time. He *had* to have still been working on it since his ultimatum. And if that's true, maybe Rose is right. Maybe we *aren't* over. Maybe my dream of having the career I've worked so hard for can also involve a sexy mechanic waiting at home for me when I come back from orbit.

I run my hands over the black leather seats and then curl them around the wheel before focusing on the problem at hand.

I don't know how to drive stick.

TWENTY-SEVEN

DEMODULATION

Flynn

I'VE ALWAYS LOVED STARING OUT THE WINDOW OVERLOOKING THE expanse of grazing land that's been in the West family for generations. A lot of that land is now overrun with oil machinery, but you can't see it from this vantage point.

An egret swoops down toward the pond, the water rippling out from its landing. Yeah, I love this ranch. Though it's been a long time since I've been back.

Holt bangs around in the kitchen making coffee. Or tar that he likes to label coffee. Seeing as my brother's coffee helped me shake off the worst of my hangover, I shouldn't complain.

It meant a lot that Holt asked me to come visit after he helped me drop Jackie's car off last night. Even if I know it's probably more to keep an eye on me than anything. And seeing as working nonstop for days to finish up Jackie's 'vette had taken a lot out of me, I'm glad for the rest.

I glance over at Holt through the cutout between the living room and family room, still amazed at the lack of resentment I feel toward him.

Holt burns himself on the pot, waving his fingers in the air. "Shoot."

I smile at his ladylike expletive and flop down hard on the couch.

"Damn it, Flynn, why can't you sit on a couch like a normal person?" He carries two mugs into the living room. "You break it, you buy it."

Yeah, my older brother missed me. "Yes, ma'am," I say with a mock salute.

"Idiot." Holt hands me the mug and sits on the nearby recliner.

I take a sip of my coffee and sputter. "Jesus, Holt. Warn a guy the next time you make the coffee Irish, will you?"

"You were damn near drowning in it last night, didn't think you'd notice." Holt's lips curl into a smirk. "Thought I'd give you a little hair of the dog. A little whiskey in your coffee today is all you get. I hid the rest of it."

"Please, like I don't know all your hiding places."

Holt just snorts.

I grab the remote before he can and click on the TV. "I'll probably head back to Clear Lake tomorrow. I've got a new rebuild coming—what the?"

"Is that Jackie?" Holt asks.

I don't answer. I simply sit up and raise the volume. The two headshots, one of Jackie that I'd seen on her NASA ID badge, and one of Brian Hampson from his baseball card, are featured in the top right corner on the screen, while the news station plays a video on the other side.

My hands grip my mug as I watch what I'd only heard about till now play out. Jackie standing up, trying to walk away. Brian grabbing her arm and dragging her around. Shoving her back in her seat.

My vision narrows. I don't even realize I'm standing until

Holt grabs my arm, now dripping with hot coffee.

"I'm going to destroy that son of a bitch."

Holt pries the now half-empty cup from my hand. "Well, I can definitely see how you'd think you'd need to do that—big man that you are and all—but I think Jackie's taken care of it." He gestures to the TV with his free hand.

I refocus on the screen where Brian is now on his knees, his face contorted in pain, while Jackie jerks him around by his index finger. She looks fierce and focused and so goddamn beautiful. Her glasses slip down her nose as she pushes Brian back.

Those fucking glasses.

The pictures and video vanish to reveal a roundtable of women. "What you just saw was a video of NASA's Darling, the newly appointed astronaut, Dr. Jackie Darling Lee, that has recently gone viral. She can be seen defending herself against a man, and not just any man, but Houston's newly acquired shortstop, Brian Hampson. PR for the Astros released a statement that the team was looking into the incident, and that the Astros would not stand for any unbecoming behavior from their players," one of the ladies says.

Another woman pipes up about how violence is out of control in professional sports.

And yet another praises Jackie's knowledge of self-defense. "Such a remarkable woman."

I shake my arm out, then wipe my hand across my shirt to dry up the remaining coffee.

"She is, you know," Holt says.

"She is what?"

"Remarkable."

I sink back down onto the sofa. "I know."

"Then why aren't you with her right now?"

"I don't deserve her, man."

"Flynn..."

I glance back at the TV, now showing footage of Brian leaving practice, his black eye partially covered by designer sunglasses. He smiles at the camera, ensuring them that the video has been blown out of proportion. My eyes narrowing, I push myself out of the chair. "That's it. I'm heading into town."

"Flynn, don't." Holt tries to block my path, but I move around him. "It'll be worse for Jackie if you confront him again and they connect you to her and then the ballplayer's black eye to you," he calls out.

At the front door I lift my keys from the hook on the wall. "They won't." And they damn sure shouldn't as I'd made sure my bribe to the building manager had included shutting off the garage's video feed.

"You want to chance that? With Jackie starting astronaut training soon?"

"Fuck." I don't know NASA's policy on idiot exes, which I guess I'm now a part of along with that dickhead Hampson. I curse again, not wanting to have anything in common with that fucker.

I loop my key ring back on the hook, too restless to go sit down again. "I guess I'll just have to ride my other Mustang then."

————

Jackie

I've made it. I think. Almost.

Okay, technically I've made it. The sign on the metal archway, between two lengths of fence, has the words West Ranch scrolled out of iron.

But just as I reach the gate, I stall.

Again.

This whole manual transmission thing is harder than I thought. I don't even want to think about all the middle fingers waved in my direction or horns honked as I'd coasted in the slow lane on the highway. I let everything pass me, even sixteen wheelers, so I could keep the amount of shifting to a minimum. The upside, I hadn't stalled all that much until I got off the interstate. The downside, it's almost dark, the fifty-minute drive taking twice that amount of time.

I push down on the clutch and brake to start the ignition again. Apparently, I can direct astronauts flying thousands of miles away in space on how to hotwire billions of dollars' worth of complex equipment while they wear the equivalent of snow gloves, but I can't shift and clutch fast enough not to stall out on a dirt road.

Awesome.

I get the car moving again, the Corvette not liking the bumpy ride. I fight to keep it in first and avoid any obvious holes or ruts. Those big pickup trucks everyone in Texas drives make a lot more sense now.

Between the snail speed and the length of the driveway, it takes me a while to reach the house. There's a lot of land.

I pass a few outbuildings along the way and see a huge barn behind the white clapboard house. I say house, but really, it's a mansion. The style is that of an old farm house complete with a wraparound porch and Queen Anne posts. Unpretentious in every way except when it comes to size. Three stories and multiple columns of windows.

I guess farming cattle is a lucrative business.

I'm pulling up to the main house when I stall again. This time not from the bumpy road but from the mini orgasm coursing through me from the single most magnificent sight I've ever seen.

Flynn on a horse.

He's riding hard toward the barn, slowing his horse as he hits the main road. Next thing I know, I'm standing next to my car with the door open. I have to glance back in to make sure I remembered to pull the brake. I didn't.

I jump back in and yank the brake up, scrambling to get out again before Flynn rides by.

But Flynn must've already seen me, as he's stopped a few yards away. The sun setting behind him, both his and the horse's chests heaving with exertion make him look like some sort of angelic horseman. A really, really hot cowboy angelic horseman.

I open my mouth, but nothing comes out. My mind blanks.

Well, that's not entirely true. It's just laser focused on Flynn's thighs gripping the saddle, the sweat soaking his shirt, and his hands loosely holding the reins, as if he rides horses on a daily basis. As if he's a real cowboy.

I shudder from an orgasm aftershock.

TWENTY-EIGHT
CHECKERED FLAG

Flynn

I LEAN BACK IN MY SADDLE, TRYING TO EASE MY SUDDEN erection. It isn't easy. I've been at half-mast since the moment I'd seen Jackie's blond hair behind the wheel of the car I rebuilt. Then she'd stepped out of the vintage 'vette, one long leg at a time.

Damn.

I shift again, but my zipper is trying to indent itself on my dick, so the only option for relief is to dismount and will my hard-on away.

I switch the reins to one hand and swing my leg over the side of my horse, my boots kicking up dust as I land. Willing away my hard-on. I'm pretty sure greeting her with both hand and dick waving is not the best way to win Jackie back.

Jackie shades her eyes against the sun and gestures to the animal. "That your horse?"

"Yeah. This is Boss." I reach up and stroke Boss's neck. "He's a Mustang."

"Like your car?"

I'm surprised she makes the connection, though I stop myself from reading too much into that. Genius that Jackie is, I'm sure nothing really escapes her notice.

"The horse came first." Sweat trickles off my forehead into my eye. I bring the hem of my shirt up to wipe the sting away.

When I look back up, Jackie's leaning against the side of her car.

I take a step forward. "Hey, you okay?"

She runs a hand across her forehead. "Yeah," she says, her voice strained. "Yes, yes. Fine."

The sun beats down on us, even this late in the day. Not so much as a whisper of a breeze offers relief from the heat. Boss nudges my shoulder, impatient for his rubdown and feed.

Jackie pushes back off the 'vette and takes a step toward me, shoving her hands into her back pockets. "We should talk." She rocks back on the heels of her Converse. They have rhinestones on them. "I know you punched Brian."

Fuck. I run my hand through my hair. My chance of convincing Jackie I support her astronaut career probably just lessened if she knows I went out and publicly assaulted her ex. No doubt I'm in for a sexy-as-fuck lecture about brains over brawn.

My dick twitches at the thought.

"Yeah. Sorry."

"Don't be." She shrugs. "He's an asshat."

I chuckle. "Another Rose term?"

She nods.

We stare at each other for a moment, the silence making me twitch.

"Do you like it?" I finally ask, gesturing to the car.

She brightens, a wide smile jostling her glasses. "I love it." She turns her attention to the 'vette, her right hand running along the roof. "But you shouldn't have. It probably cost a fortune."

Unease creeps in, but I force it away. "We should talk." Boss pulls on the reins. "Follow me to the barn?" I tilt my head down the road.

She nods, her glasses slipping down. I start walking Boss to the barn and Jackie follows at a distance.

Once Boss is in his stall, I give him a feed bag and a quick brushing. Jackie's quiet the whole time, but her eyes never leave me. I can feel her stare, even when my back is turned. I wonder what she's thinking. I wonder what it will take, if anything, for her to accept my apology.

I'd already given her the 'vette. It had been the only thing I could think of that could say everything I wanted to say but didn't know how. That I believe in her. That I support her dreams. That I love her.

I pause at a truly horrific thought. Did she drive the 'vette all the way here just to give it back? She can't. I *need* her to accept that car. I put the brush down and close the stall gate.

"Jackie—"

Jackie launches herself at me. I stumble back a step, the stall gate keeping me upright. She's everywhere. Her hands are through my hair, then one glides under my shirt, scraping her nails across my chest and around my back. Her other hand follows but takes a detour past my belt, grabbing my dick, which is now back to full attention.

When her fingers palm me though the denim, her glasses slip down her nose, tilting to one side. I pluck the glasses from her face with the other, placing them on the bale of hay by the stall. Then I move us both across the aisle and back her up against the adjacent wall, shoving a thigh between her legs, giving me the leverage I need to free my hands.

I want to touch her. I *have* to touch her.

Things have gone from zero to sixty in the blink of an eye and I love every goddamn second of it.

"I'm rich," I say, on a breath between kisses, though I don't remember making a conscious decision to do so.

"Okay." She pants, lifting her mouth to mine again.

I pull back. "I mean, I have a lot of money, Jackie. My family does. From the ranch."

She nods, seemingly unconcerned, eyes focused on my mouth.

"Like millions." My hands are still full of her ass, but they've stilled, waiting for what I'm saying to sink in.

She tilts her head to the side, arms still lopped around my neck, considering. "*Like* millions, or actual millions?"

"Actual millions."

"Huh. Who knew cattle farming was so lucrative."

My lips twitch. "Cattle farming?"

"Is that not the term?" She frowns. "When people raise fish for food it's called fish farming. I saw a documentary on it."

"I see."

She loses her frown, her gaze going over my shoulder. "It was quite fascinating. It reminded me of—"

"Jackie?" My hands squeeze her ass.

"Hmm?"

"We were talking about my millions."

She narrows her eyes at me. "Actually, you were about to tell me the correct term for cattle farming."

"Ranching. And it isn't just from cattle. The Wests are the wealthiest oil family in Houston. That's where the money comes from, actually."

"Ranching?" She pinches her brow. "But that doesn't give a clear indication of what goes on. At least when one farms, there's a direct correlation to a business that deals in growing crops and raising livestock. Ranching just means to run a ranch. That's so ambiguous."

I'm amazed, but somehow not surprised, that she is more

concerned over correct terminology than oil rights. "I love how smart you are." I lean down and run my stubbled cheek along the sensitive column of her throat. "It's so damn sexy, darling." I pull back when Jackie squirms in my hold, watching a pretty blush spread down her neck. "I also see that you truly don't care about my millions."

Peering up at me, she asks, "Why? It's not my money." She purses her lips for a moment. "Although I do like how this new fact fills in a lot of gaps."

She's got that far-off look in her eyes, like she's running through her mental file cabinet.

"What gaps?"

"The fact that you own a million-dollar house on an oversized lot in one of the most coveted neighborhoods in Clear Lake and drive a half-million-dollar car."

I actually sputter. "How do you know all that?"

"I'm looking to buy a house and a car," she states, like it's the most obvious answer. "You can't do any of those things properly without researching."

"Research." I run my hand through my hair. "I should've known."

"Yes. And as cars are fairly important to you, I've also watched numerous car movies and done extensive research on all the makes and models I saw in your garage."

"You did?" No one has ever taken an interest in my work before. Beth sure as shit didn't. Holt and Rose support me, but that's as far as it goes. But Jackie, a NASA flight controller, and now astronaut, has taken the time to learn about muscle cars. For me.

"The most recent 1969 Mustang Boss that was sold, fixed in what car enthusiasts term 'cherry' condition, was auctioned off for five hundred thousand dollars in Naples, Florida earlier this year. Although it was black, which I think is a cop-out. Your green, called Black Jade, is a much more unique, yet original, color."

It's like my dick has wings and wants to fly.

"What? Did I get something wrong?" Jackie asks, taking in my shocked expression. "I'm pretty sure my sources were highly credible—"

I crash my mouth against hers, my hands tunneling under her shirt. No more talking, no more revelations. My dick can't take it anymore. My heart either. I tell my brain to shut the hell up and savor this moment. These feelings.

I tug her shirt up and over her head. I reach one hand over my shoulder to yank off my own shirt, while Jackie reaches back and unclasps her bra. As soon as it falls away, my hands wrap around her tits, her skin so warm, so soft.

Her hands make quick work of my belt while I palm her breasts before feasting on them with my mouth. But when she starts to shove my jeans and boxers down, I reluctantly let go of her breast to reach back and grab my wallet. I flick it open with one hand and slip the condom out.

She watches, licking her lips as if hungry, as I roll on the condom over my cock.

I set her down, just long enough to grab her waistband with two hands and yank. Her top button pops off and her zipper wrenches open, allowing me to jerk her pants and panties down her long, strong legs. She manages to step one foot out before I'm on her again, lifting her against the wall and thrusting home.

"Fuck."

My curse is met with her moan. Jackie's head tilts back, her long neck exposed, the cords visible as she arches back in pleasure. Her eyes are closed and her hair creates a wild, tumbleweed-like halo around her face. My chest tightens like a rubber band pulling taut around my heart.

She's so fucking beautiful.

Jackie lifts her head and looks at me, her gaze focused but soft. One of her hands cradles my cheek, her thumb swiping lightly against the scruff on my jaw. "Flynn," she whispers. "I've missed you, Flynn. So much."

The band around my chest snaps, as does my control. I lift her higher in my hands then release her, the fall of her weight thrusting me deeper inside her.

She screams my name, her fingertips biting into my skin.

"*Christ*, Jackie." I pause, enjoying the moment of her clenched around me before an urgency to move has my hips pounding into hers hard and fast.

I tangle my hand in her hair, twisting until her face is at just the right angle for my kiss. My tongue dances with hers while she uses her hands to push up on my shoulders, helping me thrust harder, deeper than before.

We find a rhythm, wild though it is, and ride it out. It's better than racing, better than riding. Fuck.

Jackie is the best feeling in the world.

She clamps down on my dick, her whole body frozen while she contracts around my wet cock. I thrust once, twice more until my own orgasm hits, grinding myself into her, trying to hammer my way inside her, just like she has into my heart.

TWENTY-NINE
MISSION COMPLETE

Jackie

MY HEAD RESTS AGAINST THE BARN WALL, MY FACE TILTED UP. Dust particles dance in the beams of light shooting through the barn doors, like a meteor shower in space. We're both breathing hard, sweating from exertion. The smell of sex and perspiration mixes with hay and horses. I think of all the sex scenes set in barns from my cowboy romances. That plus the image of Flynn on his horse earlier and my inner walls clamp down on Flynn in an aftershock of pleasure. Flynn groans.

I lean forward to dust kisses along his collarbone and shoulder, while my fingertips dance in swirls up and down his back. As our breaths even out, I can hear the horses shuffling in their stalls, machinery running in the distance.

"I'm an astronaut," I say softly, not wanting to break the spell, but also needing to know if this was a fleeting moment of insanity for him, or the beginning of something like I hoped.

"I know." He rests his forehead against mine. "And I couldn't be prouder."

I breathe in deeply through my nose, a wide smile overtaking my lips. "Really?"

"Really." His pulls back just enough to place light kisses on each of my eyelids. "I love you, Jackie."

My heart races at his words, wanting so desperately to trust in their truth, but still remembering the way my dreams were so coldly dismissed the last time we spoke.

"You love me?" I can't help the uncertainty in my voice.

He sighs, looking thoughtful before answering. "My mother didn't really love my father."

I feel my eyes widen in surprise. "She... didn't?"

"No. She wanted a certain lifestyle. So she convinced my dad to leave the ranch and turn his love of cars into a career." He steps back, slipping from me. He waits until I'm steady on my feet before withdrawing his touch just long enough to take care of the condom, tossing it in a nearby garbage can. He tucks himself back into his jeans, then steps into my arms again. "They traveled the world, lived a lush lifestyle. When Holt was born, supposedly they stayed at the ranch for a while, but it didn't last. They left him with Grams and Gramps to continue on their way. I came along and it was the same thing. They'd come home for short stretches, enough for us to remember who they were, but not much else. Seven years later Grams died, and Gramps put his foot down, saying that they needed to come home."

My hands never stop trailing along his skin, keeping contact. Letting him know I'm here, that I'm listening.

"I was young, but even I remember how unhappy my mom was, though my dad seemed to be able to blow off the worst of her moods." He snorts. "But when Rose was born, things changed. Got harder." His large hands squeeze my waist as if strangling the memories flashing through his mind. He takes a deep breath and gentles his touch.

"Mom moved out for a while, lived in town. We barely saw

her. Dad tried to take over for Gramps, who was getting too old to be running things alone. But after a while, after Rose asked after her momma one too many times, Dad went to try and bring her back."

He's quiet for a while, his concentration on his touch. Running his hands over my cooling body. When his fingertips slide down the bridge of my nose, I risk breaking the peace of the moment by speaking.

"And did she? Come home, that is?"

"For a bit." He shakes his head. "But I think she was just using that time to convince my father to make another tour on the racing circuit." He laughs unpleasantly. "Which is crazy because by that time he was past his prime for a racer." He sighs. "But he went."

Flynn squats down on his haunches in front of me, untangling my jeans and panties, and helping me slide them back up my legs.

"He didn't win enough to be invited to the best races, the more prestigious ones. Then one day we got the call that they'd died in a crumpled mess of metal on an unsanctioned racetrack. I guess since there weren't many rules in unsanctioned races, my mom decided to jump in the car with my dad." He straightens in front of me. "Probably just chasing another thrill."

I circle my arms around him, drawing our bodies together. "I'm so sorry, Flynn," I say, knowing my words, any words, are inadequate.

"She wasn't the best mom, and he wasn't the best dad, but they were my parents. And I grew up hating them." He tightens his embrace. "It's probably why it took me so long to give in to opening my own shop. It reminded me of them too much." He eases back and dips down to catch my eyes. "And it was why I freaked out that day you told me about the interview."

"Flynn, I—"

"Knowing that someone else I loved would leave me to do something dangerous, I just… I sort of lost it."

"Oh, Flynn. I'm so sorry." I try and sort through my emotions to find the right words to make him understand. "I don't… I mean, it isn't that I want to *leave* you, it's just…"

He shakes his head. "You have nothing to be sorry for, darling. And I know you aren't making a decision like my parents did." I must look skeptical because he continues, "I do, really." He brushes a kiss on my lips. "But when you told me about the interview and how it was the last step toward being an astronaut, all that went through my head was the possibility of losing someone I love. I wasn't thinking straight." Another kiss. "Please believe me, I never wanted you to say no to your dreams. I've always believed in you, even after I acted like a complete dick."

I smile at him. "The car."

He smiles back. "I was hoping you'd get what that meant."

"Well, thanks to you, I speak car now, so I have a pretty good idea what it means when a man rebuilds a car for a woman." I reach up and touch the edge of his smile with my fingertips. "Especially a badass astronaut car." I look around, squinting. Flynn retrieves my glasses from the bale of hay next to us and helps slide them on. "Thanks." I blink a few times, my eyes focusing.

"I love you." His words send tingles through my body.

"I believe you." I rest my forehead on his.

He smiles, tugging on the end of my hair.

I place my palms on his chest, feeling the steady beat of his heart. "And I love you."

Flynn's body stills for a moment before slowly wrapping my hair around his hand, forcing my chin up.

"Before you kiss me again, I have something else to tell you."

"And what's that?" he asks, his eyes intent.

"I devised a new protocol," I whisper against his mouth. "A relationship procedure."

"Procedure, huh?" His mouth brushes mine, his other hand fisting my shirt.

"Mm-hmm." My hands lower to his hips, skimming around to his back. I dip my fingers under his waistband, grabbing his ass.

"So what's this new procedure called?"

I whisper it, suddenly embarrassed, hoping he won't laugh.

His smile is slow and so sweet my chest tightens.

"Operation Happily Ever After," he murmurs, touching his nose to mine. "I like it."

EPILOGUE

Five Years Later

Flynn

I CHECK MY WATCH FOR THE FIFTH TIME. THEN I ADJUST THE telescope Jackie got me for Christmas this year, making sure the coordinates are set.

I drove to the ranch for this, so I'd have less ambient lights mucking up the sky. I'd already driven Holt crazy asking him repeatedly if he'd cleared the north field of cattle for me, turned off all the motion and flood lights around the property, and had him double and triple check the strength and batteries of three different portable internet sticks I'd bought. He finally pushed me out the door twenty minutes ago and I drove out in the middle of one of the fields. Nothing but grass and sky for miles. Forty minutes ahead of schedule.

I pull out the origami heart from my wallet I never took out. It's become a sort of talisman I touch whenever I miss her, or I'm nervous for her. So it's gotten *a lot* of wear.

Jackie's done a lot of exciting but scary stuff these past few years on her way to fulfilling her dream. And tonight is a big part of it. I check my watch again.

I don't want to miss her.

Five minutes pass. My leg starts bouncing, shaking the fold-out chair I'm sitting on.

Another five minutes.

I'm about to slug back the flask of whiskey I brought when Elton John's "Rocket Man" lights up my laptop, the sound drifting across the empty field.

I toss the whiskey to the ground and pounce on the accept call link.

"Flynn?"

And there she is, the most beautiful girl in the world. Now the universe. Her long hair is pulled back in a ponytail that's floating away from her head. She's grasping a handhold mounted on the wall, trying to keep herself centered on the camera. Her titanium wedding band that matches mine, but thinner, encircles her left ring finger. I had them custom made. Titanium, the material used in spacecraft, with a strip of meteorite in the center. Even on land, she'll have a piece of space with her.

"Yo." Thankfully my voice sounds calm and collected and not laced with the anxiety I was drowning in just seconds ago.

Jackie rolls her eyes at my greeting. "You all set?" she asks, floating the camera over with her to the window. I see darkness and stars and then the camera lens adjusts and the Earth comes into focus.

"Wow."

"I know, right?" Jackie sighs. "I still can't get over it." She's looking out a window in one of the International Space Station modules, nose almost touching the glass. She's in profile, so I can see both the view and her. And though the view is amazing, it's her that captures my attention.

The bright, florescent lights of the station highlight the

freckles dusted across her cheek. The slender slope of her nose is more pronounced without her sexy glasses perched on top.

To be a mission specialist in the ISS you need twenty-twenty vision. So Jackie opted for Lasik. She got a raft of shit from her fellow astronauts when she continued wearing her frames after the surgery with just glass for lenses. But she'd said she felt naked without them and seeing how I love getting her naked when she's wearing them, the teasing hadn't bothered her.

This is the first time she's gone any length of time without them. And though I truly love those sexy-as-fuck glasses, I love her more, and the expression of awe and wonder so clearly displayed on her face right now.

"You should see it soon," she says, breaking my train of thought.

I look up at the sky. "I don't see it yet." I scan the stars. "I see the Big Dipper."

"That's actually Ursa Major."

"Listen here, Miss Smarty Pants," I say, looking down at my laptop, "everyone knows that's the Big Dipper."

She nods, as if conceding the point. "I guess it *is* the Big Dipper, but the Big Dipper is really an asterism, which is part of the constellation Ursa Major."

"Oh yeah?" I love the way she tilts her head when she gets sidetracked on one of her brainy tangents.

"Yep. It's also called the Big Bear. Roman Mythology states that the god Jupiter fell in love with a mortal, Callisto. Juno, Jupiter's wife, turned the woman into a bear in a jealous fit. When Callisto's son saw her as the bear and tried to kill her, Jupiter intervened by turning him into a bear as well and casting them both into the stars to keep them safe."

"Well, speaking of casting into the stars, I think I see it."

She perks up, checking her watch. "Yes, we're heading over right about now." Her voice is giddy, and if it weren't for the lack of gravity, I bet she'd be doing that adorable jump/clap right about now.

She turns the camera to the window again, and on my laptop I can see North America, dark except for the concentrated lights from urban areas.

I glance back up, a light streaking across the sky.

I prop my laptop so that she can still see me as I look through the telescope. There, among the stars, is the International Space Station, traveling over seventeen thousand miles per hour, roughly five miles a second.

Though crazy expensive and probably the most technically advanced on the market, considering the lecture she'd given me about it on Christmas morning, my telescope can only make out the basic shape of the ISS, and not Jackie peering out a window. But I know she's there.

My girl. My astronaut. My wife.

"Hi, Flynn," she says softly.

"Hi, darling."

———

GO to www.SaraLHudson.com for a bonus epilogue!

Space Cowgirl: Houston, All Systems GO

Astronaut Julie Starr knows nothing is earned without blood, sweat, and frizzy hair. On her way to becoming the youngest Commandeer ever, she isn't about to let a stalker derail her goals. Or a chivalrous, wealthy, rancher for that matter either.

Holt West doesn't mess with flirts. And that's exactly what the smart-mouthed, out-of-this world beauty is. He has enough on his plate trying to get back into his family's good graces, he doesn't need to be distracted by curly hair or long legs clad in leather pants.

But when Holt's brother and Jules' best friend decide to get hitched, they're thrown together as best man and maid of honor. Jules take the opportunity to hide out from her stalker while doing her bestie a solid by planning the wedding of a life time. She's an astronaut for god's sake, how hard can planning a wedding be?

Holt goes overboard, taking on a full scale renovation at the West ranch for the wedding. Ensuring that a certain feisty, control freak, maid of honor sticks around that much longer.

Between Jules vying for a record-breaking promotion and Holt fighting a losing battle with his heart, can the two of them get it together enough to plan a wedding, stop a stalker and say yes to the ride of their lives?

Or is this mission a no-go?

———

Chapter One

Jules

Spinning. So much spinning.

Lights flash beneath my eyelids and the temperature of my surroundings heat to an uncomfortable level. My lungs struggle for breath. When the end comes, it's violent in its abruptness. There's a sudden loss of time and space perception before my ass is slapped like a bull about to buck in the arena.

My dance partner grunts in appreciation and raises his hand to get another brief feel of my ass, but I swerve beyond his reach. Keeping in time with the beat, I continue out of his path and off the dance floor, in search of a drink.

I like to dance. I like to dance with my eyes closed even more. It reminds me of reentry inside the claustrophobic Soyuz capsule. Dancing and speeding through the atmosphere toward the planet we call Earth are both beautiful in their carefully orchestrated violence.

At least the way I like to dance is.

Or live for that matter.

"Jules!" My new friend Rose waylays me as I head to the bar. "Damn girl, you can dance. I swear, if this were Vegas I'd make a move on you."

I hook my arm in hers and continue to where I can get some much needed alcohol. "Why just Vegas?"

She shrugs, her constant mischievous grin in place. "I don't know. It seems to be where my latent lesbian tendencies dwell." She looks me up and down from the corner of her eye. "But I could always give you a go. Maybe Big Texas will resurface some hoo-ha fantasies."

Laughing, I rap my knuckles on the bar, getting the attention of one of the bartenders. I've been gone a few months, and though I stopped being surprised by how the world continues to spin while I'm in zero gravity, this time was different. So much of *my* world has changed.

At the far end of the oak bar top, Jackie's perched on the lap of a hot piece of ass. Flynn. Apparently my best friend took my recent pep-talk, a.k.a. blackmail, to heart and found herself a social life. A social life complete with hot mechanic sexy times.

I can't complain. It's obvious Jackie's new boyfriend worships her genius brain as much as her long, long legs, and her new friends welcomed me home like I'd known them all my life. Like real family should.

"What can I get you, sweet cheeks?"

Before I can open my mouth to answer the cute bartender smirking my way, Rose pipes up. "Sweet cheeks? Oh Billy, you need some new material. Sweet cheeks may work on the bleached-out, rhinestoned-up cougar clientele you usually associate with." She waves towards the crowded mass. "But this here is the living legend, America's sweetheart, Astronaut Julie Starr."

Billy takes a long look at me, eyes and mouth widening.

"Show some respect and get some new material for the recently returned to Earth hero, will ya?" Rose snaps her fingers at Billy's slack jaw.

I laugh and wave away Rose's words. "Really, no need. Sweet cheeks works." I twist to look down at my ass. "After all, my ass *is* pretty damn sweet."

Billy recovers, as does his smile. "Well ladies, this calls for a drink on the house."

"Beer for me," I say. But he gives me a funny look and places three shot glasses on the bar.

Rose elbows me in the boob. "Hey, if the man wants to give you free liquor, you take the free liquor." As if she didn't just give me an inverted nipple, Rose fluffs her wavy blonde hair and adjusts her bra, leaving her plentiful cleavage just this side of indecent.

I shrug, not even bothering to touch the chaos on top of my head. I'm back in the land of humidity and already sweaty from spinning on the dance floor; no telling what my mop-top of curls will look like if I try a come-hither hair flip. I'd probably look like an electrocuted poodle.

"Think Jackie wants one? Or Trish?" I ask, looking down the bar again.

"I think Jackie's too busy sucking my brother's face off." Rose rolls her eyes. "Ugh, so gross."

I glance over at the couple making out like it's her last night on Earth. And for Jackie, I'm sure that time won't be too far off. She was recently promoted to astronaut and her training starts soon. I can't wait for us both to be on the ISS together. I'm going to angle hard to be on her first mission. "Where's Trish?"

"Probably trying to lose her tail."

"Tail?" I straighten up. "Someone hassling her?"

"Calm down there, bruiser," Rose says, patting my arm. "I meant Ian. Ever since the dude locked eyes on her, he's been following her around like a puppy dog." She snorts. "Well, a really fine-looking puppy dog who tries to pretend he isn't infatuated when in reality he's one step away from stalkerville."

A chill races down my spine at the word stalker. I focus on the three shot glasses in front of me, trying not to think about the stock pile of disturbing messages that I'm sure await me in my social media accounts. I'll deal with that later. Or not.

I vote not.

I don't even ask what's in the shots. As soon as Billy lowers the shaker, I pick up the glass closest to me and knock it back. I knock back the next as well, but when I reach for the third, Rose blocks me and snatches it up.

"Back off, astro-girl. This one's mine."

While Rose shoots her shot, I wink to Billy in apology for taking his. He smiles and winks back. "I can always pour myself another. Perk of the job and all." He leans over the bar and into my space, his slow, drawn out smile making no bones about what he wants. "You want a third, Astronaut Starr?"

"No, she's good."

The warmth from the alcohol has nothing on the fire streaming through my veins at the sound of the deep voice behind me. Taking my time, I turn toward the speaker, knowing exactly who I'll find.

And yep, there he is, pure sex poured into cowboy boots. Boots that have actually seen a hard day's work on a cattle ranch and aren't just for show. Dark blue Levis topped off with a tight, black t-shirt that looks surprisingly new. The front is tucked behind a modest-sized belt buckle, scratched and dull instead of shiny and decked out in bling. An honest to goodness cowboy hat acts as the cherry on top of this sexy-man sundae. Not one of those stupid, bigger-than-a-Cadillac, ten-gallon things that a lot of these cowboy posers wear, but a low profile, black hat that's worn well and hard, just like the man sporting it.

Yummy.

I bat my lashes and bring my hand to my chest. "Why Holt West, I do declare."

————

I try not to smile at the southern syrup dripping off Miss Starr's words. But with my mind on her tall, lithe form, it's kind of hard. When I first saw Julie standing at the bar next to my sister, all I could see was her firm rear end pushing the limits of her tight leather pants. That's right, we're in a Texas Saloon and the lady is wearing leather pants. God love her.

Her Ziggy Stardust t-shirt looks like it's been through a meat grinder. It drapes over one shoulder, showing off a thin black bra strap and the bottom of the shirt is tied at the waist. The knot in question rides up, giving me a glimpse of her navel as she leans back, both elbows on the bar behind her, crossing her shit-kicker biker boots at the ankles.

My sister has no such qualms and she openly snorts at Jules' sarcastic southern twang. "Nice, Jules." Rose looks at me. "What're you doing here? A bit far away from Lonesome Dove, isn't it?"

A long-suffering sigh escapes me. I know I don't leave the ranch very often. I can't. I've got a business to run and people depending on me. But now that I've patched things up with my brother, and him being all but attached at the hip to his new girlfriend, Jackie, I want to make more of an effort to be involved. With Rose. With Flynn Their friends.

Rose leans in and gives me a quick hug. I don't tell her enough, but for all her smart mouth ways, I love her the most. She's the most positive force in my life. Always has been. Even after Gramps' death and then our parents, her smiles light up the room. Hell, even when Flynn and I acted like grade-a jerks, her positivity was the glue that kept us from becoming completely unhinged.

"Miss Starr." I nod in Julie's direction.

"You can call me Jules, hot stuff." She lifts her chin at someone behind me. I turn to catch some guy with a pseudo mullet leering in her direction.

"Friend of yours?" I ask, hoping she doesn't hear the tightness in my voice.

"That's Doug. I let him twirl me around on the dance floor a while ago."

She watches the guy walk away. "Good footwork, but too handsy for me to give him a second round."

I swallow the jealousy I feel towards douche-bag Doug. She can dance with whomever she wants. I don't care. She lifts her chin at yet another douche bag. This one with actual rhinestones on his belt buckle.

I step up to her, cutting off her line of sight to the rest of the crowd. One of my boots on either side of hers.

All I get in response is a raised eyebrow.

"Geez, caveman much, bro?" Rose swivels in place and raises her hand in Flynn and Jackie's direction. I guess the lovebirds finally came up for air. "While I truly enjoy you metaphorically banging your fists on your chest, I've already witnessed this ride with Flynn." She blows a kiss at us before walking away. "Good luck, brother dear," she calls out over her shoulder.

I'm grateful for the dim lighting. For a guy, I blush easily, and it's annoying as all get out.

I turn my head back to Jules to find her slugging back a beer, her wide mouth wrapped around the opening. Another twitch in my pants has me shifting in my boots.

"Where'd that come from?"

She raises a finger, telling me to wait. And I do, while she chugs back the entire thing, slamming down the bottle and then licking her lips. Her wet, full lips.

"Listen, Paco, I already have a dad, I don't need another. Hell, I don't even want the one I have." Her brows furrow, like she doesn't know where that last bit came from. But I soak it up. Jules is hard to get a read on, so I'll take everything she gives, even if it's alcohol induced. "I can drink what I like, when I like. Especially when the bartender tells me a fan of mine bought it." She smiles seductively. "Don't want to disappoint the fans, now, do I?"

"Paco?"

"Hey. Paco is a cool-as-shit name. Sheesh, you racist or something?"

"I'm *not* racist. That's just not my name." I can actually feel my blood pressure rising. "And you should know better than to accept drinks from strangers. Jesus, Jules. That's drinking 101."

Jules remains unfazed by tone. "Billy gave me the beer from the fan. I'm sure he vetted the dude." She tilts her head to the side in thought. "Or girl. Chicks dig me."

I blanche at this. The twitch I've been fighting in my pants becomes a full-blown salute at the thought of Jules naked with another woman.

"In fact, your sister propositioned me just a bit ago."

Annnnnnd, the salute drops.

"Sheesh." I rub my hand down my face.

She laughs. "I know, right? I'm on fire tonight." She pushes up from the bar, her height putting the top of her head level with my nose. Which is some feat, as she isn't even wearing heels. She's at least five foot eight, maybe five foot nine, coming in a few inches below my six foot one.

Jules makes a move to step past me, but falters, her shoulder banging into mine.

"Whoa, there." I reach out and steady her, but she brushes my hands away.

"I'm not one of your horses, cowboy. 'Whoa' someone else, I'm good." Then she saunters away, a little unsteady, but still hot as hell in those tight leather pants. She's right, she isn't one of my horses, but I still can't help wanting to get her in the saddle.

———

Twenty minutes later and I'm concerned. I haven't been here long enough to know how much Jules drank, but her eyes look unfocused and she's leaning heavily on the wall next to the table the group commandeered earlier. Getting a table on a crowded Saturday night hadn't been so much luck as having an inside advantage— Trish is one of Big Texas's bartenders.

I refocus on the petite, southern lady, wondering why my manhood won't twitch in her direction. Trish is exactly my type. Polite, dainty, a nice, sweet smile on her lips. She's dressed in a denim skirt and wearing heels so high she must have to balance on her tip toes just to walk around. She's friendly, seems laid-back, the perfect woman for sharing a cup of coffee on the ranch's porch before I start a long day of hard labor. She's the kind of woman who would probably bake me banana bread just because she knows it's my favorite.

And yet she does nothing but conjure up friendly, sisterly feelings as she sits on one of the bar stools, while some guy named Ian, who I don't know very well, gazes at her like a puppy would a bone. He catches me looking at Trish and glowers.

I turn my attention back to Jules. She's still propped up against the wall, long legs crossed just like her arms are over her chest. Uninviting, but alluring. Like the kind of girl who would chew you up and spit you out after a night of hard loving. I have a feeling if I told her I like banana bread she'd scoff, make an anatomically incorrect gesture, then determinedly devour a raw steak in front of me to make me feel like an idiot for liking baked goods. Jules isn't easy and her smile is more sexy than sweet, but she's the one that my whole body locks on, the one certain parts of my anatomy salute.

Suddenly, Jules scrunches her eyes closed, then opens them in a series of blinks. The tight curls around her face shake as she straightens from her place on the wall and steps towards the table.

"Hey Jackie, I—"

She never finishes her sentence because she falls forward, luckily catching herself on the back of Jackie's barstool.

I move fast around the table, but Flynn gets to Jules before I can, his hands under her arms, lifting her up. I try not to think about how close his fingers are to her breasts, and instead focus on her face, which is slightly pale and sweaty.

"Jules! You ok?" Jackie asks, her hand cupping Jules cheek.

"Fuck. I think I may have miscalculated my alcohol tolerance since landing." She's trying to laugh it off, so I can't tell if her slightly slurred speech is from amusement or from the amount of drinks she's had.

"I've never seen you like this. You're usually such a tank." Jackie looks up to Flynn, the panic in her eyes telling me more than her words that this isn't normal Jules behavior. Jackie jumps down off her stool. "Let's get her home, Flynn."

Flynn nods, though I know it's reluctantly. It isn't that he wouldn't do anything for Jackie's friends, but he told me earlier that he had something special planned for Jackie tonight, and I'm sure they don't include playing babysitter to his girlfriend's drunk bestie.

"That's ok, I'll take her."

All eyes turn to me, and quite a few smirks. Stupid busy-bodies.

"I've got my truck, it's no problem," I say, shrugging off their interest.

Jules steps away from Flynn only to fall into my arms. She snakes around my waist and pats my butt cheek. "No problemo, eh, Paco?" Then she snort-laughs into my chest.

I know she's drunk, and I'm a complete jerk for thinking this, but by God I love her body against mine. Not to mention her hand on my ass.

"I don't know …" Jackie frets. "What if she needs me?"

Carefully, I place my hands at Jules' waist, holding her steady. "I'll take care of her, Jackie. Promise."

Flynn's hand comes down on my shoulder. "Thanks, man," he whispers. Then louder, "Let us know when you guys are home safe."

"Yeah, let's go home," Jules says, while she squirms up my body, climbing me like a tree. She wraps her leather-clad legs around my waist, gripping the back of my head with her hands. As she is no petite lady, that puts her boobs right at eye level. On top of which, I have no choice but to grab her backside to keep her from falling.

"Ride 'em cowboy," she mumbles, her head falling forward, her breath tickling the underside of my ear.

Holy heck, I'm in trouble.

———

To get updates on new releases, free books and more— sign up for my newsletter at www.saralhudson.com.

ACKNOWLEDGMENTS

There are many people that made this book possible. But first and foremost— Lynn and Daryl Hudson, my parents.

Since I was little, my parents have supported me. They gave me love, education, a willing ear and more often than not, a helpful checkbook.

Mom and Dad you are the reason I am what I am today. And as I'm pretty awesome, you should be proud. :)

My husband, Ken. Who would have thought you'd knock up your prom date?— albeit fifteen years later.

Your encouragement and willingness to nuke chicken nuggets for the kids while I work has only made me love you more. You inspire me, both with your horrible dad jokes and your consistent need to say "boobs" every time I take a shower. As if they'd somehow disappear if you didn't.

You're amazing and I love you.

To my fellow authors who have given me insights, support and advice. Particularly Kirsten Oliphant and Jami Albright. Thank you for putting up with my many, many questions. You guys rock.

My editor Karen Simmering, who gave me that extra bit of confidence even when you had to teach me a lesson on tense.

And of course, *Space Junk* would not be what it is today without the person who brainstormed, beta read and drank through every line, scene and chapter. The amazing Ms. Leslie Marshman.

You, my dear hippie, are my ride or die, and it is an honor traveling the publishing road with you.

Next writing night (aka drinking session) is on me.

ABOUT THE AUTHOR

Sara L. Hudson was an east coast wild child until her NASA engineer husband wrangled her up and shipped me down to Texas.

Now she lives in Houston with her smarty-pants husband, their two adorable kids and fur-baby, Jack.

Sara has her master's in Creative Writing from Bath Spa University, England and was previously published as a news reporter and columnist.

Sara is also a professor of English Composition, Literature and Humanities, her favorite course to teach being the one she created on the World of Romance Novels.

Because the world needs to love and laugh more.

xx Sara

www.saralhudson.com

facebook.com/SaraLHudsonWriter
instagram.com/sara_l_hudson
tiktok.com/@author_saralhudson
amazon.com/Sara-L-Hudson
bookbub.com/authors/sara-l-hudson

Printed in Great Britain
by Amazon

23053174R00175